HOLIDAY DEFENDERS

DEBBY GIUSTI
SUSAN SLEEMAN
JODIE BAILEY

D0210212

 HARLEQUIN® LOVE INSPIRED® SUSPENSE

If you purchased this book without a cover you should be aware that this book is stolen property. It was reported as "unsold and destroyed" to the publisher, and neither the author nor the publisher has received any payment for this "stripped book."

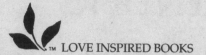 LOVE INSPIRED BOOKS

ISBN-13: 978-0-373-44626-1

Recycling programs for this product may not exist in your area.

HOLIDAY DEFENDERS

Copyright © 2014 by Harlequin Books S.A.

The publisher acknowledges the copyright holder of the individual works as follows:

MISSION: CHRISTMAS RESCUE
Copyright © 2014 by Deborah W. Giusti

SPECIAL OPS CHRISTMAS
Copyright © 2014 by Susan Sleeman

HOMEFRONT HOLIDAY HERO
Copyright © 2014 by Jodie Bailey

All rights reserved. Except for use in any review, the reproduction or utilization of this work in whole or in part in any form by any electronic, mechanical or other means, now known or hereinafter invented, including xerography, photocopying and recording, or in any information storage or retrieval system, is forbidden without the written permission of the editorial office, Love Inspired Books, 233 Broadway, New York, NY 10279 U.S.A.

This is a work of fiction. Names, characters, places and incidents are either the product of the author's imagination or are used fictitiously, and any resemblance to actual persons, living or dead, business establishments, events or locales is entirely coincidental.

This edition published by arrangement with Love Inspired Books.

® and TM are trademarks of Love Inspired Books, used under license. Trademarks indicated with ® are registered in the United States Patent and Trademark Office, the Canadian Intellectual Property Office and in other countries.

www.Harlequin.com

Printed in U.S.A.

Praise for Debby Giusti

"This story stirs the heart for the real soldiers
serving our country today and
presents a good mystery while doing so."
–*RT Book Reviews* on *The Officer's Secret*

"Quite suspenseful with a good mystery
and well-defined characters."
–*RT Book Reviews* on *The Captain's Mission*

Praise for Susan Sleeman

"Sleeman's intriguing plot proves that it's possible to
meet life's challenges."
–*RT Book Reviews* on *Double Exposure*

"The mystery will keep you involved until the end."
–*RT Book Reviews* on *The Christmas Witness*

Praise for Jodie Bailey

"As a military wife, Bailey generates characters
and a plot that are multi-layered
and wonderfully unpredictable."
–*RT Book Reviews* on *Crossfire*

"Bailey creates strong characters and palpable suspense
in this tale that will keep you guessing."
–*RT Book Reviews* on *Freefall*

DEBBY GIUSTI

is a medical technologist who loves working with test tubes and petri dishes almost as much as she loves to write. Growing up as an army brat, Debby met and married her husband—then a captain in the army—at Fort Knox, Kentucky. Together they traveled the world, raised three wonderful army brats of their own and have now settled in Atlanta, Georgia, where Debby spins tales of suspense that touch the heart and soul. Contact Debby through her website, www.debbygiusti.com, email debby@debbygiusti.com, or write c/o Love Inspired Suspense, 233 Broadway, Suite 1001, New York, NY 10279.

SUSAN SLEEMAN

grew up in a small Wisconsin town, where she spent her summers reading Nancy Drew and developing a love of mystery and suspense books. Today she channels this enthusiasm into hosting the popular internet website TheSuspenseZone.com and writing romantic-suspense and mystery novels.

Much to her husband's chagrin, Susan loves to look at everyday situations and turn them into murder-and-mayhem scenarios for future novels. If you've met Susan, she has probably figured out a plausible way to kill you and get away with it.

Susan currently lives in Oregon, but has had the pleasure of living in nine states. Her husband is a church music director and they have two beautiful daughters, a very special son-in-law and an adorable grandson. To learn more about Susan, please visit www.susansleeman.com.

JODIE BAILEY

has been weaving stories since she learned how to hold a pencil. It was only recently she learned that everyone doesn't make up whole other lives for fun in their spare time. She is an army wife, a mom and a teacher who believes chocolate and a trip to the Outer Banks will cure all ills. In her spare time, she reads cookbooks, rides motorcycles and searches for the perfect cup of coffee. Jodie lives in North Carolina with her husband and her daughter.

CONTENTS

MISSION: CHRISTMAS RESCUE

DEBBY GIUSTI

For God so loved the world that
He gave His Only Begotten Son,
so that all who believe in Him may not perish
but may have eternal life.
—*John* 3:16

Dedication

To my own
Mary, Joseph and Elizabeth.
Remember when you acted out
the Nativity as children?
Those sweet memories inspired this story.
Merry Christmas.

ONE

Elizabeth Tate pulled back the living-room curtain and stared into the night. All she saw in the windowpane was her own reflection and the twinkling lights from the Christmas tree.

Unable to shrug off her unease, she dropped the curtain into place and headed down the hallway to check on Joey and Mary Grace.

Ever since her sister-in-law had died thirteen months earlier, Liz frequently stayed overnight at her brother's house to babysit his four- and six-year-old children when he was on assignment for a story. His job as a newspaper investigative reporter often took him out of town. Tonight he was working on something closer to home, although he hadn't shared the details with Elizabeth. All she knew was that it involved the rather controversial *"Z" Notes* whistleblower blog he wrote on the side to bring public attention to unethical or illegal corporate practices. Normally, Liz treasured the time she could spend with Zack's little ones. Tonight she was anxious and worried.

Perhaps it was Zack's warning to remain vigilant that had her conjuring up all types of scenarios. None of them good.

Ever since he'd launched *"Z" Notes,* she'd been concerned about her brother's safety. Exposing corruption at any level wasn't for the faint of heart. Usually Elizabeth could overlook the downside of his work by reminding herself of the good he was doing. And besides, his dedication to his work meant that she had the joy of being deeply involved in her niece and nephew's lives. As an elementary school teacher, she loved all children, but Mary Grace and Joey held a special place in her heart.

Slipping into their bedrooms, she sighed with relief, feeling both comforted and reassured that they were nestled in their beds, fast asleep. From the looks of contentment on their sweet faces, they were probably dreaming of Christmas, only two days away. By then, her nervous unrest would be a memory and another reason for Zack to poke fun at her concern for his well-being.

Called back to the living room by the shrill trill of her cell, she reached for her BlackBerry and smiled at her brother's picture on the screen.

"Hey, bro. What's up?"

"Lizzie, listen to me carefully and do exactly what I tell you. Pack a bag for the children. A couple outfits each. Some underwear. Extra warm clothes. Don't forget Mary Grace's toy Nativity set and Joey's lamb."

"But—"

"You have to leave the house and go somewhere safe. Hide out until I contact you."

She pushed the cell closer to her ear. "Is this a joke?"

"I wish it were."

The urgency in her brother's voice brought a renewed volley of concern.

"What happened, Zack?"

"An ambush. The guy I was supposed to meet—" He hesitated. "The whistleblower's dead."

Liz gasped. "Where are you?"

"On the run. There're four of them. They want information I've uncovered. Grab my laptop and take it with you. Be careful, Liz. Don't let them find you or the kids."

"Where can we meet up?"

"We can't. They're on my tail. You've got to hurry. Take the children and escape."

A roar filled her head. She tried to think. "But where should we go?"

Zack hesitated. "I...I'm not sure."

"The Lassiter police can help, Zack. I'll call them."

"No." His firm reply frightened her even more. "You can't trust them. You can't trust anyone, except—"

"You're scaring me, Zack."

"As much as you won't like it, sis, there *is* one person you can trust. Nick Fontaine's back from his military deployment. I'll call him. He's the only person I can depend on."

She shook her head, vehemently opposed to her brother's suggestion. "I don't want Nick's help."

"There's no one else."

"Then I'll handle this myself."

"You'll need Nick. Hurry. You don't have much time."

"Zack—"

"Stay safe, and take care of my babies."

The connection ended.

Her hands trembled. She stared down at the now-blank screen and tried to comprehend what her brother had just said.

A man murdered? Zack on the run?

She needed to notify the authorities, except he'd been adamant about not telling the very people she wanted to call.

Her stomach churned. Tears stung her eyes. Blinking them back, she glanced at her watch: 10:00 p.m.

How long had she been standing there, stalled, unable to grasp the reality of the moment?

"Oh, God, help me," she moaned. "Help Zack."

Knowing she didn't have a minute to spare, Elizabeth ran into Mary Grace's bedroom and started packing things into a canvas bag. The Nativity set—a gift Zack's wife had stitched for their baby girl's first Christmas—sat on the nightstand. Liz shoved the plump, hand-sewn figures of Mary, Joseph, Baby Jesus and a donkey and camel into the quilted carrier designed as a stable, complete with a Star of Bethlehem appliqué. Closing the Velcro fasteners, she dropped the entire set into the larger, canvas tote before she raced to Joey's room. The lamb he slept with—another bit of her sister-in-law's handiwork— was still clenched in his arms.

The serene calm on the child's face contrasted sharply with the surge of adrenaline that made Liz light-headed. Raking a hand through her hair, she pulled in a lungful of air. Surely she was dreaming.

The memory of Zack's fear-laced voice echoed in her head. "Hurry," he had warned.

Glancing again at her watch, she groaned. Twenty minutes had passed. Why was she moving so slowly when time was passing so quickly?

She shoved Joey's outfits in the bag and added his favorite storybook. It was sitting on top of a craft box filled with crayons and paper, so she threw that in, too. Zipping the bag shut en route, she raced back to the kitchen and grabbed Zack's laptop, along with the small tote she had packed for herself in case she decided to spend the night at her brother's house. Her hands shook, and she struggled to unlatch the back door, then stumbled into the adjoining rear garage where she'd parked her SUV.

A December storm had dumped four inches of snow earlier today. The weatherman promised a white Christmas for this part of Tennessee, but right now survival was her only concern. Keep the children safe.

If only she knew where to take them.

She plopped the totes and computer in the rear between the kids' car seats, grateful Zack had loaded them in her car earlier. Just in case, he'd mentioned. Had he known there might be trouble?

Why, Zack?

Why tonight?

Why this close to Christmas?

Why, when the children have already lost their mother, would you do anything this dangerously foolish?

Anger swelled within her and mixed with frustration and fear that left her gasping for air.

She shook her head. She needed to focus on getting away. From whom, she wasn't even sure.

Racing back into the house, she yanked heavy winter coats from the closet, along with fleece hats, mittens and boots that could be pulled on over the children's flannel, footy pajamas.

What else?

Lights from the tree twinkled in the living room.

She unplugged the cord and shivered in the darkness. The only illumination was a small band of light, spilling from the hallway.

Footsteps sounded on the front porch.

Her blood chilled.

She stared at the door, paralyzed with fear. Why had she delayed so long?

Two knocks.

"Lizzie?"

A voice she knew. Her inner resolve to be independent crumbled, and relief flooded over her.

She pulled open the door. Nick Fontaine stood before her, tall, muscular and even more handsome than she remembered.

In spite of her best intentions, her knees went weak, and her heart skidded to a stop.

Ten years. She hadn't seen him in all that time, yet she'd never forgotten him. How could she forget her first and only teenage love—not to mention the first boy to break her heart?

"Zack called." He pushed past her into the house, the scent of his aftershave and the cold outdoors coming with him. He closed the door, locked the dead bolt and turned to stare at her with unfairly beautiful dark eyes.

Overpowered by the bulk of him, she took a step back.

"My truck's parked on the next block," he said matter-of-factly. They weren't exactly the first words she'd expected to hear from him after ten years with no contact. But then, she should have known better than to expect anything from him ever since he'd walked out of her life the night of her high school prom.

Even after all these years, she couldn't cast off the feeling of betrayal. Going to prom with Nick had been a dream come true, and when he'd stood on her front porch and said he loved her, her heart had soared with joy. It had broken the next day, when she learned that he'd left town without even saying goodbye, never to return again.

"I don't need your help, Nick."

"Zack thinks you do."

"What do brothers know about kid sisters?"

"You're in danger, Lizzie."

She bristled, hearing the name he'd whispered between kisses the night he'd left her.

"It's Elizabeth, and I think you should go."

"Not until you and the children are in your car, headed for safety."

Why was he so determined?

She reached for the door. He didn't need her ten years ago, and she didn't need him now. End of discussion.

A car engine sounded outside. Nick stepped to the window and tugged back the curtain ever so slightly. She peered past him, and her heart froze as four men crawled from a utility van parked in front of the house.

In a blur of motion, Nick hurried her out of the living area. She pointed him to her nephew's room. "Joey's a sound sleeper. He won't wake up and be frightened seeing you like his sister might be. Make sure you bring his lamb."

Hurrying into the other room, she scooped Mary Grace from her bed and met Nick in the hallway, with Joey in his arms. Leading the way into the kitchen, Nick grabbed the pile of coats and pointed to the back door. "Garage?"

She nodded.

Leaving the warmth of the kitchen, Mary Grace blinked open sleepy eyes.

"We're going for a ride," Elizabeth reassured the child as she woke Joey and helped both of them into their coats. Once bundled up, Liz placed them in their car seats and climbed into the rear between them.

"Keys are in the ignition," she told Nick as he slipped behind the wheel.

He started the engine and glanced back at her before he hit the garage remote control. The panel door lumbered open. Shouts sounded from the side of the house.

"Dear God, protect us," Liz prayed as she covered the children's heads with her arms and pulled them close.

Nick backed the SUV out of the garage and turned onto the rear access road before he shifted into Drive and floored the accelerator. Four men with drawn weapons ran toward the car.

Elizabeth wanted to scream. Instead, she whispered words of comfort to the children and tried to shield them with her body.

A shot rang out.

"Keep the kids down," Nick warned.

The SUV screeched onto the main road. The force of acceleration threw her head against the seat. Hot tears stung her eyes, and she struggled to keep the nervousness from her voice as she soothed the children.

Nick's hands gripped the wheel so tightly his knuckles had gone white. A muscle twitched on the side of his neck. She saw him glance at her reflection in the rearview mirror and then turn his focus back to the road.

The SUV tore through the neighborhood of white lights and evergreen wreaths. An inflatable Santa Claus and Jolly Snowman nodded in passing. After a series of sharp turns, they left the subdivision and sped away into the night.

Everything had changed seemingly in the blink of an eye. An informant was dead. Zack was in danger, and she had to depend on Nick Fontaine—a man she'd never wanted to see again—in order to save her niece and nephew and herself. Elizabeth hadn't been able to trust Nick ten years ago. Why should she think she could trust him now?

TWO

Nick could barely take his eyes off Lizzie's reflection in the rearview mirror. She'd grown even more beautiful over the years, but it hadn't been her pretty face that took him by surprise earlier.

Rather it had been the look in her blue eyes that cut him to the core when she'd opened the door at Zack's house. Betrayal and abandonment flashed across her face for an instant before she'd raised her chin and glared at him with accusation.

As much as he wanted to explain what had happened ten years ago, he had to focus on the children's and Lizzie's safety first. They could delve into past issues after the danger was over.

When Zack called, he'd been on the run and worried about his family. Without a moment's hesitation, Nick had raced down the mountain to his old friend's house.

The two guys had reconnected a number of times over the years when Nick came back to Tennessee on leave, always meeting at Nick's mountain cabin, on Nick's turf. He'd never gone back to Lassiter. Never would have, if not for Zack's plea for help.

Nick couldn't say no to his old friend, especially when he'd learned Lizzie was in danger along with two adorable kids. The promise Nick had made to Lizzie's father, Judge Tate, years earlier, that he would never step foot in Lassiter again— a promise that Lizzie never knew about, made under duress— wasn't as important as keeping the three of them safe.

"Where are you taking us?" she asked from the rear.

He glanced again at her reflection. Long honey-brown hair, arched brows, full lips and crystalline eyes he'd seen too many times in his dreams.

"We're going someplace safe."

"I need to know where," she insisted, her voice raised ever so slightly.

He lowered his gaze to the little guy strapped in beside her who still clutched the stuffed lamb in his arms. Long, thick lashes drooped over his full cheeks.

Nick raised a finger to his lips. "Shhh. Someone's falling asleep."

Lizzie glanced at the boy. The strain that furrowed her brow eased, and a hint of a smile teased her lips.

"His name's Joey," she said, her voice thick with emotion.

"I seem to recall Nick telling me that big sister is named Mary."

Turning to her niece, Lizzie stroked her fingers through the child's curly hair and gave her a reassuring smile.

The little one smiled back. With her bow-shaped mouth, upturned nose, golden hair and blue eyes, she'd steal many a boy's heart when she grew up.

"My name's Mary *Grace,*" she informed him without hesitation. "Aunt Lizzie calls me Sunshine 'cause I brighten her day. I'm six years old."

Nick inwardly chuckled. Little Miss Sunshine was cute as a button. "You're so grown up. I'm sure you help your dad around the house."

"Daddy says I need to help take care of Joey, too."

"Because he's younger or because he's your brother?" Nick played along and paired his seriousness to hers.

"No." She shook her head emphatically. "'Cause he doesn't talk."

Nick threw a questioning glance at Lizzie, who remained silent.

"Joey hasn't talked since Mama died," Mary Grace explained.

Nick felt a stab of remorse at the children's pain. How could a so-called loving God allow their mother to be taken?

Nick's own dad had died some years earlier. After three deployments with the military, Nick had been up close and personal with death, but what rocked him to the core was senseless loss of life, like Zack's wife.

And Jeff.

His army buddy shouldn't have died. If only Nick hadn't—

"Aunt Lizzie, where's Baby Jesus?" Mary Grace asked, her eyes suddenly wide with concern.

"Here, honey." Lizzie unzipped the tote she'd packed for the children and removed the Nativity play set.

Mary Grace tugged on the Velcro fasteners and pulled out Mary, Joseph and the infant babe, along with a lopsided donkey and a two-humped camel. With a contented sigh, she rested her head on the back of her car seat.

Once the child was asleep, Elizabeth glanced over her shoulder at the road behind them. "Any chance we're being followed?"

Nick studied the darkness. "I've kept to the side roads and doubled back a few times. So far I haven't seen anyone on our tail."

Seemingly satisfied, Lizzie settled into the seat and glanced at Joey to ensure he was asleep, before she lifted her gaze. "I'm worried about Zack."

Nick was, as well, but he wouldn't tell her. She needed something to hold on to, something that provided hope.

"Your brother's been snooping into other people's business since before we graduated high school. He'll be okay."

She rubbed her arms and stared out the passenger-side window. "You don't understand. He's placed himself in danger too many times since Annabelle died. Sometimes I think he's running away from her death, trying to overfill his life so he doesn't have time to remember how good it was when she was alive."

Nick could relate. He'd run away from Lassiter and the townsfolk who never let him forget his father was a failure, and who seemed convinced that Nick was following in his dad's footsteps. Back then, no one believed in Nick. No one except Zack and Lizzie.

"Your brother has never worried about danger," Nick said, unwilling to dwell on his own past failures. The army had changed him, thankfully for the better.

"Maybe not, but Zack needs to be careful, especially with two young children."

She was right, of course. "Tough break to lose a spouse. Cancer, right?"

She nodded. "Thirteen months ago. Everything happened fast. Annabelle was fine one minute and gone the next."

A weight settled on Nick's shoulders. He knew too well how quickly life could change.

"But then…" Lizzie stared at him from the backseat. "I'm sure you understand about leaving without notice."

Her words were a stab to his heart. His gaze locked on hers for a long moment but then broke away. They both knew the history of their past. No reason to bring it up again. She'd moved on. So had he.

Headlights pulled his focus to the road behind them. A vehicle moving quickly. He swallowed down a rise of concern.

"We're being followed."

She glanced over her shoulder.

"Get down, Lizzie," he warned.

Slipping lower in her seat, she placed her hands protectively on the children.

"Is it a van?"

He shook his head. "I can't tell."

They crested a hill. On the far side of the ridge, he cut the lights and made a sharp turn onto a smaller two-lane that led into a warehouse parking area. Doyle Manufacturing. The largest employer in the county. Nick braked to a stop behind a tractor trailer and killed the engine.

"What are we doing?" she whispered.

"Hiding." He peered past the semi to the main road. "I want to see who's behind us."

Headlights crested the hill at a rapid speed. The vehicle came into view. A utility van.

Nick's gut tightened.

"It's them, isn't it?" Lizzie had unbuckled her seat belt and scooted forward in her seat.

Her closeness affected him. For a long moment, he closed his eyes and tried to shrug off the sensations playing havoc with his emotions. Steeling himself, he blinked his eyes open and started the engine.

"At least we know which direction they're headed," he said, hoping to reassure her.

With a sigh, Lizzie buckled her seat belt. "I don't like this, Nick."

"Everything's going to be okay." Of course, he hoped it would be, but his internal warning radar was on high alert. Something very wrong was happening in Lassiter, Tennessee.

Pulling onto the two-lane, he steered away from the main road the van had traveled. Staring into the darkness, he saw the faint outline of the mountain ahead in the distance.

The killers wouldn't follow them there, especially not on a snowy night. At least, that's what Nick hoped.

If he were a praying man, he'd ask for the Lord's protection. Regrettably, he couldn't rely on God. He couldn't rely on anyone or anything except his own instincts to keep Liz and the children safe.

He glanced back. Her head rested on the seat, and her eyes were downcast. Perhaps she was praying.

Lizzie didn't realize the pain he had endured when he'd left Lassiter. In hindsight, her father had been right years ago. Lizzie deserved better than a nineteen-year-old punk aimlessly drifting through life. Nick may have done well in the military, but she still deserved more than he could offer. When this was over, he'd remove himself from her life once again. But in the meantime, he'd do whatever it took to keep her safe.

THREE

Liz's eyes flew open when the car braked to a stop. She glanced first at Nick and then at the expansive A-frame rising up at the end of the driveway. How long had she been asleep?

Nick stepped from the car, opened the back door and leaned over Mary Grace, which put him much too close. Liz unbuckled her seat belt, needing to distance herself from the man who made her equilibrium falter.

Inwardly she chastised herself, ashamed at her own inability to stay awake earlier. Violent men were after them, yet she'd closed her eyes and drifted to sleep. What if Nick hadn't been a trusted friend of Zack's and someone suspect instead. Would she have dropped her guard then?

Nick unclasped the harness buckle on Mary Grace's car seat and, with strong, powerful arms, lifted the sleeping child into his embrace. For half a second, Liz remembered after prom when they had stood on her front porch, saying good-night, wrapped in each other's arms.

Enough nonsense. She hurriedly unlatched Joey's harness and carried the child out the door Nick held open.

"Where are we?" she asked, breathing in the cold mountain air.

Her gaze fell again over the wooden A-frame with its expansive windows and welcoming front porch. The majestic valley spanned out below them, wrapped in snow that reflected the light of the moon.

Everything was clearly visible at this elevation—the constellations, the North Star and the moon shining down like a giant lamp in the night sky.

She turned back to Nick. "Is this where you grew up?"

He nodded. "My dad's cabin."

"But—" She glanced again at the sturdy structure, so pleasing to the eye and in perfect balance with the natural setting. Years earlier, she had visited Nick's childhood home with Zack. In her mind, it would always remain a dilapidated shack, surrounded by clutter and as tired and listless as Nick's father had been.

"You must have hired a builder."

"I did the work myself, piecemeal, over the years, when I was home on leave."

"Where did you get the building supplies?" It couldn't have been in Lassiter. In all that time, she had never seen him, or even heard word of him coming to town.

"I found what I needed in Cambridge, on the other side of the mountain."

She glanced again at the fine craftsmanship of the structure, marveling at Nick's ability. "I...I didn't know you were a builder."

He laughed, the sound filling the night. "There's a lot you don't know about me, Lizzie."

It's Elizabeth now, she thought, but she failed to correct him. For some reason, Lizzie sounded right coming from Nick.

A cold wind blew, and she cuddled Joey closer. "We need to get the children inside."

Nick reached for the totes and laptop before heading toward the house. After climbing the stairs, he stamped his feet and keyed open the door.

"Watch your step." He took her elbow and helped her up the slippery stairs.

"Will they follow us here?"

"I hope not, but we still need to be cautious. Let's get the children settled and then try to uncover who your brother was meeting. That might help us determine who's after us and why. Once we get information, we can contact the authorities outside the local area. Zack told me not to trust the Lassiter police. If there are dirty cops, there's no telling how they'll manipulate our story to make it fit their own needs."

"Zack called the guy a whistleblower."

"Good to know. Our job is to find out what secrets he planned to share that got him killed."

Nick held open the door. She slipped inside, noting the massive stone fireplace on the far side of the room. The faint scent of tomatoes and green peppers hung in the air as if he'd cooked Italian hours earlier.

She glanced down at her watch. Quarter past midnight.

Nick must have driven around on back roads for some time, trying to elude the killers. He had remained vigilant while she snoozed.

Shame on her for not staying alert to protect the children, yet nothing gave her pause to worry about her own safety where Nick was concerned. Quite the opposite; she'd felt an immediate sense of relief when he'd touched her arm and guided her away from the window after they'd spotted the van parked in front of Zack's house.

She shivered inadvertently, thinking of what could have happened if Nick hadn't arrived in time. He'd left her hanging in the past, but he'd come back at the perfect moment.

To protect Zack's kids. No reason to think it had anything to do with her. And even if it did, she'd never be foolish enough to trust him with her heart again. He would keep them safe, and that was all.

"Cold?" he asked. Concern filled his gaze. "I'll turn up the heat." After adjusting the thermostat, he pointed to the overhead loft. "My bedroom's upstairs. The kids can sleep there."

She followed him along the circular stairway, marveling at the breathtaking view out the floor-to-ceiling windows. The cabin contained a mix of sleek modern furnishings interspersed with a few antiques. All quality pieces and so unlike anything she thought the former Nick would have purchased. Tonight, she saw Nick in a new light and realized she didn't know anything about the man he had become.

The only thing she didn't see, which gave her pause, was a Christmas tree or any other holiday decorations.

Upon entering his bedroom, Nick laid Mary Grace on his king-size bed and, without prompting, slipped off her coat. The child snuggled under the thick comforter and crisp sheets.

Liz settled Joey on the opposite side of the bed. Just as Nick had done, she removed the little one's jacket and pulled the covers over his shoulders, grateful both children were in their pajamas. Hopefully, they would sleep until morning.

Or until something—or someone—disrupted their slumber.

"Please, Lord, keep them safe." She pressed a kiss on first Joey's and then Mary Grace's forehead.

Nick stood at the foot of the bed. "They'll be okay for the night," he assured her.

She nodded, not wanting to give voice to her own concerns. Everything had happened too quickly. Not that many hours ago, the children had been in their own beds dreaming of Christmas.

Then Zack had called, and their peace and security had vanished like the wind that was starting to gain strength outside.

"Let's go downstairs," Nick suggested. "I'll fix coffee. Are you hungry?"

"No, but coffee sounds good." She followed him to the first floor and watched as he filled the water reservoir and basket. The rich scent of the ground beans filled the kitchen area.

While the coffee brewed, he used a remote control to lower the blinds that covered the huge windows. "They'll block out the indoor light so no one suspects we're here. Zack and I were inseparable in high school. Memories linger in small towns. Someone might make the connection."

The tightness in his voice made a chill scurry along her spine.

"I'd build a fire except smoke coming out the chimney would signal that the house is occupied."

He wasn't taking chances. The cabin was isolated, tucked high on the mountain. They were well hidden, unless someone knew where to look.

"I suggest we both take the batteries out of our cell phones."

Elizabeth bristled at the suggestion. "But what if Zack tries to call me?"

"We can activate your cell every few hours and check for incoming calls."

She glanced down at her BlackBerry. "You think someone will trace us through our phones?"

Nick nodded. "It's possible. I've got a burner phone that can't be traced. We'll use that if we need to make any calls."

"Let me try to contact Zack first." Elizabeth punched his number on speed dial.

"Don't worry," she said when the call went to voice mail. "The children and I are being well protected." Hopefully he'd know that Nick was keeping them safe.

After disconnecting, she turned off the device and removed the battery. Nick did the same to his cell and tucked his smartphone and the throwaway model in his pocket.

Grabbing binoculars off a nearby shelf, he peered through a small side window. "I can see almost the entire stretch of access road. The snow's already covered our tire tracks, which helps. Hopefully we'll spot any unwelcome visitors in time to react."

"Which means we're safe."

He nodded. "At least for now."

She stepped closer and glanced out the same window. Once again, the view of the snow-covered terrain bathed in the iridescent glow of the moon's reflection took her breath away.

"Everything looks so peaceful."

He nodded. "That's what I like about the mountain. I relax completely when I'm here."

"Are you stationed close by?"

"At Fort Rickman. A couple hours south of Atlanta."

"It's nice you could come home for Christmas."

"Actually, I'm on convalescent leave."

"What!" She startled, unable to sort through the concern tugging at her heart. "You were injured?"

"Nothing serious, but the docs thought I needed to recuperate for a month or so."

"I...I didn't know. Zack never mentioned—"

"No need," he quickly added.

"He could have at least—"

Nick touched her hand. "High school was a long time ago, Liz. I understand."

"Understand?" What was he talking about?

She was the one who didn't understand why he'd betrayed her trust.

FOUR

Nick was grateful for the buzzer that rang when the coffee was ready. Seeing the surprise written on Lizzie's face when he'd mentioned convalescent leave had him hoping she might still have feelings for him. Then he realized his mistake. The past was long gone.

He pointed her toward the kitchen. "I've got milk in the fridge, and the sugar bowl is on the counter." He pulled two mugs from the cabinet and filled them.

"Black works for me," she said, accepting the cup he offered.

He took a sip. Hopefully, the hearty brew would clear his mind. He was way too aware of Lizzie—Elizabeth. He needed to stay focused and on task. The mission came first. He understood that in combat. He needed to remember that now. He couldn't let Lizzie's nearness veer him off course.

"Let's take a look at Zack's computer." Nick ushered her toward the table in the great room.

Her eyes widened as she ran her hand over the smooth surface. "The wood's beautiful."

"Thanks. As they say, one man's junk is another man's treasure."

He smiled at her raised brow and went on to explain, "I found the table in a flea market north of here, near the Kentucky state line. Solid oak and built in the mid-1800s, but covered with layers of chipped paint. Bringing the wood back to its original beauty was a work of love."

"And the chairs?" She pointed to the set of Windsors with spindle backs sturdy enough to support even someone his size.

"Another find that required hours of labor but was worth the effort."

She scooted into one of the chairs while he opened Zack's

laptop. Sitting next to her, he pushed the power button and waited for the password request.

"Annabelle's birthday." Elizabeth provided the date.

After he punched in the digits, the screen saver came into view, showing Zack's wife, cradling an infant in her arms, no doubt Joey. Their toddler daughter stood cuddled at her side.

The depth of the family's loss tugged at Nick's heart. "Mary Grace looks just like her mother."

Elizabeth nodded. "And Joey takes after Zack."

Nick smiled. "A future investigative reporter, perhaps?"

"I hope not." The seriousness in her tone reminded Nick— as if he needed a reminder—that Zack's search for the truth had placed his life in danger.

"I'll pull up his documents."

Working quickly, Nick looked for anything that might shed light on the identity of the murdered informant or Zack's current investigation. He read through a series of files with information Zack had probably used in past blog posts. Some of them focused on the Lassiter police department and possible corruption, which wouldn't put Zack in good stead with the local authorities. Whether that played into what had happened tonight, Nick wasn't sure.

He double-clicked on a file Zack had opened yesterday. A list of names unfolded across the screen. "Recognize anyone?"

Liz leaned closer and pointed out two names. "These guys were a couple years behind me in high school. I see them around town occasionally, but I don't know them personally."

"Can you think of anything they share in common other than attending the same high school?"

She shook her head. "Unfortunately, no."

After working through the majority of the files without success, Nick stretched back in his chair and rubbed his neck. "Zack isn't making this easy."

Liz scooted away from the table and stood. "You keep searching. I'll check on the children."

Nick was relieved to have some breathing room. Being close to Lizzie required self-control. He wanted to touch her hand and feel the softness of her skin.

He chuckled inwardly. Silly for him to think she'd feel the same attraction, almost a magnetic force that was stronger than he could handle at the moment.

Everything about Lizzie was a distraction and seeing her concern for the children was even more so. She'd make a great mom and should have a houseful of kids of her own. Instead, she taught a classroom of other people's children. No doubt, she was a terrific teacher, but she needed a family, as well.

Maybe caffeine would help clear his head.

"Want some more coffee?" he called up to her as she climbed the stairs to his bedroom.

"A glass of water would be good." He heard the smile in her voice and his chest tightened, wanting to do anything to make her happy.

Her face had been washed with worry since he'd arrived at Zack's house. No wonder. Hard to look beyond the danger they were in. If they could elude the killers until Zack could hand his information over to the proper authorities, then this mission would end on a good note.

It had to end well.

Shaking off the ominous feelings that came with his thoughts, Nick dropped his cup into the sink and poured water into two glasses. He gulped half a glass and refilled it before carrying both to the table.

The local all-night television channel aired news on the hour. He hit the remote and lowered the volume. A commercial played across the screen.

Hearing Lizzie's footfalls coming down the stairs, he turned. She smiled at him, and he felt buoyed by her gaze.

"Both children are sound asleep," she said.

"They're great kids."

"The best." She glanced at the table. "Thanks for the water."

He handed her the glass. Stepping closer to take it, she glanced up. The look on her face was telling. Lizzie had stepped too close.

His heart pounded in his chest. The *thump, thump, thump* was so strong, she'd surely think a snare drum was coming from the TV.

She didn't mention his heartbeat. Instead, she focused on his lips, her eyes scorching him with their gaze.

The world faded away, and all he saw was Lizzie, even more beautiful than he remembered. More than anything, he wanted to reach for her and pull her close. Everything inside him yearned for her kiss.

She leaned in closer, almost as if she wanted the kiss as badly as he did. But then she glanced at the television, the spell of the moment broken.

Her face darkened. She gasped. Nick followed her gaze to the photograph plastered on the plasma screen.

A photo of Zack.

The newscaster's voice, although faint, could be heard in the stillness.

"Zack Tate, noted investigative reporter and author of the controversial blog *"Z" Notes,* is wanted in connection with a man found murdered in the roadside park off Phillips Road."

"No," Lizzie moaned as she walked closer to the television. Nick picked up the remote and increased the volume.

"The unidentified man was shot to death and found in the rear of the park rest stop a short time ago. A police spokesperson said evidence found at the site of the murder makes Zack Tate a person of interest. He's considered armed and dangerous, and the public is asked to use caution and call the authorities if they spot Tate."

Nick put his hand on her shoulder, offering support.

The newscast continued. "Most people know Tate from his blog. Over the years, many of the stories he's featured have been highly inflammatory toward local authorities. The police have long said Tate paints law enforcement in a less than favorable light, which has hindered their effectiveness within the community."

"No wonder the cops are upset," Nick said. "Zack exposed their duplicity."

Lizzie shuddered when Annabelle's name was mentioned.

"Tate's wife died thirteen months ago, and an unnamed source questions whether foul play could have been involved. His two young children, age six and four, are missing along with his sister, Elizabeth Tate, a teacher at Lassiter Elementary. She's also wanted for questioning."

Nick didn't like hearing Lizzie's name mentioned in connection with the murder. If law enforcement wanted to question her, she would be in added danger if the police turned a blind eye to the law.

When the newscast went to a commercial break, Nick lowered the volume and threw the remote on the couch. "Zack was right. Everyone's on the take. He's being set up to take the fall for the informant's death. They want so badly to smear his name that they're even creating suspicions about his wife's death."

"At least the police haven't apprehended him yet."

The police wouldn't find Zack if the four thugs had already grabbed him. Not that Nick would share that thought with Lizzie.

"His past blogs hit too close to home," he said. "Someone must have decided he needed to be silenced. Maybe the meeting with the whistleblower was a setup to lure Zack in. Dirty cops can't be trusted, especially if someone threatens to expose their underhanded dealings."

She rubbed her arms. "What's our plan if the killers come looking for us?"

"We'll grab the kids and then head out the back door off the kitchen. I'll park your SUV on a small path that leads higher up the side of the mountain. With the long access road, we should have time to spot an approaching vehicle and get away."

"But they'll keep following us."

"The access road dead ends here at the cabin. If they don't know about the mountain path, they'll think we left before they arrived."

"At least that's what you're hoping."

She had given voice to his own concerns. Nick glanced at his watch. They had a few hours before dawn. Hopefully they'd be secure here, at least for now.

They still needed to uncover information that could lead them to Zack, or give them leverage against the men trying to kill him. Knowledge was power, and they had to uncover the corruption that had placed him in danger and led to the taking of another man's life.

Just so the violence ended there. Nick wouldn't let anything happen to Lizzie and the children. He'd protect them with his last breath, if need be. If only they could be safe.

FIVE

Lizzie's head was still reeling from seeing Zack's picture on the news. Hoping to calm her racing pulse, she pulled back the blind and watched Nick maneuver the SUV out of the driveway and onto a path that rounded the cabin.

The night was pristine and still and devoid of anything that seemed threatening. Feeling a need to breathe in the freshness of the outdoors, she opened the front door and stepped onto the porch.

Her gaze took in the expansive mountain landscape dotted with evergreens, heavy with snow. Moonlight wove through the bare branches of the hardwoods and bathed the snow-covered walkway in light.

Something on the side of the path caught her eye. Relief swept over her, seeing the camel from Mary Grace's Nativity set. The child doted on the various figures and had played with them constantly during the holiday season as if to draw closer to the mother she missed.

Lizzie hurried down the steps and ran to where the object lay. The plump camel must have fallen to the snow when Nick carried the sleeping child inside. Bending, she picked up the stuffed animal and clutched it to her heart, finding comfort in the tiny toy. Turning back to the house, she stared for a long moment at the A-frame, once again appreciating the simple lines of the mountain lodging and Nick's expert craftsmanship.

A sharp wind cut through her clothing. Shivering in the night air, she hurried toward the porch.

A twig snapped behind her.

She stopped short and listened. All she heard was the rumble of the car engine on the far side of the house.

Snow crunched, signaling a footfall.

Run!

Liz stumbled forward, needing to get inside and lock the door. She had to protect the children.

Her heart pounded, and she gasped for air, hearing another footfall.

Cold winter air took her breath and clamped down on her lungs. Fear clogged her throat.

Someone was behind her, closing in.

Racing to the stairs, she struggled to maintain her footing. She slipped, righted herself and took the stairs two at a time.

A hand grabbed her shoulder.

Her heart burst.

"I've got you." A voice, low and menacing.

Liz's knees went weak.

Tears stung her eyes.

She had opened the door to danger and allowed the killer— or killers—access.

Liz screamed for the one man who could save her.

"Nick!"

Nick parked the SUV in the rear of the cabin, satisfied it was well hidden from sight, yet still close enough to the house for easy access. If need be, he and Lizzie could carry the children to the car and drive them away from danger before either the killers or the cops arrived.

Good police he'd welcome on the mountain, but Zack had warned about cops on the dole. If they approached the police directly, it would be too hard to determine who was good and who was bad. Better not to deal with any of them.

A voice screamed his name.

Nick's heart crashed against his chest.

Lizzie.

Racing at breakneck speed, he rounded the house and stopped short when he saw the burly mountain man. Full beard. Fur cap pulled low over his head with woolly flaps that covered his ears and tied under his chin. His left hand clasped Lizzie's upper arm. His right hand held a rifle.

"Burl?"

The old codger kept a tight hold on Lizzie's arm but turned

in surprise at the sound of Nick's voice. Recognition spread over his weatherworn face.

"That you, Nick? I thought you were still fightin' in Afghanistan."

Nick stepped closer and pointed to Lizzie. Her eyes were wide with fright, her face pale and drawn. She stared at him like a wounded animal caught in a trap.

"You need to let the lady go."

"Is she causing you any harm, Nick?"

Only to his heart, but that wasn't what the old guy meant. "She's a guest, Burl. I invited her here."

The mountain man dropped his hand and took a step back as if flustered by his evident mistake. "Sure am sorry I caused you any concern, ma'am. Nick trusts me to look after his property when he's gone. Fact is, I've been laid up with the influenza for a few weeks and couldn't make my rounds. Now that I'm better, I wanted to check the house. Thought you might be breaking in." Burl sniffed. "Can't be too careful."

Liz stared back at him. "And I...I thought you were—"

Nick climbed the steps and put his hand on her arm, hoping to reassure her. "You're safe, Lizzie. Burl didn't mean any harm."

"That's right, ma'am. I was just making sure the cabin was okay."

Nick glanced at the road that led up from the valley below. "Let's go inside. We need to talk, Burl."

"I hope you're not too upset, ma'am."

"Just startled." She let out a ragged breath. "The night seemed peaceful. I never thought—"

"It's okay, Lizzie." Nick pushed the open door wide. "How about a cup of coffee, Burl?"

"That'd be mighty nice."

Nick ushered Liz into the cabin. She rubbed her arms, no doubt appreciating the warmth that greeted her.

Burl left his rifle at the door and followed them inside.

"I'll get the coffee while you two talk," she volunteered.

"Thanks." Nick pointed to the table where the old man lowered himself into a chair, sniffed and peered down at the computer. "You're working late."

"Just checking some information."

"I'm sorry about spooking your lady friend. I didn't know you were back." He whistled. "Course, it's almost Christmas. 'Spect that's the reason."

"Sorry you had the flu."

"Don't worry, Nick. I'm still strong as an ox," Burl said with a definitive nod. He then proceeded to talk about his illness until Liz brought them all mugs of coffee.

"I've got a favor to ask," Nick said when Burl took a sip of the hot brew.

"What can I do for you, neighbor?"

"A few guys from town have been giving me a hard time. They're a mean bunch, and I don't want them hurting my…" Glancing at Liz, he smiled. "My lady friend. Wouldn't be appropriate to have them show up when she's visiting."

Burl nodded. "I hear what you're sayin'."

"They're driving a beige utility van. Might be as many as four of them. Watch yourself, Burl. They're packing and they're mean."

Burl's gaze narrowed as if he was seeing the killers in his mind's eye.

"You still have minutes on that mobile phone you bought at the Mega Mart?" Nick asked.

Burl patted his chest pocket. "Don't use it much, but it's good to have. 'Specially if I get into a pinch."

"I could use your eyes for the next couple days, Burl. If you see anyone coming up the mountain, anyone at all, but especially someone in that van I described, give me a call. I'm using that throwaway phone I told you about."

"So they can't track you?"

Nick nodded. "Exactly."

"I won't let anyone pass until I get the go-ahead from you, Nick."

"No need to let them see you. They're bad dudes. You've got both my cell number and the number for the burner phone programmed in your device?"

The old guy nodded. "Sure do."

"Let me know if I've got company coming. Even if it's not the van."

"You can count on me, Nick."

Burl slurped down the rest of his coffee in one long swig. After placing the mug on the table, he rubbed his hand over his mouth, scratched his chin and then pushed back his chair.

"Mighty fine coffee," he said to Lizzie. His gaze shifted to Nick. "Good seeing you, Nick. I'll be in touch."

"One more thing." Nick pulled up the file containing the list of names, and motioned Burl closer to the laptop. "Do you know any of these folks?"

The mountain man peered at the monitor. His lips moved as he silently read each name. "I know Everett Meeks, Sam Bellows and Hugh Garrett."

"Are they from Lassiter?"

"Those three are. Can't say about the others."

Nick pointed to the people Lizzie had recognized. "Do these names mean anything to you?"

Burl shook his head. "'Fraid not."

"I'm trying to find a common link between these folks, Burl. Anything come to mind? Do their children go to the same schools? Maybe they attend the same church or work for the same business?"

Burl rubbed his chin. "Don't know about their religious views or their kids."

"Does anything else come to mind?"

"Doyle Manufacturing."

"They work for Colin Doyle?"

"That's right."

"Any idea what type of jobs they have?"

"No clue." Burl hesitated for a long moment. "Does the list have something to do with the men in that van you're worried about?"

"I'm not sure."

"Sorry I couldn't be more help." He patted his pocket containing the cell. "I'll call you if I see anything."

"Keep this between us, Burl. If someone asks, tell them you haven't seen me."

The man glanced at Lizzie. "I haven't seen her, either."

Nick nodded. He escorted Burl to the door and watched as he grabbed his rifle and disappeared into the night. Nick needed his help, but he didn't want any harm to come to his old friend. Burl was a good man with a big heart, and Nick wouldn't have mentioned the danger except he needed someone to watch his back. Burl would do that. He'd guard the mountain road with his life.

SIX

"Can you trust Burl?" Lizzie asked when Nick stepped inside and closed the door behind him.

"Absolutely. He won't divulge our whereabouts, and he won't let anyone up the hill without notifying me." With a definite nod, Nick added, "I'd trust him with my life."

Which is exactly what Nick might have to do.

She glanced down at the tiny, handmade camel. "In that case, I'm glad I went outside, after all. He wouldn't have even known you were here, otherwise. And my little Sunshine would have been upset about losing one of her animals."

Nick nodded. "She likes Christmas?"

"What child doesn't? But the Nativity set has special meaning. Her mother made it for Mary Grace's first birthday."

"The scruffy lamb Joey won't let out of his grasp looks handmade, too. Was that a gift from his mom?"

"Annabelle finished some of the hand stitching when she was in the hospital. I'm afraid to think what would happen if he lost Lamb."

"Human nature to hold on to the memories."

Exactly as Elizabeth had done. She'd held on to the memory of Nick's kisses, believing they signaled the start of something wonderful between them. Only later—after he'd left town—had she learned he'd only taken her to prom as a favor to Zack.

She'd been a fool back then to give her heart so readily to a guy who didn't care. She was Zack's baby sister then. Nothing more. Just as now.

Averting her gaze, she glanced at the television. A News Alert flashed on the screen. She reached for the remote and turned up the volume.

"Police are seeking information about Zack Tate, last seen fleeing the crime scene. Tate had recently been in contact with

Nicholas Fontaine, a captain in the U.S. Army, currently stationed at Fort Rickman, Georgia."

Nick stepped closer to the television.

"Fontaine was wounded in Afghanistan but survived his injury due to a new tactical vest issued to military personnel in Afghanistan. We spoke to noted local psychiatrist David Wax who mentioned the high incidence of post-traumatic stress disorder in returning military personnel. Although Fontaine has not been diagnosed with PTSD, Wax said symptoms could develop at any time."

Liz turned to Nick, confused. "How did they connect you to Zack?"

"I'm not sure."

Fear came with the realization that made her shudder. "Someone got hold of Zack's cell phone and tracked the calls he made. That means he's been captured by either the police or the killers."

"Maybe, but also they could just be guessing. Lots of people in town knew Zack and I were friends in high school." Nick rubbed his forehead. "I'm more curious as to why the news mentioned the vest I was wearing that supposedly saved my life."

"Supposedly?"

He let out a frustrated breath. "I was issued the new vest, but I gave it to a buddy. He was going out on patrol. He had a wife and two kids, and the mission that night was dangerous. His unit came under attack, and my unit was called in to help rescue them."

"That's when you were hit?"

He nodded. "But I was wearing an old vest, the one Jeff should have had on."

"I don't understand. You gave him the newer, supposedly more protective model?"

"Exactly. We both came under fire. I took a hit to the chest and sustained a bruise, but the vest I wore—the older vest—stopped the bullet."

"Yet you were injured."

Nick nodded. "A second round penetrated my side where

the vest doesn't offer protection. The second hit did the damage, but the old vest protected me from a chest wound that would have been fatal."

He stared at her as if unable to go on.

"Your buddy Jeff," she said, realizing what had happened. "He didn't survive."

"The ceramic plate inserts in the new model were faulty and didn't stop the hit to his chest."

Nick rubbed his neck. "I started asking questions and found other cases when the supposedly improved vests had failed. Jeff's dad has ties with government at the national level. I told him my concerns at the funeral, hoping he'd push for an inquiry, but—"

"But what?"

"He was angry at the military and with anyone in uniform, including me. It was easier to blame Uncle Sam for his son's death, instead of Stratford and Castings, the company that produces the vests."

"Does that company make the ceramic plate inserts, as well as the vests?"

"I'm not sure. The information's not readily available." Nick raised his brow. "Did Zack mention ceramic plates?"

Liz shook her head. "Why would he?"

"I told him my concerns when I got back to the States. I thought he might have looked into it."

"If he did, he never mentioned it, but then Zack keeps a lot to himself."

Nick's expression was telling. He still carried the guilt of his friend's death. "Was Jeff's wife's reaction like his father's?" Liz asked.

"She was the exact opposite and even thanked me for trying to help her husband. Only swapping vests was a huge mistake on my part that cost Jeff his life."

And saved yours, Elizabeth wanted to add.

"You didn't fire the gun that killed him, Nick. And you didn't manufacture the vest that was supposed to protect him."

Knowing how tenacious her brother could be, she asked, "Did Zack ever mention the vests after you spoke initially?"

"No, but we've only talked a couple times since I redeployed home."

Liz shook her head with regret. If only her brother had been more forthright.

Keep Zack safe, Lord. Keep Nick safe, as well.

Once the newscast concluded, Nick turned off the television. "I'll load some supplies into your SUV in case we need to leave in a hurry. Why don't you recheck Zack's files? We may have missed something on the first go-round. Does he have a Facebook page or Twitter account? Is he on LinkedIn? Or any new social media site other than his blog?"

"Not that I know of."

"What about your parents? He might be holed up with them."

"Dad retired five years ago. He and Mom moved to Florida for sunshine and golf. Zack wouldn't drive that far, especially if the children were still in Tennessee."

Lizzie paused for a moment. "The only negative comments I've heard from Zack recently were about the Doyles. Zack could never let go of Dad's concern that Colin Doyle pulled a bit too much weight in town."

"Your father was a good judge. Mr. Doyle probably pushed for some special favors, which your dad wouldn't have allowed."

Sitting at the table, Lizzie placed her fingers on the keyboard. "While you pack the car, I'll search for information about Colin Doyle in Zack's documents."

As Nick loaded the supplies, she studied various files and then shook her head when he came back inside. "Nothing comes up. Maybe I should recheck the sites Zack opened recently."

Lizzie clicked the search history prompts and scrolled down the list of websites. "I didn't notice this before. It's a URL for a newspaper article."

Once the text appeared, she leaned closer to the monitor. "It's a short piece about Harold Doyle. Remember him?"

Nick pursed his lips. "Not sure if I do."

"Colin Doyle's nephew. He was in my high school." She glanced up at Nick. "According to the article, Harold gave a speech to the Rotary Club, in Tyler, Tennessee, on Veteran's Day."

"Wonder why they didn't invite someone with ties to the military?"

"Maybe that's why Zack saved the article. He never had anything good to say about Harold."

"A party boy and not too bright?"

"That's right. Yet he graduated from Lassiter High with honors. That got to Zack. He always suspected someone had doctored his grades. As I mentioned, Dad never had much good to say about the Doyles, which probably rubbed off on my brother. Of course even back then, Zack was always on the hunt for a story to investigate."

As much as Nick didn't want to dig up the past, he had always wondered if Judge Tate had ever revealed the truth. "Did your father question Harold's grades?"

"I don't think Dad knew, although Zack ranted enough to me. Said he felt sure someone in the school administration had been swayed because Harold was part of the Doyle family. Funny, though—"

Her brow knit as she stared up at Nick. "After you left town, Zack never mentioned Harold again."

Nick shrugged. "Your brother probably uncovered some new controversy that turned his attention away from high school."

"Maybe Zack was trying to determine why you ran away." Liz hesitated for a long moment. "Is there something I should know, Nick?"

"Of course not."

"You never told me why you left."

Ignoring her comment, Nick pointed to the kitchen door. "I still have a few more supplies out back to load into your car."

Leaving her without even a backward glance, Nick headed for the rear storage area. He kept bottled water and packets of dehydrated food along with extra blankets and sleeping bags, most of which he'd already packed in the SUV.

"Nick!" she called after him.

He couldn't turn back to her, and he couldn't tell her what happened after the prom.

You're not good enough for my daughter. The judge's words echoed in his memory. They were true then and they were true now.

Lizzie deserved someone who could provide her with a home and family and security for the future. He'd done well in the military, but he couldn't come back to Lassiter and be who she'd want him to be. He had to be true to himself first or he wouldn't be good for anyone. His father hadn't understood duty or honor or the importance of putting your life on the line for a higher cause, for freedom, for country.

Her father, Judge Tate, had seen through Nick's false bravado, and although his admonition had been difficult to accept, the judge had forced Nick out of the downward spiral he'd been living in his youth. Nick had never regretted the decision he'd made that night.

Until he and Lizzie had reunited.

Now he had to struggle with what common sense told him. He wanted to follow his heart, and his heart was focused on Lizzie. But a relationship between them would never work—something he couldn't let himself forget.

SEVEN

Hot tears stung Elizabeth's eyes when she heard the door to Nick's cabin shut with a bang. He had turned his back on her again and the questions she needed answered. Questions about why he'd professed his love and then left town without explanation.

She'd heard the emotion in his voice that night. In the years since, she'd tried to convince herself it had been nothing more than the shallow ramblings of a teenage boy being carried away in the moment. Didn't that fit with the revelation that he'd only taken her out as a favor to her brother? She'd called herself a fool for believing Nick and had tried to forget him.

In hindsight, she realized his bad-boy image may have been the attraction. She'd been young and impressionable and had seen Nick as better than his actions at the time.

He'd been drifting through life, but she'd always known he would make something of himself. She was proud of who he had become. Her only mistake had been giving him her heart.

Frustrated, she went to the window and pulled back the curtain. Heavy clouds covered the moon and darkened the night even more.

Staring into the distance, Elizabeth saw lights. On the access road. Heading toward the cabin.

Her heart stopped. She dropped the curtain and backed away from the window.

The kitchen door opened. Nick was yelling at her.

"Headlights on the mountain road. They're coming. Get the children."

Once again they raced to grab the little ones, taking the stairs two at a time. Snatching them from the bed, they hurried downstairs and snagged the tote bags, laptop and coats on their way out the back door. Joey stirred in her arms, but remained asleep.

Mary Grace peered at Liz over Nick's shoulder, her eyes wide. "Where are we going, Aunt Lizzie?"

"Someplace safe, honey. You don't need to worry."

Lizzie's heart broke.

They had to save the children, but would they escape in time?

Nick eased the SUV out of the hiding spot and headed carefully up the mountain. The path was narrow, and the dropping temperature could mean ice beneath the snow.

Over the past few hours, the wind had picked up and drifted snow that quickly covered their tracks from the cabin to the car. Perhaps someone on high was watching out for them, after all.

He glanced at Liz as she patted the children to sleep. Her faith was strong. She'd probably prayed for the Lord's help. No doubt, God had listened.

If only Nick could be sure God could ever care for someone like him. The chaplain in his unit had laid the foundation for his coming to faith, but Jeff's death had made him doubt again. Reconnecting with Lizzie had made him reconsider.

She shifted in the backseat and emitted a low groan. From the rearview mirror, he could see her staring out the passenger's-side window at the drop-off that disappeared into a dark abyss.

"Tell me you've driven up the side of this mountain before," she said, her voice tight.

"Buckle your seat belt, Lizzie. Let me worry about the road."

"Or lack thereof. It's too narrow."

"Your car has good tires, which works to our advantage. Besides, I've been traveling this path since I was a kid."

"But not in a four-door SUV."

"Trust me, Lizzie. Okay?"

She shook her head, all the while biting her lip, her eyes wide.

"We don't have far," he said, hoping to offer a bit of reassurance.

She glanced out the back window. "Are they following us?"

Nick shook his head. "More than likely, they're searching my cabin." And destroying so much of what he'd built over the years. He flicked his gaze to the front passenger's seat, relieved he'd been able to grab Zack's laptop on their way out the door.

He was also glad he wore a loaded Glock on his hip. Not that the children would notice it under his jacket, but it added another layer of protection they needed.

Snow fell faster than the wipers could clear it away. Nick gripped the steering wheel and inched the car up the steep incline. His hands cramped from the strain. Thankfully, the moon had broken through the clouds and provided enough light for him to drive without headlights, which would have given away their whereabouts.

"We're almost there," he said. If only the snow didn't get too deep or the road too slick. As if in response to his thought, the wheels shifted on the icy undercoat. He turned into the skid, relieved when the car righted its direction.

Tension tightened his shoulders, and a dull ache climbed his neck and wove along his scalp. Blink, he reminded himself as he tried to see through the pelting snow.

Every so often, he glanced down the mountain. All he could see was the black night and the white snow. A winter wonderland that would be breathtaking under different circumstances. Tonight it only compounded an already-difficult situation.

A gunshot sounded in the night. Then a second and a third.

Nick pursed his lips and gripped the wheel even more tightly.

Lizzie startled at the sound, her eyes wide. "What was that?"

"Gunfire."

"Was it Burl?"

"I don't know. I told him not to take any chances."

"From what I've seen of Burl, I doubt he backs down from danger."

Nick almost smiled. She had Burl pegged. "I'll call him when we stop. Hopefully, he'll clue us in on what happened."

Inching the car around the last bend in the road, Nick sighed with relief when he saw the entrance to the cave. The road widened and led to a level plateau. He parked and opened the driver's door.

"Let's get the children inside, out of the wind and snow. The cave maintains an even temperature. With sleeping bags and blankets, we should be fine."

She eyed the dark opening to the mountain cave. "What about bats?"

He had to smile. They were on the run with at least four killers on their tail, and Lizzie was worried about small critters that were relatively harmless. "They've never caused a problem in the past. I've seen a few of them, but there's nothing to worry about."

"I don't like bats."

"If we leave them alone, they'll do the same for us."

He unbuckled Mary Grace and lifted the sleeping child from the seat. Rounding the car, he met up with Lizzie, carrying Joey in her arms.

Nick opened the rear hatch and gathered up the sleeping bags, holding the carrying straps in his left hand. "After we get the kids settled, I'll unload the rest of the supplies and hide your car."

He handed her a Maglite and grabbed a battery-powered lantern. "Wait until we're in the cave and around the first bend in the rock before you turn on the light."

She nodded but said nothing as she reached for one of the sleeping bags.

"It'll be over soon, Lizzie."

"How can you say that, Nick?"

Because he didn't want her or the children to worry.

"I've got a feeling everything is coming to a head." Whether that meant a happy ending, he wasn't sure.

"I'll lead the way." Nick stepped into the cave, inhaling the earthy scent that reminded him of the times he'd camped out in his youth. Too often, he'd needed someplace to hole up when his dad was on a tirade. The cave had been his refuge. If only it would be for Lizzie and the children, as well.

Once inside the entrance tunnel, he flipped on the lantern and aimed the light on the ceiling. "See? No bats."

Lizzie smiled halfheartedly. "Something in our favor."

"There's a large internal chamber just ahead. We can make camp and bed down there."

The area was expansive, probably twenty feet high and just as wide. Working together, they opened the sleeping bags and nestled the children into the thick down.

"Body heat will warm them up," Nick assured her.

Joey held on to Lamb, and Lizzie tucked Mary Grace's Nativity set into the bedding beside her.

"Are you okay?" Nick asked once both little ones were settled and asleep.

"I'm okay."

"Stay with the children while I haul in the supplies." He stared into her blue eyes. "You're safe, Lizzie. They won't find us here."

At least not until the storm passes, and they think about climbing the mountain. He decided not to mention that.

Nick hustled back to the car and hauled in the other items he'd packed in case they needed the mountain refuge. Now he was glad he'd been proactive.

On the last trip into the cave, he almost chuckled, seeing how Lizzie had arranged the supplies neatly along the wall. She had even placed a couple of the sturdier boxes together to be used as seats near the light.

"I need to move the car." He pointed to another tunnel in the rock that ran in the opposite direction from the entrance. "That avenue heads to an opening on the far side of the mountain. It's a natural escape route. I'll park near the exit. If anything happens, you can take the children and head down the mountain. A dirt road turns to gravel not far below. The trail is easy to follow, even with the snow, and leads to Cambridge."

"Where you purchased your building supplies. Don't tell me you used the narrow mountain pass to get there?"

He smiled. "Usually I drove around the mountain, but the road is navigable, and the town isn't far."

"Let's go there now, Nick."

"Not before we have evidence about the corruption Zack tried to expose. Then we'll need to find out about Cambridge's police officers and whether they're in cahoots with Lassiter's dirty cops."

She rubbed her temples. "I keep forgetting we're wanted for questioning."

"That's what worries me. Before we turn ourselves in to anyone, we need more information. Knowing your brother, his investigation has to be important. If the Cambridge police are working with the Lassiter police, they could easily claim we're involved in tonight's murder. We need someone on our side, but we'll deal with that once the sun comes up. Right now, I've got to move the SUV."

"Be careful, Nick."

Raising her hand, she cupped his cheek. "Please, God, take care of Nick."

Her touch filled him with hope.

"Come back to me."

"I will, Lizzie. I promise."

He hurried into the cold darkness. The trail to the rear of the mountain was narrow but navigable. He parked the SUV near the exit to the escape tunnel, hoping the children would think all this was an adventure should they have to flee again.

If only this whole operation would have a good ending. Right now, he wasn't sure what would happen. The only thing he knew was that Lizzie and the children were in grave danger.

EIGHT

What was taking Nick so long? Lizzie looked at her watch for the umpteenth time and blinked back tears. She was tired and scared and worried about Nick. Had something happened?

The wind howled outside, and in the cave, unknown sounds—creaks and groans—made her shiver. She glanced at the ceiling high above, expecting to see bats. All she saw were dark shadows. If only the lamp would provide more light.

If Nick didn't return soon, she'd have to go looking for him, yet she couldn't leave the children unguarded.

What if he never came back?

She shook her head, refusing to dwell on anything that unsettling. Nick wouldn't leave until she and the children were safe. She was sure of that. Moving the SUV was taking longer than expected. Snow and ice and the strong winds could all play into the mix, which only made her more anxious.

She glanced again at her watch. Fifteen minutes had passed, yet it seemed like an hour. Her stomach roiled, thinking of all the things that could have happened.

A noise sounded to her right.

Footsteps came from the entrance to the cave.

She raised her hand to her mouth and bit down on her fist. The swell of fear threatened her breathing. Her heart pounded in her chest.

"N-N-Nick?" Her voice was little more than a whisper.

The lack of response made another volley of dread tangle around her spine. If Nick didn't show himself in the next few seconds, she'd wake the children and head out the rear escape. But what if the tunnel had offshoots, heading in various directions? Would she know which avenue to follow?

Oh, please, Lord.

I need Nick.

Another sound startled her. This time it came from the tunnel to her left. Her heart dropped. There were four gunmen. They must have split up. Two were approaching from the front and two from the rear.

She stepped closer to the children and stood protectively in front them. The light flickered, forming shadows where someone could hide. She reached for the lantern and hit the switch. Blackness surrounded her. She placed her hands on the children. Whatever happened, she would fight to the end to save them.

The footsteps drew closer.

Her heart lodged in her throat.

In a matter of seconds, she'd be face-to-face with the gunmen.

Where was Nick?

"Lizzie." Nick's voice broke through the darkness.

He raised the Maglite, illuminating her face. She gasped for air, as if trying to control her relief, and blinked back what looked like tears.

"I...I thought you had—"

"It's okay, honey." He opened his arms, and she ran to him. He could feel her warmth and the need she had for his protection, yet she had been strong and courageous. "Everything's okay."

"But—" She glanced over her shoulder. "I heard footsteps."

"You did?" He narrowed his gaze and squinted into the darkness. "Then we've got company."

At that instant Burl stepped into the expansive interior of the cave, carrying a flashlight of his own that he'd raised to shine on his face. He took off his hat and nodded. "Ma'am."

She expelled a huge breath. "Oh, Burl, you scared me."

"Sorry 'bout that. I came looking for Nick. Need to tell him what's happened."

"Let's talk over there so we don't wake the children." Nick pointed him to the far side of the cave where Burl lowered himself to a rock ledge and fiddled with his hat.

Nick sat nearby with Lizzie by his side. Her gaze darted back and forth to the children.

"You were right, Nick," Burl said, eyeing him. "I saw that utility van, but only two men were inside." He whistled. "Bad-looking dudes."

"Did you recognize them?"

"'Fraid not. I stayed out of view, behind the trees. They forced open the door to your cabin and got me mad as a coon dog for what they were doing to your things."

Nick nodded. "That's what I suspected would happen."

"Once I saw what they were up to, I fired a couple shots to put a little fear in their hearts."

"Did it work?"

"You bet. Those boys came out of the cabin and stared into the darkness. I fired another round and got one of them in the arm. The other guy—he must have been the ringleader—pointed to the van. Don't you know, they hightailed it out of there lickety-split. Had me slapping my leg and laughing under my breath."

"You shouldn't have taken any chances, Burl."

"Happy to do it, Nick."

"Did you hear them say anything?"

"Only that they needed to get back to Tyler."

"Tyler, Tennessee?" Lizzie asked.

"More than likely."

"You know of anything happening in Tyler that might get a man killed?" Nick asked.

Burl shook his head. "I don't have a clue about anything that happens in the valley. Ask me about the mountain, and it's a different story."

Nick chuckled. "You're a wise man."

"Most say I'm a fool." He slapped his hat against his leg and stood. "Just wanted you to know what happened."

He smiled at Lizzie, then glanced at the children. "Mighty fine-lookin' kids, ma'am."

"My niece and nephew," she said. "The men are after their father. We need to keep the children safe."

"Of course you do. And you will."

Burl checked his watch. "Almost daybreak. I need to head back to my place." He peered at Nick. "Doubt those guys will return, at least not until nightfall."

Nick stuck out his hand. "Appreciate your help."

Burl accepted the handshake and added a smile.

"I'll get a few hours' sleep, and then be back on duty." He waved his hand as he headed out of the cave. "You can count on me."

Lizzie turned to Nick. "Burl's a different kind of guy."

"To say the least, but he's got our back, and that's what we both need."

Glancing at the sleeping children, he added, "There's a third sleeping bag. Close your eyes and get some rest. I'll wake you if anything happens."

"What about you?"

"I'll keep watch."

"Burl didn't think anything would happen until later."

"We can't be sure, and I won't take any chances."

"I can sleep with Joey. You take the other sleeping bag."

He held up his hand, palm out. "I'm fine. Besides, I want to go back out there to ensure our tracks are covered with snow."

Noticing the strained look on her face, he stepped closer and took her hand. "Get some sleep, Lizzie. We don't know what will happen when morning comes."

"But I'm worried about you and your health. The wound to your side must have been serious or you wouldn't be on medical leave."

"I'm healing. At least that's what the doctors tell me."

"Then humor me and take it easy for a change."

"When you and the children are safe, that's when I'll be able to relax."

He didn't stay to listen to her argue. Instead, he walked toward the entrance of the cave, needing fresh air to clear his mind and get him back on track.

After his mission to keep her safe ended, then he'd be able to think of other things. Other things like how badly he wanted to kiss Lizzie.

NINE

As the rising sun cast a pink glow across the horizon, Nick raised binoculars to his eyes and studied the surrounding terrain. The snow had stopped falling, and a surreal stillness had settled over the mountain.

He breathed in the cold morning air, appreciating the beams of sunlight that brightened the day and his mood. Last night, he'd anticipated trouble. This morning, he felt upbeat and encouraged. Maybe they'd eluded the killers, after all.

Nick checked his watch—7:00 a.m. Over the past few hours, he'd thought about Jeff and what had happened in Afghanistan. Needing closure, he pulled out his cell, inserted the battery and found the number in his phone log—a number he never thought he would call again. He tapped in the digits and waited for Mr. Santori to answer.

"It's Captain Nick Fontaine, sir. Jeff's friend. We were together in Afghanistan. I hope I didn't wake you."

"Not at all. I'm an early riser. I'm glad you called, Nick. I need to apologize."

"How's that, sir?"

"For the way I treated you. I was grieving and not thinking straight at the funeral, which I hope you can understand. Jeff was my only child. He…" Mr. Santori's voice faltered. "He was my life."

"Jeff was an outstanding solider and a great friend, sir."

"And the best son a man could have. I miss him, and for that reason, I struck out at the army, and I'm afraid you got my wrath, as well. I talked to Jeff's wife. She helped me see the truth."

"The truth, sir?"

"That you only wanted to protect Jeff. You traded your own

vest, the new model, for his older one, never realizing the new vest was substandard."

For a second, Nick didn't know how to reply. How could the man be so forgiving? Nick's intent back on that awful night didn't matter—what mattered was that his actions were the reason Jeff hadn't been protected. Uncomfortable with the direction the conversation had taken, Nick tried to turn it to the reason why he'd called.

"I believe the problem was with the ceramic plate inserts, sir. Some of them failed. The vests were made by Stratford and Castings."

"They're an East Coast company?"

"Yes, sir. Their main plant is outside Baltimore. With your connections, I hoped you'd be able to determine if they made the ceramic plate inserts, as well, sir."

Mr. Santori hesitated, and when he spoke again his voice was thick with emotion. "Jeff was a hero. He died protecting our country."

"You're right, sir. Your son was a hero. Focus on that, and forget anything that brings pain."

"The pain comes from knowing our soldiers are fighting with vests that don't offer enough protection. I'll contact a friend in Congress and pass on what you told me."

"Thank you, Mr. Santori."

"Please accept my apology. Men like you are few and far between, Nick. You chose to sacrifice your own well-being for my son's safety. I will be forever grateful."

"I was just doing my job. I wish I could have done more."

Mr. Santori's involvement might bring the substandard vests with the faulty plates to the attention of the powers that be. Hopefully, before more soldiers were injured.

He was pleased with Mr. Santori's promise to help, but still bewildered by the rest of the call. Did he really believe that Nick had done the right thing, even though the results had been so unexpectedly tragic? Others had tried to reassure Nick—his commanding officer, the men in his unit, even Jeff's wife—but he hadn't wanted to listen. Mr. Santori's anger at the funeral had only bolstered his opinion that he was to blame for making the wrong choice.

He didn't know what to do with Mr. Santori's apology, or his explanation that his words had come from his grief rather than a genuine belief of wrongdoing on Nick's part. He could definitely relate to the anger and pain Jeff's dad had described. Nick had felt them himself at losing his friend. Had he allowed his own self-chastisement to get out of hand, to build into a weight of guilt he wasn't meant to carry?

Mr. Santori had forgiven him. Was it possible for Nick to forgive himself?

Lizzie woke to find Nick gone. She crawled from the sleeping bag, careful not to wake Joey. The coolness of the cave and the cloying scent of the musky earth surrounded her. Wanting to ensure Nick was okay, she headed to the entrance and blinked at the bright sunlight as she stepped into the clearing outside.

The beauty of the new-fallen snow and the sparse landscape of pines and jagged rock greeted her. No wonder Nick loved the mountain.

"Lizzie."

At the sound of his voice, relief swept over her.

"You're up early," he said from a rock perch to her right.

"And from the looks of the rolled-up sleeping bag, you didn't rest at all."

"I've been checking the valley." He held up the binoculars in his hand. "Everything looks calm this morning. They'll probably wait until nightfall before they return."

"But you expect them to come back?"

"I'm sure they're still looking for whatever it was they wanted to find. Now that it's daylight, let's check Zack's files again. We should have a few hours of battery life left on his laptop."

"The children will sleep for a bit longer. They'll be hungry when they wake."

"I've got a small camp stove we can light. There's enough draft in the cave and it's large enough that we don't have to worry about fumes. I'll boil water for coffee and make something hot for the children. Instant oatmeal sound okay?"

"Perfect."

After a quick glance at the valley, he lowered the binoculars and hopped down from his perch. "Let's head inside."

He put his arm on her back, and together they walked into the cave where, good to his word, he quickly prepared instant coffee that provided warmth. Adding sugar and dried creamer made it more than palatable.

The oatmeal filled a hole in her stomach, although it did little to ease the nervous anxiety she felt each time she thought of Zack. Did he have food and shelter and something warm to wrap his hands around?

"Oh, please, God," she whispered, surprised when Nick looked up.

"I know you're worried." His gaze was filled with concern.

She nodded. "I was thinking about Zack."

"I tried to call him this morning but didn't get a response."

"Do they have him?" she asked, almost afraid to hear Nick's answer.

"He's okay."

"How can you be sure?"

"I know Zack."

"You knew him years ago, before he lost his wife and became so reckless, despite his two children, who should make him be more cautious."

"Zack was born to be an investigator, Lizzie. His work gives meaning to his life."

"His children should come first," she insisted.

"And they do, but he has a job to do. For me, that's the military. For him, it's exposing corruption and righting wrongs."

"You mentioned the military." She pulled in a ragged breath. "Aren't you afraid when you go into combat?"

"Of course I worry about what could happen. Everyone does. Anyone who says otherwise isn't being truthful. My mission is to defend my country. To fight for what's right, for freedom, for truth. I wouldn't be able to look myself in the eye if I didn't do my job."

Nick was telling her that he lived with danger and always would. Was this the way life would be if she were with Nick? Always afraid? Always looking over her shoulder?

Lizzie shook her head ever so slightly. Why was she even thinking about a future with Nick? He'd just told her how important the military was to him. He had a job to do that didn't include her. Was that why he'd left her behind all those years ago—because he'd known that he wanted to go serve his country, and that that would mean letting her go so his mission could come first?

Mary Grace stirred. Her eyes blinked open, and concern momentarily clouded her face. She dug her hand into the sleeping bag, pulled her Nativity set free of the bedding and smiled at Lizzie.

"Morning, Sunshine. We're having a campout and a special breakfast." Lizzie kept her voice light. "How about something warm to eat?"

"My tummy's hungry."

"I'm sure it is. Get up quietly so you don't wake Joey."

Mary Grace climbed from the sleeping bag and gave Liz a hug. "When will Daddy come to get us?"

"Soon, honey. I hope very, very soon."

If only Zack would think of the children and stop placing himself in danger.

She glanced at Nick. He wouldn't change, either, and she could never ask him to be anything other than the brave man he was. Nick was good and strong and determined to make a difference.

She had to stop blaming him for hurting her in the past. He'd chosen a path that didn't include her, but it was a noble and honorable path. She shouldn't blame him for choosing it over her. As soon as the danger had ended, he'd return to Fort Rickman and the military. Future deployments and assignments around the world would take him far from Lassiter and far from Lizzie. That was the reality she needed to accept. No matter how much she wished their reunion could grow into a relationship, her time with Nick would be short-lived.

She needed to steel her heart. Nick Fontaine would walk out of her life again.

TEN

Nick enjoyed watching Mary Grace eat breakfast. She followed the oatmeal with dried fruit and laughed when it stuck to her teeth.

"I need to brush," she said after swallowing the last bit of dried banana.

"My mistake," Nick said with a chuckle. "I forgot to include toothbrushes or toothpaste in with the supplies."

"Daddy says I need to set a good example for Joey."

As if hearing his name, the little guy opened his eyes. He looked as confused as Mary Grace had been when she'd first awakened.

Lizzie moved closer and smiled down at him. "Morning, Joey. We're camping out—it's an adventure! Would you like some breakfast?"

He nodded his head, sat up and smiled at Nick.

"Hey, Sport. Did you sleep well?"

Again the nod. He stretched his arms above his head and then reached for Lamb, still buried within the sleeping bag.

"I set up a makeshift latrine at the end of the escape tunnel and hung a tarp for privacy," Nick explained. "There's a basin, bottled water and soap for washing up, if you want to take the children."

Liz herded them into the tunnel, taking the totes with their outfits. Once they returned with clean faces and hands and dressed for the day, Nick helped Joey with his breakfast.

After eating, the children sat with their legs crossed on the thick down sleeping bags and played with their handmade toys. Mary Grace handed her brother the stuffed figure of Joseph and plopped Mary onto the back of the hand-stitched donkey.

"Let's pretend we're going to Bethlehem, Joey. I'll ride and you walk Joseph next to the donkey."

The two children hopped their figures over the sleeping bags and stopped at the stablelike carrier.

"Knock on the door of the inn and see if there's room for us to spend the night," big sister instructed her brother.

Joey pretended to knock and then shook his head. His wide-eyed, innocent expression revealed how totally immersed he was in the playacting. Even without talking, he seemed to have a childlike comprehension of what had happened more than two thousand years earlier.

"The innkeeper said we can stay in the stable," Mary Grace announced, always the spokesperson.

"Some people believe the stables of old could have been caves," Lizzie mentioned. Both children accepted the comment and glanced around the stone walls of their own makeshift lodging.

"Maybe just like this cave," Mary Grace said with awe in her voice.

Joey nodded and pulled Lamb closer to his heart.

"Aunt Lizzie, can we ask Baby Jesus to bring Daddy here so he can play with us?"

"Of course, honey, but he has a job to do, so maybe we should ask Jesus to bring him here when his work is done. Besides, I don't think we'll stay in the cave much longer."

The little girl pondered Elizabeth's comment before adding, "Tomorrow's Christmas. Let's ask that Daddy can come back to us—wherever we are—in time for Christmas."

She reached out her hand to her aunt, who grasped it in her own and then, in turn, Lizzie stretched her other hand toward Nick.

He didn't understand.

"We hold hands when we pray," she explained. "I thought you might want to join us."

"Sure." He stepped closer and took her hand, enjoying the feel of her soft skin and long, delicate fingers. "Praying is a good idea."

"Sunshine, why don't you lead us?" Lizzie said.

Joey placed the lamb on his lap and then took Nick's and his sister's hands.

"Jesus," Mary Grace began, her eyes closed tight. "Joey and I want Daddy to be with us for Christmas. Tell him to hurry. Thank You for loving Daddy and for loving us, too."

Joey nodded.

"And Aunt Lizzie and Nick. Thank You for letting Aunt Lizzie have someone grown-up to help her. We love You, Jesus."

"Amen," they all concluded, except Joey, who nodded.

Nick continued to check the mountain road throughout the day. The children alternated between playing with their handmade toys and creating Christmas decorations with construction paper and art supplies Lizzie had packed in the tote. By midmorning, paper chains decorated the cave, along with cutout Christmas trees and wreaths. Nick took a turn with the scissors while Lizzie made peanut butter sandwiches for lunch.

Later in the afternoon, Nick turned on the battery-operated radio he had packed with the supplies and adjusted the volume. "Time for the hourly news. Let's see if the police are revealing any new information."

"More snow is forecast later today," the announcer said, "with temperatures dipping below freezing tonight."

"Daddy wanted a white Christmas," Mary Grace announced. "Mama loved snow. He said we can look at the snow and remember how happy it always made her."

"Your dad's right," Nick said, all too aware of the huskiness in his voice.

His own mother hadn't been interested in her son's well-being. Instead, she'd run off with a drifter who'd promised her whatever she wanted to hear. No telling where he had dumped her and where she could be now. If only God had listened to his childhood prayers to protect his mom.

If only God would listen to Mary Grace and Joey's prayer for their dad.

Nick glanced at Lizzie, who sat near the children and played with the cloth toys, surrounded by the cutout Christmas decorations. She was trying to be strong for the children, but he could tell that Lizzie was worried about her brother.

So was Nick.

Even more than that, he was worried about a utility van, and whether he could keep three special people in his life alive if the men returned to the mountain.

Even as Lizzie played with the children, her attention was on the radio. Inwardly, she was wound so tight she thought she might explode, yet she had to be strong for the children.

"The police are still on the lookout for Zack Tate in connection with the killing of a Tyler man identified as William Arnold, a father of two. Mrs. Arnold says her husband planned to meet investigative reporter Tate in a late-night rendezvous. She admitted he seemed worried."

Nick turned to Lizzie. "Do you know the victim?"

She shook her head. "The only person I know from Tyler is the school librarian I work with."

"Call her."

"She's probably heard the news report by now."

"Tell her the truth. You're not involved, and you're worried about your brother. Find out what she knows about William Arnold."

Lizzie pulled out her cell and inserted the battery. She found the woman's number once the cell activated.

"Helen, it's Elizabeth Tate."

"Where are you? Have you seen the news? Your brother, Zack—"

"I know. That's why I'm calling. I'm trying to figure out what's going on. I haven't seen Zack all night. Do you know anything about William Arnold, the man who died?"

Silence filled the line.

"Helen, I need your help."

"I know he has a wife and children who won't have a father this Christmas."

Elizabeth nodded, feeling a sense of loss for the family, but also knowing she had to learn more about the victim. "Where did he work? Was he involved with law enforcement? Could he have gotten into debt or had his house foreclosed on? There must be something that was wrong, Helen. You've got to tell me what you know."

Elizabeth looked at Nick and shook her head.

"I only know that he needed money," Helen finally admitted. "You're right about his house. It was in foreclosure. The bank had given them a few months grace period, but they have to move out by the first of the year."

"So money was an issue?"

"I think they just got behind. He worked for a local company that was bought out a few months ago. The new owners brought in their own middle-management people. William was able to keep working, but he took a sizable pay cut and was put back on the production line."

"What's the company?"

"Barringer Products. I think BP partnered with a larger company that has something to do with government contracts."

Lizzie pulled the phone closer to her ear. "Do you know the name of the other company?"

"I don't have a clue. Everyone's been fairly closedmouthed about the takeover. Some people made out very well in the sale."

"You mean folks who formerly owned BP?"

"That's right. The CEO was ready to retire so the sale was timed perfectly for him."

"Who bought the company?"

"I don't know."

"Could you find out? My brother mentioned a whistle-blower, which means there was something suspect going on."

"If the police question me, I'll have to tell them the truth."

"I wouldn't want you to lie."

"I'll make a few phone calls."

"Hurry, Helen. I'm afraid time is running out."

ELEVEN

Nick booted up Zack's laptop and checked the battery power options to gauge how long they had to review the files. Once again he searched Zack's documents, but found nothing about Barringer Products.

Unable to make sense of the smattering of information on the laptop, Nick left the computer on a rock ledge and turned to Lizzie. "Could there be any other place that Zack stored his files?"

"He liked to keep everything at his fingertips and on his laptop. I'm surprised he didn't take it with him last night."

"Maybe he knew there might be trouble."

"If so, he shouldn't have gone." Lizzie glanced at the children, still playing with the toys their mother had made.

Nick motioned to her. She raised her brow.

He scooted back against an edge of rock that blocked his view of the children and secluded them as Lizzie stepped closer.

The worry on her face eased, and she smiled, sending a barrage of emotion rolling over him. Even after all this time holed up in a dank cave, she looked fresh and bright. He took her hand and pulled her close, thinking only of her eyes that burned into him and her mouth that opened ever so slightly. He couldn't take his gaze off her.

"I called you over to reassure you, but I'm not thinking of that now."

She leaned closer. "What are you thinking about?"

"How my sprits lift when I'm with you. You make me optimistic and ready to conquer whatever faces us. We can do it, Lizzie. We can track down the corruption Zack was trying to uncover that will lead us to your brother."

"I told Zack that I didn't need your help, but I was wrong.

I didn't know where to go or what to do." She glanced around the corner at the children. "I don't want to think about what could have happened."

"But it didn't." He pulled her closer, keeping his gaze on her face, on her smooth skin, on her lips. This wasn't the time or the place, but he couldn't help himself. He needed to hold her in his arms.

He wrapped his hands around her and pulled her into his embrace. She stared up at him with a coy smile that made him think only of Lizzie.

This was crazy—he knew he shouldn't do this, knew she deserved better than him. But the longer he spent around her, the harder it was to resist the urge to hold her. Warmth spread through him, and he held her tight, rubbing his arms over her back and her shoulders, surprised by the feelings that exploded within him. How could he bear to walk away again from Lizzie when she was all he'd ever wanted? He started to lower his mouth to hers.

The trill of her phone interrupted their almost kiss.

She pulled back and shook her head. "Bad timing." Reaching for her cell, she noted the name. "It's Helen."

"What did you find out?" she asked as soon as the call connected.

The seriousness of Lizzie's expression worried Nick.

"You're sure?" Lizzie paused for a long moment. "Thanks, Helen."

She disconnected and gazed up at Nick. "Guess who bought BP?"

Nick shook his head. "No clue."

"Doyle Manufacturing."

"So what's the Tyler plant doing that caused one of their workers to contact Zack?" He glanced down at the laptop. "There's got to be more information. Tell me what Zack said when he called you."

"He said the killers would probably come to his house and for me to get the children to safety and to take his laptop."

"Anything else? Tell me everything."

"He said to be sure to take Mary Grace's Nativity set and

Joey's lamb. To pack some outfits, their underwear and to get out of the house."

The children started to squabble. Lizzie sighed and hurried toward them. "What's the problem?"

Mary Grace crossed her arms over her chest as she pouted. "Joey won't share his lamb."

The little guy hugged his stuffed animal and shook his head.

"You each have your special toys, Sunshine. You're being so nice to let Joey play with your set, but you know how much he loves Lamb."

"But Lamb's sick. He needs to go to the doctor."

Lizzie tried to hide her smile. "Why do you think he's sick?"

Joey clutched the toy tighter and glared at his sister.

"Lamb has a tumor. I felt it. Just like mommy had."

"A tumor?"

"Daddy said mommy's sickness started with a lump inside her. It turned into a tumor. That's what made her sick."

"Oh, honey." Lizzie wrapped her arms around Mary Grace.

Tears clouded the little girl's eyes. "Daddy said not even Santa can bring Mama back. Why can't he, Aunt Lizzie?"

"Your mama's in heaven with Jesus."

"Baby Jesus?"

She nodded. "That's right."

"Doesn't she want to be with us?"

"Of course she does, Sunshine, but her time on earth ended. She still loves you and Joey more than anything. She'll always love you, but instead of being on earth, she's in heaven."

Mary Grace wiped her eyes on her sleeve and sniffed. "Daddy said I have to be strong."

Lizzie rubbed her hand over the child's back. "You are brave, honey."

Nick moved closer and pulled Joey into his arms. "Does Lamb have a boo-boo, Sport?"

The little guy fingered the lamb's stomach near the seam in the stitching. He looked up with big eyes at Nick as if wanting him to help.

"I've had some medical training from the military," Nick said, playing along. "Want me to check it out?"

Joey nodded.

Nick felt the hard interior. "Feels like something's in there, Sport. I'll take it out so Lamb can feel better. You hold on to him, okay? I'll use my pocketknife and just pull a couple stitches loose."

Nick opened the stitching ever so slightly and wiggled the hard *lump* out of Lamb's stomach. "We'll let Aunt Lizzie sew that opening closed when we get back to your house. Okay?"

The little guy nodded again.

"At least now your lamb feels better, and Aunt Lizzie and I have something to look at." Nick held up the flash drive he'd removed from the lamb.

Her eyes widened.

"Shall we slip this into your brother's laptop?"

Lizzie rummaged in the box of supplies and pulled out two small boxes of raisins. "Children, have a snack while Nick and I look at Daddy's computer."

Nick seated the flash drive in the USB port and hit the prompts to pull up the documents.

"Voilà," he said when the file list appeared.

He found Barringer Products and opened the file.

What he read surprised him even more, but before he could tell Lizzie, the burner phone trilled.

Glancing down, his gut tightened. Burl's name flashed on the call screen.

Raising the phone to his ear, he knew what Burl would say before he heard his voice. "Did you see them?"

"Four this time. In the van. They're moving fast up the mountain, although the snow and slick conditions will slow them down. You want me to blow out a tire or two?"

"I want you to use caution and stay out of sight. Thanks for the warning."

Nick ripped the flash drive from the port and handed it to Lizzie. "Put this someplace safe. It has all the information and explains what Zack was investigating."

"Which was what?"

"No time. That was Burl who called. The killers are on the way up the mountain. Get the children. You need to escape out the rear tunnel and head down the hill to Cambridge. Remember Jean Simpson?"

"She taught English and drama when we were in high school."

"That's right. She lives on Main Street, in the heart of the downtown area. Follow the mountain road into town. Pass the square and the big church on the next corner. Jean's house will be the third bungalow on the left after that second intersection. Tell her what happened and give her the flash drive. She'll know who to contact. Now that we have evidence law enforcement will have no choice but to listen."

"Do we have to leave again?" Mary Grace grumbled.

"I told you we wouldn't stay here long. Get your Nativity Set and pull on your boots. Joey, you, too."

Lizzie helped the children, her hands trembling.

Trying not to let them see her nervousness, she quickly ushered them into the tunnel. Nick picked up Joey and carried him, while Mary Grace ran next to Lizzie.

The escape passage was narrow and dark, but the Maglite provide ample illumination.

"Tell Jean everything," Nick advised. "Don't hold anything back. I trust her."

"I can't go alone. You've got to come with us, Nick."

He shook his head "Not this time. I want to stop these guys once and for all."

"But there're four of them and only one of you."

"I'll hold them off so you and the children can get a head start down the mountain."

They pushed through the narrow opening at the end of the tunnel and stepped outside, inhaling the crisp mountain air.

"Hurry," Nick warned.

Once the children were buckled into their car seats, Lizzie held out the keys to Nick. "You drive. I'll sit in the back."

He grabbed her hand and shook his head. "I'm not going. You can do this. Tell Jean I sent you. Make sure the flash drive gets to someone in law enforcement, someone who's not on the take."

She shook her head. "I'm not going."

"Lizzie, please."

"Not unless you go with us, Nick."

He hesitated for half a heartbeat then steeled himself to say what he needed to say to make her leave. "It was nearly time for us to go our separate ways, anyway. Be realistic. We didn't have anything that would keep us together in the past, and nothing will now, either. It was nice reconnecting, but we're not meant for anything long-term. I'm returning to Fort Rickman in a few days. You'll return to teaching."

"But—"

"No buts. You've got to save the children."

She heard Nick, but she didn't want to believe him. Except the harshness in his voice made her realize he was being totally honest.

How foolish to think Nick cared for her. He was only interested in the army and returning to Fort Rickman.

After climbing behind the wheel, she started the engine, wanting more than anything to run back to his arms and beg him to change his mind. But she had to shove those thoughts aside, even though the pain of never being in his arms again was almost too great to endure.

Lord, help me. She eased the SUV onto the path and started down the hill. When she finally glanced back, Nick was gone from sight.

Tears burned her eyes, and she blinked to keep them from blurring her vision. Twilight had settled on the mountain, and the path was slick. She had to get the children to safety.

When would this nightmare be over? Nick said Jean Simpson could be trusted, but Lizzie wasn't sure who to trust anymore. Like a fool and for a second time, she'd wanted to give her heart to Nick, but he wasn't interested.

Glancing back, her stomach dropped. The top of the mountain was obscured from view. What she had with Nick was over.

Forever.

She flicked her gaze to the children in their car seats. She had Mary Grace and Joey. They were all that mattered right now.

Getting them to safety.

Keeping them safe.
Please, Lord, let me do exactly that.

Nick's heart broke as he watched the SUV disappear down the mountain. He'd seen the pain on Lizzie's face when he told her they didn't have a future together. He hadn't lied, but that didn't mean he wanted the words to be true. More than anything, he wanted to spend the rest of his life with her. But she deserved someone better, just as her father had told him years ago. No matter how much Nick wished things could be different.

He hurried through the cave and climbed to the perch he'd found this morning on the rocks. He'd lie in wait for the four gunmen to defend the mountain and buy time for Lizzie and the children.

Would he be able to stop the killers?

Only God knew the outcome. Nick could use someone else on his side. He raised his eyes to the darkening sky.

Lord, I could use Your help. Cover me and get Lizzie and the children to safety.

TWELVE

The lights in town were bright as Lizzie drove along the snow-covered street and followed the directions Nick had given her. She passed City Hall and the big church on the next corner all lit up for Christmas, but when she pulled in front of the house Nick had indicated, it sat dark and abandoned-looking.

Unwilling to reveal her discouragement to the children, she drove farther down the block and spotted a small church on the right. People were flocking there, and twinkling lights glowed from the large tree outside. The windows of the church were inviting with their warmth, and she knew she would find help inside.

Taking a chance, she parked the car and asked a lady on the sidewalk if she knew Jean Simpson.

The woman pointed to the side door of the church. "Jean's in the education center."

Peering through the car window at Mary Grace and Joey, the woman smiled. "I just dropped off my children so they'd have time to get into their costumes. I'm going home to pick up my husband. We'll come back for the service and the Christmas Eve program."

"Program?" Lizzie asked.

"The live Nativity. Jean's in charge. She'll tell you where your little ones need to go."

Lizzie unbuckled the children and headed inside where she was directed to the teacher she vaguely remembered, now in her late sixties, but trim and fit and with a welcoming smile when the threesome approached her.

"Nick Fontaine said you could help us." Liz quickly explained what had happened, glad that no one was around to overhear.

"You must be cold and hungry."

Lizzie shook her head. "We're okay. Nick took care of us."

"Of course he would."

Lizzie knit her brow. "What do you mean?"

Jean took her hand. "He's a good man."

Nodding, Liz blinked back another volley of tears that threatened to reveal her true feelings.

The older woman's gaze was filled with compassion. Turning to the children, she pointed them toward a table filled with plates of baked goods. "Get a cookie while I talk to your aunt."

The little ones hurried to the table and eyed the assortment before making their selection.

"I don't want to be presumptuous," Jean said, her attention once again on Elizabeth and her voice low so the children couldn't hear. "But it seems you care deeply about Nick."

Painful as it was to admit the truth, Liz nodded.

"He's always loved you—you must have known that—ever since high school."

Lizzie shook her head. "But he left town without a word to me."

"Because your father told him to make something of his life and had him promise to never return to Lassiter. Your dad was thinking of your future when he said Nick wasn't good enough for you. With Nick's family history, the truth in your father's words hit him hard."

Lizzie's ears rang. Surely she wasn't hearing Jean correctly. "Nick promised we'd always be together, that he loved me."

Jean nodded. "And he did love you. Probably still does. Your brother broke into Lassiter High School that night to uncover grades that had been altered."

Suddenly, Liz understood. "Harold Doyle."

"Exactly. Zack was right about the administration doctoring grades, which is the reason I retired early. But he tripped an alarm, and the police arrived on-site that night. Nick has always been the type of guy who would do anything for a friend. Zack was on scholarship to college. He and Annabelle planned to marry. Nick knew your brother's future would be ruined if he was arrested, so he made sure Zack escaped, which delayed Nick. The police apprehended him leaving campus."

"Nick sacrificed himself just as he's doing right now for me." She looked at the children. "For us."

Lizzie held up the flash drive. "I've got the information Zack uncovered that needs to get in the right hands. Lassiter police are on the take."

"You can trust Cambridge law enforcement. In fact, the chief of police is here helping out."

"My first concern is keeping the children safe."

Jean nodded knowingly. "Sometimes hiding in plain sight is the best option." She motioned for the children. When they drew close, she stooped down to Mary Grace's level. "The girl who was supposed to play Mary is sick, and I don't have a replacement."

The child's eyes lit up. "That's who I am when Joey and I play with the Nativity set my mother made."

"Then you'll be perfect for the part."

"What about my brother?" Mary Grace pointed to Joey. "He doesn't talk."

Jean's smile was bittersweet. "But he has a lamb. He'll make a wonderful shepherd."

She gestured to a man in police uniform, who quickly approached. "Anything I can do to help, honey?"

Jean blushed as she introduced Lizzie to Chief Todd Carter and then pointed to a corner alcove. "You two can talk there while I find costumes for the children."

Moving into the private area, Lizzie dropped the flash drive into the chief's hand and quickly explained what had happened.

He listened attentively, nodded a few times and, when she was finished, he raised his cell to his ear. "Tracy, notify the deputies to meet me at the foot of the mountain ASAP."

Lizzie thanked him, then hurried back to where the retired teacher was digging through a box of costumes. "Thank you so much, Jean."

Lizzie hugged the children. "Stay with Ms. Simpson. I'll get Nick, and we'll be back in time to see you perform."

"Are you sure?" Mary Grace asked.

Lizzie smiled and traced a mark on her chest. "Cross my heart."

Satisfied, Mary Grace turned to Jean. "Can we get into our costumes now?"

Racing outside, Lizzie glanced at the mountain where Nick was fighting for his life. Now she understood why Nick had left town. Her dad knew he needed a shove in the right direction. If only he hadn't added the comment about Nick not being good enough. He was exactly who she wanted, who she had always loved. If only Lizzie could get to Nick in time.

THIRTEEN

Lizzie drove past the Cambridge police amassing at the foot of the mountain, knowing she couldn't wait for the captain to arrive. She had to help Nick. Accelerating up the mountain, she felt her heart stop when she crested the peak. Two men lay in the snow and two more shoved Nick toward the utility van parked in the clearing.

Blood stained his jacket, and he favored one side.

Anger swelled within her. She wouldn't let anyone harm the man she loved.

Seeing her approach, one of the two remaining gunmen stepped into the clearing and raised his weapon.

She floored the accelerator. The tires spun on the ice before taking hold.

The man jumped out of the path of the SUV, but not in time. The side bumper caught his leg and sent him flying. His head hit a boulder, and he collapsed in a heap. His weapon sailed through the air.

Lizzie jumped from the car and ran to where his gun landed and disappeared into the snow.

She dug frantically in the icy drift. She had to find the weapon. Sirens sounded in the distance, but all she could think about was saving Nick.

Nick had never expected to see Lizzie again. Telling her they weren't meant for each other had been the hardest thing he'd ever done, next to the night he'd left Lassiter for good.

Now she had come back to him.

Only she shouldn't be here. He wanted her safe and protected and not in the middle of a gunfight.

He'd fought for his life to give Lizzie and the children time to escape. He'd taken down two of the thugs and then had been wounded again in the side, where he'd been hit in Afghanistan.

Sirens filled the night. Help was on the way, but would it arrive in time?

The last man standing raised his weapon. Nick's heart dropped, seeing the gun aimed at Lizzie as she knelt in the snow.

'No," he screamed. He lunged, grabbed the guy's arm and struggled for possession of the firearm.

The thug slammed his other fist into Nick's side. Air rushed from his lungs. His grip on the gun eased ever so slightly.

The guy jerked free. He staggered backward, holding the weapon.

Nick started to rise.

The killer aimed at Nick. His finger tightened on the trigger.

Lizzie screamed.

Sirens drew closer.

A shot sounded.

The gunman clutched his heart and fell to the snow.

Nick looked at Lizzie. She appeared as surprised as he was.

A noise caused them to turn. Burl stepped from behind a boulder. "Looks like I got here just in time."

In the next second, everything broke loose. Four police sedans pulled to a stop in the clearing. Lights flashed. Cambridge officers sprang from their cars, weapons drawn.

Lizzie was crying and running toward Nick. "You're hurt."

"I'm okay," he reassured her, opening his arms and reaching for her. Her tears wet his neck, and his blood stained her jacket, but they were together, and that's all that mattered.

"I love you," he said, pulling her close.

"Oh, Nick, I've always loved you."

EMTs bandaged Nick's wound and said he was lucky. Just a few inches more and the bullet would have done serious damage.

Burl stayed around long enough to talk to the police and apologize to Nick for taking a while to get up the mountain.

"Your timing was perfect," Nick said with a wide smile.

He held Lizzie's hand after the EMTs finished bandaging his side and cleaned the blood from their clothing.

"Check out the warehouse in Tyler that Doyle Manufacturing bought a few months back," Nick told Chief Carter. "I have a feeling you'll uncover information that will lead you to Zack Tate. You'll also find a stockpile of faulty ceramic plates. Harold Doyle took over the warehouse operation and used the substandard plates to prove to his uncle that he could save money for Doyle Manufacturing."

Shaking his head in frustration, Nick continued. "Or maybe Harold pocketed the profits for himself. Either way, BP had planned to destroy the plates before they sold the company, but somehow that detail got overlooked. Harold shipped the faulty plates to Stratford and Casting, claiming they were the improved inserts for the new tactical vests that went to our active duty forces."

He glanced at Lizzie. "Soldiers in Afghanistan were issued the less-than-effective vests, like the one I received when I was there. The one I gave to my friend Jeff."

As the police worked the crime scene, Nick and Lizzie said goodbye to the chief and headed back to town. They had a performance to watch.

After parking in front of the church, they hurried inside, just in time to see Mary Grace walk up the aisle, carrying a doll baby that represented the Infant Jesus. She took her place at the front of the church, where shepherds, including Joey still clutching Lamb, stood to welcome the Newborn King.

Jean waved from the sidelines when she saw Nick and Lizzie, then gently prodded a little boy dressed as a camel to where he needed to stand near the makeshift stable.

Once the children were in place, the pastor, a big man with a resounding voice, read scripture from Luke's gospel.

"While they were there, the days of her confinement were completed. She gave birth to her firstborn son and wrapped him in swaddling clothes and laid him in a manger."

On cue, Mary Grace placed the doll in a small wooden cradle filled with straw. Lizzie smiled and nestled closer to Nick's uninjured side.

Wrapping his arm around her shoulder, he listened attentively to the Christmas story and accepted as truth the coming of the Christ Child. As if he'd been given a new birth like the Infant Babe, Nick's heart fully opened to the Lord's love.

He offered a prayer of thanks for Zack. The chief had called on their way into town. Tyler law enforcement had found Zack bound and gagged, but alive and unharmed, in the warehouse. Knowing his old friend had been rescued, Nick could finally relax. With Lizzie in his arms and the children safe, Nick had everything he'd ever wanted.

FOURTEEN

Chief Carter asked Nick and Elizabeth to remain in town until the dirty cops in Lassiter could be rounded up. Jean invited them to spend the night at her house, and the next morning, the children woke early and hurried down the stairs. Lizzie and Nick were drinking coffee in the dining room.

"I told Joey that Santa wouldn't know where to take our toys." Mary Grace peered under the tree, disappointment evident on her face.

"You never know about Santa," Nick said with a smile. "Didn't you ask him to bring your dad back?"

"Not Santa, Nick. We prayed to the Baby Jesus."

"My mistake."

A knock sounded at the door. Nick crossed into the living room and opened it to find Santa, looking surprisingly like the Cambridge chief of police, dressed in the traditional red suit and beard.

"Ho, ho, ho," Santa said with a wink. "I hear Mary Grace and Joey spent the night at Ms. Jean's house with you and their aunt."

"That's right, Santa." Nick held the door for the jolly man to enter.

"I've also heard that they're very good children."

"They're always good," Lizzie assured Santa.

"That's why Santa brought presents." He lowered a large bag filled with toys to the floor. "But I've got something even more special."

Zack stepped into the house. Mary Grace squealed and ran into her father's arms. "Daddy!"

Joey stood for a long moment and watched from across the room.

"Sport, don't you want to give your dad a hug?" Nick worried the little boy had been through too much.

Zack waited, giving Joey time.

Wide-eyed, the little guy handed Lamb to Nick for safekeeping, then opening his arms, he ran to his father.

"Daddy," Joey squealed.

Tears ran down Lizzie's cheeks. Nick took her arm and gently ushered her back into the dining room to give the children and Zack time to reconnect.

"That's the first time Joey's spoken since Annabelle died." Dabbing her eyes, she peered around the corner into the living room. Joey was chatting as if he needed to catch up on all the things he hadn't said in the past thirteen months.

Reassured by the family reunion, Liz turned her attention back to Nick. "We wouldn't have this happy Christmas morning if it weren't for you. You put it all together, Nick, and told the police where to look to find Zack."

"All the pieces were on the flash drive. The chief said Harold is under arrest, and Colin Doyle is being questioned to see if he knew what was going on. They're also weeding out the dirty cops."

"I suppose you're going back to Fort Rickman after Christmas."

"I've got extra leave. I thought I'd stick around for a while longer."

"That would be nice."

"I'm glad you think so." He drew her close, his eyes twinkling. "I don't have a gift, but there's something I want to give you."

He pulled a small heart cut from red construction paper out of his pocket.

She smiled. "You made it when you were playing with the children."

Nick nodded, throwing her a lopsided grin. "It's my heart, Lizzie. You've always had it."

Her eyes filled again, this time with tears of joy. "I asked God this Christmas to free me from the past. But it found me—

You found me, Nick. I'm not sure if you realized that when you left, you took my heart with you."

He pointed to the ceiling. "Do you see what I see?"

Lizzie followed his gaze to the beam above them and the clump of mistletoe that hung from a bright red ribbon.

"You know what that means?" he teased, his eyes playful.

"I'm not sure."

"It means I'll have to kiss you. At least once, maybe twice, probably three time to make sure."

"Make sure what?"

"That you know I love you."

"Hmm." She smiled. "You might have to kiss me more than three times to ensure I get the message."

"Whatever you say, ma'am. Like any good army guy, I aim to please."

Then his smile ended, and his lips lowered to hers. Lizzie lost count of his kisses, but she didn't tell him to stop. She'd never tell him to stop because she'd been waiting her entire life for this Christmas filled with love.

* * * * *

SPECIAL OPS CHRISTMAS

SUSAN SLEEMAN

A man's heart plans his way,
but the Lord directs his steps.
—*Proverbs* 16:9

Dedication

To Paul and Cailin, for believing.

Acknowledgments

Paul, you never question this calling or me disappearing into my office for hours…even over Christmas break. You support me and, believe me, I know I'm blessed. I love you.

Cailin, you gave up time with Mommy over Christmas break, and you never asked why. But you did discover you and your daddy have a love for Australian TV shows, and that's pretty cool. Thanks, Boogie Ma Shoo Shoo… I love you.

Glenda Cook, when I say there's a new book, you say, "How long before I get to read it?" There are great English teachers in the world and then, above all of those, there's you. Thank you.

Dad, you gave me everything money can't buy, and those are the best things. And Mom, you never fail to be there when I need you.

Emily and Elizabeth, you are amazing editors. I love what you have to say and I love the way you think! Thanks for letting me be a part of this team!

Sandra, I'll never stop saying thanks for giving me a chance. And for brainstorming with me when I get stuck. Now that's when it gets fun.

Dawn Lucowitz, Kimberly Buckner, Donna Moore, Christina Nelson, Lesley Cooper, Laura Ott, Laura Harris, Heather Edge, Shalawn Avery, my FCA family, my Culbreth family…and the list goes on… Thanks. For praying, for cheering, for reading, for promoting, for listening and for loving.

ONE

Captain Travis Chapman readily served wherever his country needed him. All Green Berets did.

But this?

"I realize this operation is a bit unusual." Colonel David Waters grabbed a marker and approached the whiteboard in the small Fort Bragg briefing room.

Unusual? Try earthshaking.

Travis tugged at his collar and swallowed down the unease threatening to bring up his breakfast. He had to find a way out of this assignment. For once, he didn't care what the team needed. This was personal. He'd do anything else. Go anywhere other than the Army Research Institute in Orlando.

Getting quickly and quietly behind enemy lines and creating insurgencies. *That* he knew and thrived on—it was how he lived and operated day to day. But working with Claire at the institute? With the woman who'd left him feeling as if a grenade had exploded in his chest, his heart still a torn mess two years later?

Not that.

He shifted in his chair and watched Waters ink Combat Action and Tactics Simulator on the board in bold red strokes. He turned, his dark brows thick as caterpillars drawn together, his perpetual scowl fixed on his broad face. "As I mentioned, your familiarity with CATS makes you the ideal candidate for this Op."

CATS. Claire's pet project to develop a lower-cost alternative to the army's current simulated training program. Travis had spent weeks by her side working out kinks in it. Discussing enhancements for the prototype. Getting to know her and...

Not going there again.

"Is there a problem with this assignment, Captain?" Waters's penetrating gaze raked over Travis.

Travis sat up straighter and dug his nails into his palms, the pain biting into his skin and keeping him on task. "No, sir, but with all due respect, are you sure this Op is appropriate for our team?"

The crease between Waters's brows deepened and his eyes remained riveted on Travis. "Didn't mention the team. Just you and your qualifications. You know the facility and CATS."

And Claire.

Even now, with Waters watching him intently, Travis could get lost in thoughts of her. The smell of her perfume with a hint of lavender in direct contrast to her down-to-earth personality almost lingered in the air. He could see her sparkling eyes behind designer glasses and wondered for the thousandth time what would've happened if she hadn't rejected him.

Waters shifted on the balls of his feet, his impatience written on his face. "Is there something you need to tell me, Captain?"

I once believed in a forever kind of love and, thanks to Claire, now I don't. Yeah right. Like he'd tell Waters that.

"No sir. I just need the Op details so I can catch my flight." He opened the briefing folder. "So are they looking for me to participate in the final testing and give the simulator a Green Beret seal of approval?"

"Negative. It's more involved than that. One of the prototypes and the equipment specs were stolen from the institute last night. Primary investigations by project director Claire Reed points to an inside job, though I must say she's having a hard time believing anyone on her team could do this."

At Waters's first mention of Claire's name, Travis's brain snapped to full attention. "Why an inside job?"

Waters raised his index finger. "First, few people outside the staff would know the value of Reed's breakthrough. She's taken a technology that has cost us billions of dollars and made it affordable, which means if it was available on the black market, even small guerilla groups would have the money to turn our own training against us."

Travis shuddered at the thought of the many insurgent groups he'd trained over the years as he imagined similar groups whose values opposed America's using the U.S. Army's exacting standards to train an unlimited number of soldiers.

"Exactly," Waters said, clearly picking up on Travis's thoughts. He rested on the edge of the table and lifted another finger. "Second, the only sign of the theft—other than the missing equipment—was a problem with the internal cameras. They were either disabled or malfunctioned last night around 2300 hours for about an hour, but the institute's external security wasn't breached."

Sounded like an inside job to Travis, too, but it didn't explain why his skills were needed. His deployments usually took him to sub-Saharan Africa in covert operations, not hunting down a thief in the United States. "Won't local investigators handle this breach?"

"No, this requires covert skills to keep the investigation under wraps. Plus, in addition to locating the thief, you'll provide protection for Reed."

"Claire needs protection?" The words shot out of Travis's mouth before he could filter them.

Waters eyed him for a long moment before replying. "Yes. We believe she's at risk for abduction and we need to put our strongest man in place to keep her out of the enemy's hands."

Questions swirled in Travis's brain, mixing with concern for Claire. "I don't understand. If the thief got what he was after, why would she be in danger?"

Waters's jaw firmed and his eyes narrowed. Travis knew his commanding officer well enough to know he wasn't going to like the next words out of the colonel's mouth. Travis braced himself for additional bad news.

"Because of the simulator's value, the project team opted to keep certain details out of the written specifications," Waters said, pausing to flex the muscles in his jaw. "That way, if the technology ever fell into the wrong hands, the prototype would be useless without this additional information. Of course, the data is on file at a secured location, but other than that, Reed is the only person who possesses the information. Security makes stealing the written documentation impossible so—"

"The only way the thief can deploy the prototype is by obtaining the specs from Claire," Travis finished as a sense of foreboding settled over him. "Which means if this really is an inside job then the thief knows she alone holds the key and will likely force her to share it."

"Hence her need for protection."

Travis knew all about obtaining information from noncompliant subjects, and he couldn't abide the thought of Claire in this situation.

And maybe being killed once she provided the information.

The room closed in on him. Feeling as if he were strangling, he dug at the knot on his tie. He wanted to help Claire, really he did, but could he let go of his personal feelings long enough to achieve this goal on his own? "Seems to me deploying the entire company would be more effective than sending one guy."

Waters shook his head hard, the steely resolve he was known for darkening his eyes. "A team of twelve would alert the institute staff to the problem. No one knows about the theft but Reed and her superiors at the institute. We want to keep it that way so we don't send the thief into hiding or force him to act immediately on abducting Reed. You'll go in under the guise of testing the latest equipment so you can stay close to Reed and quietly investigate the theft."

Stay close to Reed. Close to Claire. A distraction that could threaten his performance.

"You can handle this alone, Chapman." Waters crossed his arms and leaned back, his shoulders remaining in a hard line proving he didn't intend to back down. "You've gathered intelligence on enemies before and have plenty of experience in capturing high-value targets. Simply consider this thief high-value and you'll succeed. After your initial assessment of the situation, I'll entertain requests for deploying additional support as long as you keep in mind that this operation remains on the Q.T. until I say otherwise."

Fine. Travis got it. A covert mission it would be. Him and

Claire alone. The last thing he wanted, but he'd do it. And do it well. "You can count on me, sir."

"We always do," Waters said, then dismissed Travis.

In the hallway, Travis glanced at his watch. He had just enough time to check a handgun out of the armory then take a quick flight from North Carolina to Orlando. He'd be at Claire's side in time for lunch. That gave him a mere three hours to work through residual issues with Claire and get his head in the game. Failure to do so could put her right in the enemy's hands and cost Claire her life.

Claire Reed's dream had been stolen. Right here, in the dark of night in her home away from home. She glanced at the sign on the tall building. Bold black letters mounted on stucco painted a cheery yellow read: Army Research Institute.

Her sanctuary. Until this morning when she'd discovered the theft.

She settled her foot on a concrete planter filled with poinsettias and gently stretched the tight muscles in her leg. Christmas music pelted from the outdoor speaker belying the seventy-degree temperatures.

"'Tis the season to be jolly, fa la la la la, la la la la."

Jolly, hah!

Nothing about her day had been jolly.

She switched legs and put her weight into the stretch until stiff muscles eased and she was ready to run. Hoping her usual lunchtime jog would put her in a better frame of mind to lead her team, she pounded down the sidewalk. Her bad mood blotted out Orlando's ever-present sunshine and the four-foot-tall sandhill cranes strutting across the road. She usually enjoyed the birds' antics on her daily run through the Central Florida Research Park, but today she only cared about eliminating her frustration with the army's response to last night's theft.

"Sit tight," they'd said. "Don't tell anyone about it, and we'll get someone in place to help as soon as possible."

Sit tight, my eye. Not when someone had stolen one of her prototypes and the specs for the device, putting six years of work in jeopardy.

She groaned at the typical military response. Usually she was grateful to have such a prestigious job at thirty-one, and she loved working with this dedicated group of men and women. But today reminded her of the hassles of working for the military, such as the way the brass rarely told her what she needed to know until they believed she needed to know it. Aggravating to say the least.

Hoping to exhaust herself, she picked up her pace beyond her normal routine and plunged into a secluded parking area with taller trees blocking the sun.

Good. The darkness matched her mood and her disappointment.

How many man-hours had she put into the helmet-mounted display and software to provide a fully immersive virtual training system? A system that simulated a variety of environments a foot soldier might face. Mountains, trees, deserts. All with the hope of saving lives with realistic training that was now endangered if the army didn't act fast and recover the prototype.

Her project killed before it even had a chance to live.

Angry, she rounded a corner and pushed herself until she neared the end of the loop and her lungs screamed for oxygen. She'd soon be back at the institute and her thoughts were still a jumbled mess. She couldn't face her staff this unsettled or they'd ask questions so she ran in place to finish working through her turmoil.

As she stared over a small pond, a hand came out of nowhere and clamped over her mouth. An arm snaked around her chest, pulling her back against a rock-solid wall of muscle. Winded, she barely had the strength to breathe let alone fight, but instincts kicked in and she jabbed an elbow to the man's gut.

No response. Nothing. He didn't even grunt.

She stomped on his foot and elbowed him again.

He tightened his grip, clamping her arm against her body and dragging her backward. She dug her heels in the thick St. Augustine grass trying to gain purchase and slow their progress.

No change.

Her heart thumped an irregular beat as panic skittered up her spine.

The man picked up his pace, moving quickly down the slope toward the pond.

Alligators. No, no, no! Not this, her mind screamed as he drew her closer to the water. Step after step, the sour, organic smell alerted her to the pond's nearness.

Fear twisted in her stomach.

How could she have let this happen?

She'd screwed up. Let her thoughts of the theft distract her and she'd failed to follow basic Self-defense 101. Prevention.

After her former boyfriend Travis had learned she jogged alone, he'd taught her skills to stay safe. To know the area. Know her exact location and listen for anyone approaching. Know her escape routes. But she'd failed.

Travis. What would he tell her to do?

Her captor skirted around the pond sending a moment of relief surging through her before panic claimed her mind again, tangling her thoughts into a twisted mound of spaghetti.

Do something. Think, Claire, think!

Drop your weight, Travis had said. *Bring the creep down so you can elbow his head.*

She fell forward and jutted both elbows upward. He was strong, crazy strong, and he jerked her upright then continued moving. She dug in her heels again, tried to slow him down, but her efforts didn't faze him.

They neared a deserted parking lot where she caught sight of a white cargo van. The side door sat open like a waiting prison cell.

No. Oh, no.

If he wrestled her into the van, she might never come out. But how did she stop him?

Travis had shared a last-ditch tactic with her. It'd be painful and might knock her out, but she had nothing to lose.

Nothing.

She flopped as far forward as possible and with her remaining strength threw herself back, ramming her head into his face. Her skull connected with his jaw and her glasses flew from her face. Pain sliced up the back of her head.

He grunted, but kept moving.

No.

She slammed him again. Saw stars. Felt black tingeing at the edges of her vision, already blurred without her glasses.

God, no. Please no. Not this. Please, she prayed. *Give me strength.*

One more try. *One more.* She had to succeed in freeing herself.

She dipped forward and roared back. Her head connected as she stomped his foot and elbowed him at the same time. The perfect trifecta, making his arm slacken. With a burst of adrenaline, she spun free and bolted toward the road.

Without her glasses, the trees ahead swam before her eyes, but she dug deep and raced on. She couldn't hear his footfalls behind her, but she sensed him chasing her. He was big with powerful, long legs and was likely gaining on her. She resisted the urge to look back.

Pain razored up her legs as her lungs screamed for air. She felt like crumpling onto the thickly matted grass, but somehow she kept going.

Down an incline. Up the other side. Along a pond. Her foot sinking into wet muck. Falling.

His hand clamping her ankle like a vise.

She screamed and jerked free as she grabbed the thick grass to gain her footing. She righted herself and kicked out with every ounce of energy, connecting with his shoulder and leaving him prone. She charged up the incline.

"Help," she screamed, then decided to save her breath for running.

She ran harder.

Closer and closer to the road. Closer to help. To the faint hint of traffic sounding in the distance.

You can make it. You can make it, her mind chanted with every step until she believed it.

She ran every day. She was fast. She could outrun him and flag down help before he caught her. She really could.

She had to. She was racing for her life.

TWO

Travis turned the corner to the institute and spotted an ambulance and three police cars blocking the entrance flanked with tall palm trees. He couldn't see far enough ahead to ascertain the problem, but his gut said Claire was in trouble.

He offered a quick prayer on her behalf and pulled to the side of the road. Slapping on his beret, he got out and jogged down the street, the intense Orlando humidity hitting him in the face.

A burly male police officer manning a barricade near the entrance flipped up a beefy hand and pulled back his shoulders straining the seams on his uniform. "No one goes in."

Travis swallowed down his anxiety and forced out a smile. "Can't you make an exception? I'm late for an appointment."

"Like I said, man. No one goes in."

The urge to ignore his command and push on had Travis taking a step, but he couldn't help Claire if he was arrested. "My CO will have my hide if I don't make my meeting. You know what happens when you fail to complete orders, right? Couldn't you ask whoever's in charge if I can slip through?"

The cop waffled for a moment then nodded. "Wait here."

After he moved out of view, Travis jumped the barricade. He rounded the ambulance with lights twisting into the bright sunshine and stuttered to a stop as he sought to make sense of what he was seeing.

Claire sat on the sidewalk, her head lowered. She was dressed in running gear, with most of her ponytail ripped free, leaving honey-blond strands jutting out like porcupine quills. Raw, ugly sores marred her knees, and she rubbed her hands over her arms as if trying to rid herself from something horrible. Perhaps she heard his approach because she suddenly looked up.

Emotions flashed around them as bright as a detonated charge in the black of a desert night while the nearby chaos faded into the background. Travis knew seeing her again would be hard. But this? Seeing her wounded and afraid was gut-wrenching. He heard the vague sound of footsteps behind him—the cop coming to haul him away—and somehow, he got his feet moving toward Claire again.

"Hello, Claire," he said, making sure to keep a level tone when a vise clamped down on his gut.

She squinted at him, her gaze sharpening. "Just when I thought the day couldn't get any more difficult, they send you."

Under normal circumstances, he knew she wouldn't say such a thing. She wasn't mean, far from it, but shock pulled her uncensored feelings to the surface.

And the words lacerated him, proving she could still inflict serious pain. The only woman in his thirty-three years on this earth who could do such damage.

"Do you want me to haul him away?" the cop asked.

Travis braced himself for Claire's affirmative response, but she shook her head.

"Suit yourself." The cop's footsteps receded, but Travis wasn't alone with Claire for long.

A woman dressed in the institute's civilian uniform of khakis and polo shirt came to stand behind Claire. Travis blocked out the twenty-something woman and squatted in front of Claire.

"She was attacked," the other woman said, obviously reading his questioning expression.

"Attacked? How? Where?" he asked, barely able to stop himself from sweeping the only woman he'd ever loved into his arms.

"On her run," the woman answered. "She got away and managed to crawl back here."

Claire gestured at the woman. "Meet my assistant researcher and roommate, Julie Dickson."

"And you are?" Julie's narrow-eyed gaze ran over Travis.

"This is Captain Travis Chapman." Claire's cool and disapproving tone felt like a bucket of ice water.

"Travis?" Julie's eyebrows shot up. "He's the… Oh, no! Oh… This isn't good, is it?"

Claire looked up at her assistant, a smile lighting on her face. "Would you mind going inside and telling the team I'm okay so they don't worry?"

"Sure." Julie bit her lip for a moment. "I mean if you're sure you want me to leave you alone with…him."

"Go. I'm fine." As Julie departed, Claire ran a finger up the bridge of her nose, likely trying to push up glasses that had fallen off in the attack. The gesture was classic Claire when she was stressed or uneasy. Despite her claim that she was fine, she obviously needed comfort. Comfort she'd once have sought from him. He scooted closer. Her eyes flared with interest for a moment before she forced it away.

Interesting. She wasn't as immune to him as the day she'd claimed her job was her one true love.

Right. That day. The day she rejected his proposal. They'd devoted nearly every waking hour to CATS, but once his part of the work was done, he'd known he'd return to base in North Carolina and his heart had rebelled at the thought of leaving Claire behind. He'd been ready to make a real commitment, to build a future with her…but he should've seen the rejection coming. All that mattered to her was honoring her father. After his death in a military chopper crash, she wanted to make his dreams of a better training system for soldiers come true, and that meant her job came first. Always.

She started picking at grass clinging to her socks, but she was so disheveled it made little difference. "I assume you're here about the theft?"

"That and to serve as your protection detail, though it looks like I'm a bit late." Without thinking, he lifted his hand to move a stray strand of hair from her eyes, but she cringed.

Got it. Message received loud and clear. Nothing's changed between us and keep my big mitts off.

"Your protection isn't necessary. It was just a crime of opportunity. The guy saw a woman running alone in an isolated location and tried to take advantage of the situation." She gestured at the surrounding commotion. "I'm sure with all the cops swarming around here my attacker won't be back."

"So you think this was a onetime thing and doesn't have anything to do with the theft, then?"

She nodded but stopped when a flash of pain darkened her face. Pain he'd do anything within his power to take away.

"Tell me what happened," he encouraged softly.

She took in a breath. Blew it out. Pulled in another before starting to speak. "It was simple really. I was running. A man came up from behind and tried to drag me to a van. I remembered your self-defense moves. Had to go all the way to the head butt, but I got away." She ended with a wry smile, easing the tense lines around her mouth for a moment.

"If your attacker was trying to abduct you," he said, "we need to assume that it was the thief after the information only you possess."

She looked him dead in the eye for the first time, her expression unreadable. "You think they've already figured out the prototype doesn't work and they want to get the missing specs from me?"

He nodded. "And that's why I'll be with you 24/7 until the thief is apprehended."

"No!" She shook her head hard, not even stopping when pain pinched her eyes tighter. "Not happening. So not happening."

He refused to let her words sting. He was here to do a job and that meant tuning out the personal and getting the job done. He'd protect her no matter her wishes.

Still, it would be easier if he gained her cooperation. "Making a snap decision isn't like you, Claire. Use that wonderful analytical brain God gave you. Set aside your emotions and weigh every aspect."

Her chestnut eyes met his and emotions raced through them so fast he couldn't tell what she was thinking.

"Okay, fine," she said grudgingly. "You're right. Protection is probably a good idea, but the police can provide it."

Despite his frustration, he had to smile at her answer. He'd encouraged her to problem solve and she had. She just wouldn't accept the most logical solution.

"I can do a better job than the police." He didn't even try to sound modest. "Besides, my CO has assigned me to your detail. You may be a civilian but you work for the army. So, short of leaving your job, you have no choice in the matter."

"Not so fast. I'm sure your CO will entertain an alternative." She turned away and cupped her hands around her mouth. "Detective Purcell," she called out. "Can I have a word with you?"

A string bean of a man wearing a rumpled suit and holding a typical police-issue notepad headed their way.

Travis eyed her, looking for her motives, but coming up empty. "I don't know what you're up to, Claire, but the theft is still on a need-to-know basis and this cop doesn't need to know about it."

"Relax."

Right. How can I relax when the woman I once loved was mauled and barely escaped? When her attacker is likely to return?

When Purcell stood looking down on Claire, she gestured at Travis. "My associate thinks this may not be a random attack and that I need protection."

"Not random, huh?" Purcell shifted his focus to Travis. "Care to share your reasoning?"

Phrasing his words to keep from giving away confidential information, Travis replied, "She works on a top secret project worth millions, and someone might want to abduct her to gain access to it."

"Do you have any evidence suggesting a concrete connection?" Purcell asked.

"No, but my gut says she's still in danger."

"Can your department provide a detail?" Claire asked, hope ringing through her tone.

Purcell frowned. "Without a direct threat we don't have the manpower for a detail."

Travis looked pointedly at Claire.

She held his gaze for a moment, her mouth set in a grim line.

"Then welcome to Orlando, Travis," she said with unmistakable belligerence in her voice. "I'll accept your help, but that doesn't mean I like it."

THREE

Claire stood at the head of the table while her team discussed a testing schedule for Travis. For the first time in the past hour, his dark eyes weren't locked on her. She scrunched her eyes closed, hoping when she opened them he'd be gone. But he was there. In her conference room. Being charming. Handsome. Captivating. Everything she remembered him to be and more—and everything she couldn't have.

Which is why she'd been so rude to him outside and why she needed to keep her distance until she could figure out how to spend time with him and not open her heart again. That meant ending this meeting and sending him to the testing room. While he ran through several CATS simulations, she'd gain time to process his arrival and, as a bonus, she'd cement his cover story with her staff.

She clapped her hands. "Okay, people, let's get back to work. Be sure to make Captain Chapman feel at home."

He came to his feet, his body radiating power and demanding attention, but he immediately disarmed her staff with a smile, much the same way he'd once disarmed her.

"Please." He directed a pointed look at Claire. "Captain Chapman is a mouthful. Call me Travis."

An intern posed a question, and Claire adjusted her spare pair of glasses to watch Travis answer. He held his shoulders back, accenting his flawless posture and the perfect fit of his dress uniform. Even after hours of travel and waiting while she'd showered and changed, plus sitting through this staff meeting, the navy fabric was still crisp and neat with perfect seams. He wore his hair longer than standard army regulations as a shorn haircut could give him away on his covert missions. Sandy-brown strands held just enough curl that once upon a time she hadn't been able to keep her fingers out of them.

Julie approached him and his smile widened, one corner crookedly tipping higher. Claire remembered a similar smile when they'd first met. A smile that had made her feel as if she were the only person in the room.

Enough. An hour with the guy and you're back where you were two years ago.

She'd worked too hard to get over him, and she needed to remember he wasn't here because she'd suddenly decided their relationship was a good idea. He was here to make sure the thief didn't obtain the missing information and to recover the prototype.

She crossed the room and ignored Julie's questioning gaze. As Claire's roommate, Julie knew about Travis, but Claire hadn't met Julie until after the breakup so she'd never heard the full story.

Claire forced herself to look at Travis. "Since your dress blues are constricting, I'm assuming you'll want to change for testing."

He nodded and Claire turned to Julie. "Would you show Captain Chapman to the locker room and then set up the testing gear?"

That's it. All business. Stay polite yet firm and you'll be okay.

"Sure," Julie said pleasantly. "Follow me." She set off for the door, but Travis didn't budge.

Instead, he leaned close and looked at her through solemn black eyes. A look she knew was the closest he would ever come to acknowledging she'd somehow hurt him. "Call me Captain Chapman instead of Travis one more time and there will be consequences," he informed her in a no-nonsense tone.

"I thought it best to keep things formal between us."

He met her gaze and held it, the hurt already fading. "Try all you want, sweetheart, but calling me *captain* isn't going to make our history go away."

She opened her mouth to argue, but there was nothing she could say. Plus, her team would question why she addressed him so formally after his request to be called Travis.

"Fine. Travis it is." She jerked her head at the door. "Julie's waiting for you."

His serious expression gave way to a smile. "I know the testing's a ruse, but I'm actually looking forward to seeing how our plans came to life."

She didn't bother denying his claim to the project. His feedback and ideas had helped make CATS a supreme training tool and despite the drama between them now, she was thankful for his input. "Then your assignment won't be such a burden for you."

An eyebrow went up and he looked as fierce as the virtual enemies she'd created for CATS. "Don't forget you're going to try to solicit alibis for last night from your team while I test CATS."

"You really do believe the theft is an inside job, don't you?"

"Yes, and I'll keep on believing it until we prove someone broke in here." He took a few steps then turned back. "You never pull any punches, Claire. So try to be subtle in your questioning."

She planted her hands on her hips. "I can do subtle."

"I've never seen it, but then we pretty much went straight to kissing and there's nothing subtle about that." He chuckled and strode away.

Ugh! She fisted her hands, but Julie continued to study her intently so she forced herself to relax.

She needed to develop better acting skills fast, or she wouldn't make it through Travis's visit without having to share painful memories with Julie. More importantly, the skills would keep Travis from discovering that even though she'd ended things with him—and continued to believe she'd made the right decision—he still had the ability to make her head spin.

After he departed, she set about her daily routine, all the while trying to figure out a way to deal with the feelings Travis had raised. As her workday came to a close, she still hadn't come up with a way to be around him without all the turmoil. She'd simply have to beat her feelings into submission while doing her best to focus on finding the thief.

Remember that, she warned herself as she stepped into the large testing room. She found Travis crouched in the stealth mode of a cat hunting prey. Wearing a helmet and CATS goggles, he slowly eased left then right, his balance perfect, his movements sure. Claire knew exactly what he was seeing—he was at the spot in the simulation that placed him on a rocky outcropping designed to resemble the mountains of Afghanistan.

She could easily imagine him in a real battle, though not necessarily in Afghanistan. The third Special Forces group concentrated on covert operations in sub-Saharan Africa. The alpha team he commanded was dropped into unfriendly countries and left to infiltrate groups and gather intelligence. They frequently lived as locals and operated without military support. That meant no uniforms, leaving them outside the jurisdiction of the Geneva Convention. The enemy could torture or kill them on sight.

The thought sent a violent shudder over her body and reminded her of the very reason she'd broken off with him.

Keep that in mind when he trains those heart-stopping eyes on you.

He suddenly stood and set down his rifle, indicating the segment had come to an end. He removed his helmet and put it on a rack. When he caught sight of her, a boyish grin spread across his face, and her mouth threatened to reciprocate before she clamped down on her lips.

He jogged across the room, grabbed her in a hug and swung her in circles before putting her down and keeping her loosely enclosed in his arms. "You did it, Claire. Really did it. Everything we talked about come to life before my eyes." He leaned back still grinning from ear to ear, his body fairly vibrating from adrenaline. "What a rush!"

She let herself be caught up in his smile. In the way it felt to be held by him again. To catch a whiff of the minty soap he used. To feel protected and cherished. To feel everything she claimed she no longer wanted in her life.

He tweaked her nose as he'd often done when they were dating. "I'm so proud of you, honey."

She basked in his praise for a moment longer before coming to her senses and stepping free. "I'm glad you liked it."

"Liked it? I loved it! This will revolutionize training. We can give hands-on skills to young recruits on every base and save lives."

Right. Saving lives. That's why she'd embarked on this research in the first place. Her career military father had often lamented losing green recruits and wished for better training. She hadn't been able to do anything to save him from a chopper crash, but she could fulfill his wish.

She took another step back for good measure, garnering a raised eyebrow, which she ignored.

"I need to review the testing results with my staff before they head home," she said, making sure her tone was all business. "They'll have questions for you, and it would do them good to see your enthusiasm for the project. Do you want to get changed first or head up to the observation deck with me now?"

"If everyone is going home soon, I can't leave you alone up here while I'm in the locker room so I'll change now."

"You can't honestly think someone will attempt to abduct me right here."

"It's not likely, but I'm not taking any chances."

Julie stuck her head out of the observation room. "You two joining us for the debrief?"

"I'll be right there," Claire called out. "Get changed and meet us inside," she said to Travis, then slipped into the room.

Julie looked up from a computer monitor, the glow reflecting on her excited expression. "Check out these stats."

Claire reviewed Travis's simulation data and resisted beaming with pride. "He's good, isn't he?"

"Good? He's amazing. He made it all the way through the simulation without taking any kill shots. No one else has even come close to that."

Kill shots. In real life, Travis came under fire all the time and the longer he served as a Green Beret the greater likelihood he'd be shot. Maybe fatally. The same way his buddy Jeter had been killed. Thankfully, Travis was by her side instead of on that mission with Jeter or Travis could have died, too. That's why she'd had to end things before she lost him the same way she'd lost her father.

When she'd broken things off, she'd caught Travis by surprise and he'd demanded an explanation. She'd known he'd try to dispel her fear and draw out the inevitable end to their relationship so she'd looked for a reason he couldn't dispute. Her job was the answer. She really couldn't afford the distraction of a long-term relationship at that stage of the project so she'd shared her need to focus on saving lives. She'd hurt him, but as a soldier he couldn't dispute the necessity of her work. And she was still convinced she'd done the right thing.

And if you know what's good for you, you'll keep on letting him think that way.

"Why aren't you impressed?" Julie demanded.

I am, but I don't want to be. "Maybe we need to make the training scenarios more difficult."

"Hah! One guy out of hundreds who've tested CATS succeeding at this level does not mean we need to make it more difficult. We simply need to appreciate the incredible abilities that Travis possesses. No wonder they sent him for the final test."

Claire didn't know how to respond without lying so she said nothing.

Julie's gaze zeroed in on her. "Looks like you're having a hard time with him being here."

"A bit," Claire hedged, as she didn't know if it was appropriate to talk about Travis with Julie when Claire was her supervisor.

A fine line they'd walked for some time now.

Claire had met Julie at a conference right after her breakup with Travis, and after common interests forged a friendship between them, they became roommates. Then Julie took a job at the institute and Claire eventually became Julie's supervisor. Claire withdrew a bit from the relationship and tried to keep the most personal details of her life private. Luckily, it didn't affect Julie at all. She was such an easygoing person that she readily accepted the change in roles and Claire often had to remind herself to hold back. Like now when Julie seemed genuinely interested and wanted to help.

Business, Claire. This is business.

Julie shifted in her chair. "I hope your unease doesn't mean you sent Travis home for the day and we won't be able to question him about the simulation."

"I'd never let my personal concerns get in the way of CATS." Claire hoped she sounded more convincing than she felt. "He'll join us after he changes."

"Ooh, back in his dress blues, huh? That'll be no hardship to look at."

"Julie! Eric wouldn't be too happy to hear you say that."

"He hasn't put a ring on my finger yet, so there's no harm in looking if I want to." Julie winked.

Right. If only Claire could say the same thing, but she was certain looking would get her in all kinds of trouble that even with her best effort was going to be impossible to avoid. Plus, she couldn't afford to be distracted now. It would take all of her focus to find the prototype and keep it out of the hands of unscrupulous soldiers who with the proper training would pose a serious threat to U.S. armed forces.

FOUR

Travis ushered Claire into the house she'd bought a year ago. The aromatic pine wreath on the door reminded him that Christmas was just a week away. Too bad the sweet scent did nothing to diminish the sour taste lingering in his mouth over her continued unease around him. Nor did it do anything to lighten the agitation he felt in her presence. That never left his mind when he wasn't busy worrying about her safety.

He followed her to the family room with contemporary furniture in neutral colors, but his attention went straight to a wall-to-wall glass door overlooking her backyard. The lawn backed to a green space of brush and trees tangled into a thick jungle where Claire's abductor could take cover. The unobstructed view to the lush green space was nice. Great, in fact. *If* you weren't trying to defend the place. A fence would've been better. Not that he believed the man who risked attacking Claire in broad daylight would let a fence stand in his way. And that meant Travis needed to keep his focus on his job.

He turned to face Claire. "I'd like to inspect your security measures."

"Security measures?" She laughed. "This is a house not a military base."

"Let me check your locks, then," he said before he let that smile take him back in time and he did something he'd regret.

"Help yourself."

He dropped his duffel near the sofa, the thud reverberating through rafters in the vaulted ceiling. "Since I'll be bunking on the couch, I hope you don't mind if I leave my bag here."

"I still think you'd be more comfortable in my guest room."

"Yeah, so you've said. But my assignment isn't about comfort. The couch is next to the patio door, which my initial impression says is your most vulnerable point of entry. Any intruder would have to get past me to reach your bedroom."

She shivered and wrapped her arms around her waist, her gaze darting around the room as if it no longer felt like a safe haven.

He hated that he'd worried her and despite his self-preservation warning him to stay away, he rested a hand on her shoulder. Surprisingly she didn't back away.

"I'll do everything in my power to ensure that no one hurts you, Claire."

"Thank you." A sincere smile crossed her lips, lighting her face and firing his pulse.

A slideshow of the playful, loving woman he'd fallen for started rolling through his mind. Her laughter. Her joy. All of it reminded him that this lighthearted woman still existed— just not for him. He swallowed hard and forced his mind back to the job. "I'll check out those locks."

Ignoring her continued focus on him, he went down a small hallway. Things were happening so fast between them and he didn't know what to make of it. Only a few hours together and he felt like raising the white flag of surrender and finding a way out of the Op. But he wasn't a quitter.

He called on years of training to focus and carefully evaluated two modestly sized bedrooms before stepping back through the family room to the master. He could feel Claire's eyes tracking him and he wished she'd find something— anything—else to do, but she trailed him as he checked every nook and cranny of the house.

"Everything good?" she asked still watching him.

Good? No. Far from it. "Where's your safe room?"

"My what?"

"Where you take shelter from tornadoes." With few basements in a city boasting volatile summer weather, most residents had designated an internal room for shelter.

"Oh, that. The laundry room, why?"

"I want to establish a place for you to go in the event of an intrusion. I also suggest you sleep in your clothes in case we need to use the room or flee the house."

"Okay." That fear crept back into her eyes, making her seem vulnerable and alone.

He forced himself to turn away. "Show me the room."

She led the way to a room barely bigger than the appliances. He made a quick assessment then looked straight at her, making sure his expression conveyed the importance of his upcoming directions. "If I'm somehow disabled or if I tell you to come here, you head to this room and lock the door. No questions asked. No dallying. Straight in here. Got it?"

She gave a certain nod, but the fear lingered.

"I plan to trade this doorknob with the one for the guest bedroom," he continued. "Though it's not a dead bolt, it's better than nothing. I'll also rig up a bar to make it more secure." Hoping to eliminate this heavy tension between them before he exploded, he grinned. "Don't worry. I'll repair any damage my bumbling skills cause before I leave town."

A wobbly smile lifted one side of her mouth and though he wanted to give her additional safety instructions, he thought it best to pass the advice on in small snippets before she totally freaked out.

His stomach rumbled, giving him the perfect change in subject. "I haven't had a decent Cuban sandwich since I was here last. Our favorite place still deliver?"

She nodded. "I'm guessing you'd like your usual classic Cuban with a side of rice and beans and Jupina to drink."

He loved that she remembered how much he liked the sweet pineapple soda and sandwich Cuban immigrants brought to Florida. They'd often shared such a meal and longing surged through him for the easy relationship they'd once had. The relationship he couldn't manage to keep his mind off of.

How could a woman who stood five-seven on her tiptoes wreak such havoc in his life?

He had to get away to compose himself. "Sounds perfect. I'll work on changing locks while you order. Is your toolbox in the garage?"

"Yes," she said, seeming distracted.

Despite the desire to know what she was thinking, he hung his jacket on the back of a chair, then went to the garage. Jerking his tie loose, he inhaled deeply of the humid air and blew out his tension. He located a small toolbox and set to work swapping out the locks and constructing a bar to brace the door. He'd just tested it when the doorbell rang.

Adrenaline surged through his veins and his hand automatically shot to his holstered weapon before he remembered their dinner order. He motioned for Claire to stay put on the sofa while he retrieved their food from the deliveryman.

When they were seated at her glass dining table, he bit into the grilled sandwich of pork, ham and pickles then groaned at the tangy goodness. As he swallowed, he searched for a safe topic. "Did you have any luck discovering alibis while I was having fun with CATS?"

She set down her sandwich and wiped her mouth, taking her time as if she didn't want to talk about the theft. "Not a lot. Since my attacker obviously wasn't a woman, I started with the guys on the team."

"You can't rule the women out. They could've hired a guy or teamed up with someone they know."

She frowned but nodded her agreement. "I hadn't thought of that. I'll talk to them tomorrow."

"What did the guys tell you?"

"Not much." She narrowed her eyes. "You of all people know how men are about engaging in small talk."

"What, me?" He jabbed his thumb into his chest. "I can be social."

She rolled her eyes. "Only when forced."

"Okay, granted, I'm not big on small talk, but I speak when it's important."

"That you do." She seemed to get lost in thoughts of their past he knew better than to pursue.

He quickly moved on. "So, no luck at all then?"

"I ruled out two of the guys."

"And your team's what…fifteen people? Maybe we should prioritize them so you can give it another go tomorrow with the most likely suspects."

She sat back, an appraising look on her face. "And how do you propose we do that?"

"The way I figure it, the theft is most likely about money or revenge. Either revenge on you or the army. If we make a list of people with these motives who have the ability to disable security cameras or alter the footage, we should have a place to start."

"I'll get a notepad." She left the room and quickly returned with a pen and legal pad.

"We should start with money," he suggested.

"Let's see." She sat, her hand hovering over the yellow pad as she fidgeted with the pen, twisting it in and out of slender fingers. "I guess Alan Burns is possible. His wife is undergoing experimental cancer treatments not covered by insurance, which means he's short on cash. And he's one of our civilian software engineers so he'd be able to modify security. Plus, he fits the physical build of my attacker and he wasn't in the office at the time of my attack."

"Good." Travis tapped the notepad. "Put him on the list."

She jotted his name down and clicked the pen several times before adding Kent Norton to the page. "Kent's a lieutenant who was passed over to head up CATS. He's on the team, but he still complains about having a civilian in charge. He was also out of the office this afternoon, and he's the right size."

"So revenge might fit him. Does he have any money issues?"

She shrugged. "Not that I know of. He came into an inheritance not long ago and used it to purchase a condo by Lake Eola."

"Wow, he must've gotten a huge chunk of money," Travis said as he recalled the expensive housing near Orlando's famous Lake Eola fountain. "We'll stick with revenge, then. He might want to get back at you *and* the army."

"Maybe me, but I don't know about the army. He seems like he lives for his career, but you never know, right?"

"Right." With the discussion firmly on the investigation and not centered on anything personal, Travis started to relax and leaned back. "Anyone else come to mind?"

Deep in thought, Claire lifted her face to the ceiling. He should look away, but he couldn't take his eyes off the sleek lines of her throat. He knew firsthand how soft her skin felt to the touch. He shoved his hands into his pockets. He didn't care if keeping his hands in his pockets violated the uniform policy. The rule was so ingrained that it felt wrong and the discomfort distracted him from Claire.

She lowered her head, her eyes awash with apprehension.

"Did you come up with someone else?" he asked, her apprehension making him dread the answer.

"Maybe...I don't know." She paused and bit her lip. "There's this guy. He's not on the team anymore, and his security access has been revoked so I don't know if he could pull off the theft."

"Would he have knowledge of the security system and the technical skills to alter it?"

"Yes. He's a software engineer."

"Maybe he could bypass it, then. Tell me about him."

"His name's Mike Robb. He's former army and worked for us as a civilian. He kind of had a thing for me. It got to be a problem, and I had to fire him."

Travis's intuition sat up and took notice, raising his concern to a new level, but he played it down. "A thing?" he asked casually.

"Okay, maybe it was more than a thing." She clenched her hands and took a deep breath. "His interest crossed the line and became an obsession. When his performance suffered at work, I had to let him go. That was about three weeks ago."

Travis's gut started churning, the sandwich he'd just enjoyed feeling like lead in his stomach. "Have you seen him since then?"

"Sort of. I mean he's called me and shown up here a few times. Plus, I often run into him when I'm out, so I figure he's following me."

"And you're just mentioning him now?" Travis's words shot out like an accusation before his chest constricted.

She eyed him for several moments, her cool expression in direct opposition to his turmoil. "After I was attacked this morning, I considered telling the cops about him. But then you were so certain the attack was related to the theft and Mike was off the team so I thought it wasn't important."

Travis sat forward and resisted the urge to get up and pace away his anxiety. "I don't care if he's involved in the theft or not. He's bothering you and I intend to have a word with him."

"Why?"

He jerked his hands free and slammed a fist on the table. "He's stalking you, for crying out loud. That's not okay."

Claire jumped and he regretted the loss of control, but he doubted any man who'd once loved a woman could hear about such a thing without exploding.

Breathing deeply, she watched him while endless seconds passed. He wanted to beg her to speak, but he waited and cringed inside over her upcoming answer.

"Let's be clear about one thing, Travis," she finally said, dead calm in her tone. "Your assignment doesn't involve my personal life. Any problems I'm dealing with that aren't connected to the theft are none of your business."

"Fine. Leave the fact that he's obsessed with you out of this." Travis grabbed the pen and wrote down Mike's name in big, bold letters then circled it with a thick slash of the pen. "He's got a personal vendetta against you for firing him, which in my mind makes him our primary suspect, and I intend to have a conversation with him tomorrow."

"Okay," she said, still calm and detached.

Unbelievable. How could she be so calm? More important, how could she keep this from him all afternoon? This guy was the perfect suspect. Or maybe Travis wanted Mike to be guilty because he was interested in Claire.

Interested, my foot. He's a stalker. Plain and simple.

Travis gave into the need and got up to pace. He'd spend the night researching Mike, and after dropping Claire at the institute tomorrow, he'd go talk to the guy.

All right, maybe he'd do more than talk. Even if Mike wasn't the thief, Travis didn't care what Claire said. He'd let the creep have it for bothering her.

And if Mike turned out to be the thief after all? Then he was an imminent threat to the woman Travis would do just about anything to protect and he'd stop at nothing to keep her safe.

FIVE

As the hours inched closer to sunrise, Travis shifted on the sofa. He should be fast asleep by now but he hated to admit Claire was right. He'd be more comfortable in the queen-size bed in her guest room than with his feet hanging over the end of the sofa. But nothing would change the fact that he was in the same house as her, leaving him more anxious and distracted than he'd been in a long time. No wonder sleep was so hard to grasp.

Pacing always helped in the past. He swung his feet to the floor and saw the clock on her DVR go out. He looked into the kitchen. Stove. Microwave. All the clocks were black. The house silent. Like a tomb.

He glanced at the window over the front door. Streetlights were on.

Someone cut the power.

Not someone. Claire's abductor.

A muffled thump—maybe a window closing or footfalls—sounded from Claire's room.

He raced to her door and heard someone crossing the wood floor. Whisper-soft footsteps, but they were there. Could be Claire checking on the power outage, but he wouldn't risk it.

He whipped open the door.

Claire was in bed. A man stood over her. His gloved hand holding a cloth hovered near her mouth. In his other hand, a gun hung limply from his fingers.

"Stop!" Travis shouted hoping to catch the man off guard but only succeeded in making Claire shoot up.

The intruder glanced at Travis then dropped the rag and aimed his weapon at Travis's heart, keeping him locked in place when his feet fairly throbbed with the need to take action and protect Claire.

If only Travis could go for his weapon holstered at his side, but the risk was too great. He'd put both Claire and himself in danger.

The assailant backed toward the wide-open window. Travis tried to make out his features, but a dark hoodie shadowed his face. When he'd hefted one leg over the sill and looked away, Travis lunged, grabbing the creep's shoulders and jerking him back inside.

As he wrestled the man to the ground, Travis caught a glimpse of Claire easing out of bed. He wanted to check on her, but her assailant bucked, and Travis had to focus or risk losing him. "Safe room now, Claire!"

With a roar, the man shot up forcing Travis's back into the door. Air gushed from his lungs. Gasping for breath, he held on and tried to knock the gun free.

The guy twisted his arm out of reach then heaved his entire weight into Travis's chest, unsettling his feet. He flailed out, but lost his balance and plummeted toward the floor. The intruder lifted his gun and fearing a shot to the chest, Travis scrambled out of the way. Footfalls pounded behind him and the next thing Travis felt was the crack of the gun over the back of his head.

Pain sliced through his skull as darkness beckoned. Sweet, soft, peaceful darkness of slumber.

No. Claire needs you.

He blinked hard and willed it away. He attempted to get to his feet, but the guy shoved him down and bolted through the door.

Travis tried to rise again, but when he heard the front door open, he assumed the attacker had fled and Travis returned his attention to Claire. She crossed the room, a large metal candlestick gripped in her hands, a fierce scowl on her face.

If the situation wasn't so dire, he'd laugh at the comical sight she made holding the candlestick aloft as if it would protect her.

"You won't need that, honey," he forced the words out, the blackness now calling stronger. "He's gone. You should call 9-1-1, though." He tried to add a reassuring smile, but the pull of darkness grew and he let it claim him.

* * *

"Travis." Panic stealing Claire's breath, she dropped to the floor and found his pulse. Good. He was alive. "Travis. Please. Are you all right?"

Silence.

What should she do?

C'mon, Claire. Do something. You have to help him.

She slipped her fingers behind his head to lift it to her lap. At the feel of sticky blood, she jerked away.

"No. Oh, no. Oh, no. Please, God, help," she prayed.

Travis had said to call 9-1-1. That's what she'd do.

She rushed to her nightstand to grab her phone. As she requested an ambulance, she returned to Travis's side. By the time she'd ended the call he was waking.

"Don't move," she cautioned. "Your head's bleeding."

"All the more reason to move so I don't mess up your carpet." He got a silly grin on his face.

If he could joke, he couldn't be hurt too badly. "I called 9-1-1. The police and ambulance are on the way."

"We should get you to the safe room while I check on Julie." He staggered to his feet.

When Claire tried to help him, he shrugged her off. The big macho hunk wasn't about to accept help. Though he was more wobbly than her shaking knees left her, she let him lead her to the laundry room. She understood his need to protect. It was innate in his lifestyle and was why he was so good at his job. And his willingness to put others first was one of his most endearing qualities.

He reminded her of her father, of all the military men and women she worked with. They'd promised to give everything, including their lives, for service to their country, and her respect for them was beyond measure.

A wave of gratitude for Travis's selfless dedication swept over her, and she opened her mouth to thank him, but he held up his hand.

"Stay here and lock yourself in." He shut the door and departed.

She twisted the lock then paced in the small room. Back and

forth, back and forth as thoughts of his efforts on her behalf reminded her of why she'd fallen in love with him in the first place. If she put the positive traits he'd displayed today in one column and the negative in the other, so far, the positive far outweighed his only negative checkmark for his dangerous job.

"But it's a huge negative," she reminded herself before she let his good traits sway her toward making a mistake.

He knocked on the door, the sound sending her toward the ceiling. "It's me, Claire."

She let him in and stood back to give him room to secure the door again, his body so close in the tiny space she could almost feel his urgency to protect her flowing through him.

"Julie's fine," he said, running his gaze over her as if searching for any injuries. "I asked her to join us, but she said this room is too small for three people so she'll keep her door locked until I give her the all clear. She asked about the intruder. I couldn't tell her the whole truth, but I said it's likely your attacker from earlier today."

"Since we aren't certain of the attacker's identity or motive, she might think he'll come back. She could be afraid that she'll get hurt, too. I should go to her." Claire started for the door.

Travis grabbed her arm, the warmth of his fingers in direct contrast to the firm pressure of his grip. "I can't let you do that until the police arrive and clear the area."

Claire eased her arm free, but the intensity that remained on her face told her not to bother arguing. "I wish we could tell her what's going on so she doesn't worry about her own safety."

"Not possible. It could compromise the investigation and my CO would never give approval."

"Then we'll have to tell her you're going to keep an eye on both of us while we're home to make sure nothing happens."

"Sure. That we can do." He started to run a hand over his head and winced when his fingers grazed his injury.

"Sit," she commanded in her best supervisory voice. "I want to look at that cut."

He arched a brow, and she could see he was thinking about disagreeing so she cast him a stern look.

He laughed, a short burst of surprise that bounced around

the small room as he settled on a sturdy hamper. "I'm always amazed that a little bit of a thing like you can get so bossy."

"Hey, you grow up in a military household and you learn from the best." She tilted his head to catch the overhead light. The blood had slowed to a trickle, but she still wanted to apply pressure. She'd need a clean cloth to do so. She opened her dryer.

"You're going to do laundry at a time like this?"

"No, silly." She pulled out a washcloth. "I need this to stop the bleeding." She moved behind him. "It's gonna hurt."

"In that case." He looked up at her with the little boy grin so in contrast with the big, brawny man that it melted her heart. "Will you hold my hand?"

She laughed and felt the terror of the night disappear with it, which she felt certain was his intention. She pressed the cloth against his head making him wince.

"Sorry," she said. "I hate hurting you when you were injured trying to keep me safe."

"No biggie."

She lifted his chin until she got a good look at him and their eyes connected. "It's a big deal to me, Travis. You're a wonderful, honorable man who deserves the very best in life and I know I hurt you. For that I'm so sorry."

He shrugged. "Again, no biggie."

Really? No biggie? She dropped her fingers.

Had he actually moved on so easily when she was still stuck wondering what might've happened if she hadn't broken things off? Maybe he hadn't really cared for her at all. That thought left her sadder than words could express and she'd love to take the time to figure out where this sadness was coming from.

But not now.

Now her full focus needed to stay on the man who'd held Travis at gunpoint and nearly abducted her. If her thoughts were divided at all, her attacker might not only succeed in his mission, but he could also kill Travis in the process.

SIX

When Travis entered the seafood restaurant where Claire said Mike regularly ate, the lunchtime rush was in full swing. Tangy spices scented the air, but Travis had no appetite. Not when he was tracking down the man who could've broken into Claire's house last night.

The house had been inky black and the intruder would've only gotten a glimpse of Travis before he fled, but Travis had to allow for the possibility that Mike could recognize him. This meeting held the potential to turn disastrous. Travis would have to be on his guard.

He searched the narrow room laden with pine boughs and twinkling lights for the man who resembled Mike's personnel photo. Travis quickly spotted the muscled guy with thinning hair sitting at a long counter near the back. Just seeing the man who was stalking Claire sent Travis's anger vibrating to a quick boil.

Stop. Breathe. Anger will get you nowhere. You're on a mission. Like any other mission.

He drew in a few cleansing breaths and crossed the room to slide onto a vacant stool next to Mike.

Travis tapped a colorful menu lying on the counter. "Can you recommend anything here?"

Mike looked up from his lunch and ran his gaze over Travis.

Here it comes, Travis thought, and waited for recognition to dawn.

Instead, he got a welcoming smile. "For a fellow army grunt, sure. The crab cakes are great."

Either Mike was a consummate actor, he hadn't seen Travis clearly enough last night to recognize him, or he wasn't their guy. The last option was definitely not something Travis wanted to entertain.

"You active duty?" Travis knew the answer but he wanted to get Mike talking.

"Nah. I decided to take my chances as a civilian." He stabbed his fork into a golden-brown crab cake. "We don't see many uniforms in the Orlando area."

"I'm visiting a woman." Travis leaned closer and gave a conspiratorial wink. "Wore the uniform to impress her if you know what I mean."

A lecherous grin distorted Mike's face, twisting it into an ugly expression. He was thinking about Claire, and Travis wanted to wipe the look off the guy's face.

Mike thrust out his hand. "Mike Robb."

Travis gripped Mike's hand and resisted the urge to twist it around the creep's back and slam him against a wall. Instead, Travis forced a smile and offered a fake name in the event Mike still talked with anyone at the institute. "Do you live around here, Mike?"

"Not far."

"I've heard there's some great nightlife in this part of town," Travis said, hoping to get Mike to divulge his whereabouts the previous night.

"That there is. I can give you the names of the best clubs if you want."

"Sounds like you go out a lot."

"Not usually. My friends don't like clubbing much. But I've been in a funk the last few weeks so I've gone out alone to drown my sorrows. Been out most every night."

Which meant he might not have a concrete alibi. "Sounds like woman troubles."

"Exactly, but I'm working on a plan to win her over."

Plan? Like stealing her equipment and then pretending to be the hero who finds and returns it? But that wouldn't explain the abduction attempts—unless he'd staged them, too so he could pretend to save Claire.

The desire for the answer almost made Travis rush ahead, but he counted a few beats until it passed. "I have a good ear if you want to talk about it."

Mike glanced at his watch. "I'd take you up on it, but I have to get back to work."

Travis felt his opportunity slipping away, and yet he didn't want to sound overeager and alert Mike to his real mission. "Maybe some other time, then."

Mike seemed to think about it as he pushed to his feet. "I'm going bowling tonight with a few guys from work. If you don't have plans you could stop by."

Perfect. "I'm not sure I'll be free," Travis said, playing it cool. "But give me the details just in case."

Mike rattled off the particulars for a nearby bowling alley as he tossed a meager tip onto the counter. "Maybe I'll see you there."

Mike departed, and Travis's intuition screamed to follow the guy. He waited until Mike climbed into a shiny red sedan before heading to his rental car. He eased into traffic and hung well back from Mike. Fortunately, the red car stuck out in the sea of white rentals populating the tourist capital of Florida, making it a breeze to follow.

Surprisingly, Mike took a direct route to the institute where he pulled to the curb well shy of the guard station. Travis stopped farther back and grabbed binoculars from his bag. He zoomed in on Mike, who'd perched a camera on his open window, aiming it at the institute.

Was he planning an attack here? Or maybe another theft?

Time ticked slowly by as Mike continued to snap photos. Travis had the urge to march up to Mike and demand an explanation, but he employed the patience he'd learned on the job. That is, until Mike put his camera away. Then Travis gripped his weapon and sat at full alert.

Mike fired up his car and drove slowly past the building. At the corner, he whipped a U-turn and crept by in the other direction. After he cleared the building, and Travis knew Claire wasn't in danger, he dropped down in his seat so Mike wouldn't see him.

Despite the ongoing danger Mike posed to Claire, Travis smiled. Looked like Mike was their man. Now all Travis had to do was prove it, and meeting Mike tonight was the first step.

* * *

Claire trailed Travis to the front door of her home, her emotions lingering near the surface as they had been since Travis arrived. She didn't want to be around him and yet she didn't want him to leave. Surprisingly, as uncomfortable as it sometimes was to be with him, he made her feel safe. Not that she'd admit it to him.

He opened the door then faced her, his expression a hazy mix of concern and eagerness to get going. "Be sure to keep the door locked and remember Officer Harper's right out front. He won't be going anywhere until I get back."

"Relax," Claire said, though uncertainty continued to crowd her brain. She was thankful an officer who was friends with her boss offered to stand watch when Travis had to go out tonight. She appreciated his protection, but honestly, she felt safer with Travis. Still, she wouldn't keep him here when Mike was waiting at the bowling alley. "You'll be with our top suspect, so he won't be coming after me. I'll be fine."

Travis searched her eyes, and she warmed at his genuine concern. Concern for her. For her safety. She loved that he was always willing to come to the aid of someone in trouble. *Check.* Down went another mark in his good-guy column. Despite her desire to keep him at bay, he was quickly swaying her toward thoughts she shouldn't even be considering. Writing out her Christmas cards and drinking a soothing cup of hot chocolate should blot him from her mind.

"I hope to be back by ten at the latest," he said and, after a final lingering look that did nothing to help Claire forget the effect he had on her, he strode down the walkway to his car.

She locked the door as if locking him from her heart then went to the kitchen and retrieved her favorite mug. She filled it with water and caught Julie watching from the family room.

"Something wrong?" Claire asked.

"Not with me." Julie stood and headed for the kitchen. "But you look worried."

Claire put the cup in the microwave and stared at the whirling turntable as she considered her answer. Clearly, Julie noticed Claire's distress, but did she want to talk about Travis with Julie? Claire had never told anyone, not even her mother, the real reason she'd ended things with him. She'd barely been able to admit it to herself much less speak it aloud, but now that he was back and raising all these feelings again, the need to talk about it with someone was pressing in on Claire.

Was Julie the right person, though? The line Claire had held with Julie made her unbiased when it came to Travis and she should be able to offer a rational opinion. Maybe she *could* help.

"I guess I'm more uncertain than worried," Claire answered hoping to slide into the discussion and see where it took them.

"Uncertain about our safety or about Travis?"

"Officer Harper's out front so I'm not worried about our safety at the moment." Claire waited for the microwave to ding, then took the cup to the breakfast bar.

Julie slipped onto a stool, perching on the edge and resting her elbows on the smooth granite counter. "I don't know how you can drink that when it's so warm out."

"Comfort food, I guess. Besides, if the cold front they're predicting comes through tonight we'll both be drinking it tomorrow."

"But that's tomorrow." Julie propped her chin on her hands, her penetrating gaze locking on Claire. "This's now."

Claire poured the chocolate powder into the mug and before she could decide how to respond, Julie shifted closer. "This is about Travis, isn't it?"

Claire shrugged, but her reluctance was halfhearted as she really did want to get this out in the open so she could make sense of her feelings. She just didn't know how to begin revealing something she'd kept to herself for so long.

"It's clear you two still have a thing for each other," Julie continued. "So why'd you break up?"

Julie was right. They did have a thing for each other. Claire had no idea what this *thing* was, but it was a good place to start the discussion. She perched on a stool and thought back to the beginning, when her father died. Memories came flooding back and she stirred the cocoa to keep from crying. The day of his funeral was as fresh today as it'd been that bitterly cold day six years ago. Standing at the freezing cemetery, her arm around her mother's convulsing shoulders as much for warmth as for comfort in their loss. Watching them lower the casket into the ground. Saying good-bye. Forever.

"Claire?" Julie asked gently.

Claire forced herself to move forward. "I told you about how my dad was killed in that chopper crash. Well I... The pain. It was unbearable."

Julie patted her hand. "I've never lost anyone so unexpectedly, but I can imagine how hard it must've been."

No, you can't. Not really. Not until you experience it. "I vowed to do everything I could to never go through it again. Which meant I couldn't get close to anyone else who served in the military and had a dangerous job like my dad. Then along came Travis..." She ended with a lift of her shoulder.

"And you fell for him."

"Big-time." Claire shook her head. "I mean, really! How could I have fallen for a guy who was the worst risk of all? He runs into danger on a daily basis. It's only a matter of time before...well...you know."

"So you broke up with him before that could happen." Julie paused to appraise Claire. "Didn't that hurt, too?"

"Yes." Tears pricked Claire's eyes and she swiped them away. "But not as badly as if I had to say good-bye to him at a funeral."

Julie nodded her understanding. "Now he's back and you're still not over him."

"Yes," Claire said as tears began to fall in earnest and she grabbed a paper towel to dab at them. "But nothing's changed. He's still putting his life on the line and I'm no more ready to risk the pain of losing him than I was two years ago."

Julie sat back, her eyes narrowing the way they often did when puzzling out a problem at work. "You have to admit if you were going to fall for anyone with a dangerous job, Travis's skills give him a far better chance of coming home at the end of the day."

Claire hadn't even considered that. "I guess, but skills or not, he's not protected from a rocket launcher or bomb strike."

"I'm so sorry you're going through this, Claire. Especially on top of this crazy guy stalking you." Julie squeezed Claire's hand and seemed sincere, but a mountain of skepticism lingered on her face.

"I hear a 'but' coming."

"Since I'm not a Christian," Julie said, sounding uncertain. "I could be way off base here, but I know you usually pray over big decisions. Have you asked God if He wants you to be with Travis, or did you let your fears get to you and make the decision on your own?"

Claire sat back and felt a flush of embarrassment color her face. She'd completely left God out of her problem. Not just once when she ended things with Travis, but for two solid years whenever she'd thought of Travis or about dating. Worse, it'd taken someone who didn't even believe in God to point it out.

How had she been so blind?

Suddenly it occurred to her that she hadn't prayed about the missing prototype, either. She'd been so worried about her lost work, and the idea of her project ending up in enemy hands, but she'd never thought to turn it over to God, to trust in His solutions…or to even consider the idea that He might have sent Travis to her—to protect her work, and to force her to face her fears.

Julie's brows furrowed. "Did I say something wrong?"

"No." Claire shook her head, not only to reassure Julie, but because she couldn't believe how oblivious she'd been. "You said the thing I needed to hear most and something I'll be spending a lot of time thinking about."

SEVEN

Mike and his friends Hank and Nick had been too busy focusing on one-upping each other to give Travis time alone with Mike. Three hours of bowling and Travis had learned nothing other than Mike was highly competitive and a sore loser.

Travis didn't care. He poured his frustration into the bowling ball and hurled it down the lane. The pins exploded, the loud whack fighting with "Jingle Bell Rock" blaring from speakers.

Cautioning himself not to gloat over the win and alienate Mike, Travis turned back to the group.

Hank looked at Travis, a snide grin on his chubby face. "So glad you came along so Mike didn't skunk all of us." He slid his ball into a neon-orange tote bag. "I'm out of here. Catch you guys tomorrow."

"Hold up, I'll walk out with you." Nick shrugged into a lightweight jacket, his slight frame the opposite of Hank's, a man who could easily fill in for Santa Claus without any padding.

"Fine, run home to your wives," Mike said tauntingly.

Hank picked up his bag and scowled. "You're just jealous there isn't a little woman waiting at home for you."

Mike fired a testy look at his buddy. "I'll be married soon enough."

"Don't you actually need a girlfriend for that to happen?"

"I've got a girlfriend," Mike ground out between clenched teeth.

"Oh, right." Hank raised his eyes in disbelief. "Claire. The woman we've never even seen."

They know about Claire? the question shot through Travis's brain.

Mike crossed his arms, his jaw rigid. "That doesn't mean she doesn't exist."

"Oh, we think she exists," Nick said casting a knowing look at Hank. "We just don't believe she's your girlfriend."

Mike spun on Nick. The anger in Mike's eyes said he was fully capable of hurting someone—maybe even Claire, the woman he claimed to love.

"You'll see," Mike said. "She's not only my girlfriend, but she'll be my fiancée before the week is out."

"Whatever." Nick rolled his eyes and clapped a hand on Hank's shoulder. "Ready, man?"

Hank nodded and they strode away.

"Sorry about that," Mike quickly fired off an apology to Travis, but kept his flaming angry gaze on his friends.

Travis slipped out of his bowling shoes. "I have to admit it was uncomfortable."

"They just don't get it. But they will. Everyone will." Mike packed up his equipment. "Once I make Claire mine. For life."

You won't get close enough to make her yours for even a minute.

Mike leaned closer and Travis had to fist his hands not to deck the guy. "But see, what they don't know is I've got this big thing in the works that's gonna insure Claire will marry me."

The soda Travis drank earlier churned in his stomach, but he forced an even keel to his voice. "Big thing? Like what?"

"I don't want to talk about the details. You know, in case I jinx it." Mike winked. "But trust me. It's gonna happen soon. Real soon."

Travis tried to gain additional details as they returned the rental shoes, but Mike clammed up. Travis even tried to set another meet with Mike, but he gave a vague response and hopped in his car.

Frustrated, Travis pointed his own car homeward as Mike's words reverberated through his brain.

Soon. Real soon.

Had Mike really stolen the prototype to stage a phony recovery of the device to garner Claire's favor? Or were his plans more sinister?

Mine. The word shot into Travis's brain, shocking him into admitting the truth.

He wasn't over Claire. Far from it. His feelings for her were just as strong as the day she'd rejected him. How could he even consider trusting her again when he could still feel the sting of her rejection? Could they make things work? Was he even willing to try after the way she'd let him down?

Hah, get a grip. A second chance at love wasn't for him. Wasn't for most of the guys in his company. Women just couldn't handle a Special Ops soldier continually leaving at a moment's notice with no idea when they'd return. He didn't like the situation, but he got it. Besides, Claire might be attracted to him but she'd made it perfectly clear that she wasn't interested in pursuing anything, whether he wanted to or not.

Feeling defeated, he parked in her driveway and sent Harper on his way. He found Claire curled up on the sofa, her Bible open on her lap.

She looked up at him, her expression flat. He couldn't get a read on her mood. "I was wondering if you were coming back."

"I could never stay away from you, Claire," he teased to hide his emotional turmoil.

She frowned. "Everything go okay with Mike?"

Travis didn't want to frighten her, and he considered not sharing Mike's plan, but she had a right to know about the threat. He provided the highlights.

"Sounds like you really think he's our guy, then," she said.

Travis did, but was it because Mike wanted Claire or because Mike was the best suspect?

"Travis?" Claire asked more pointedly.

"I have nothing concrete to base it on, but he seems slimy to me."

"He *is* slimy, but that doesn't mean he's a thief, or that he attacked me."

"He's our best lead."

"Yes, but we still have Kent and Alan." A smug smile played on her lips. "While you were off playing private investigator, I thought of a way to get their alibis without raising their suspicions."

"How?"

"I'm giving special Christmas presents to the team this year to say thank you for successfully concluding this phase of CATS. We can meet with Kent's and Alan's wife to get gift suggestions, and ask a few other questions while we're at it." Her eyes sparkled with enthusiasm for her idea.

"Perfect." Loving her lighter mood, Travis perched on the arm of the sofa. "I thought this whole thing with Mike would bother you, but you're taking it well."

"I'm trying to do a better job of trusting God." She suddenly snapped her Bible closed and set it on the cushion next to her. "Can I ask you a question?"

"Sure," he said, not liking the way her eyes had turned uneasy again.

"I've been thinking about when Jeter died." She shivered.

Jeter. Travis focused on the ornate nativity scene on the sofa table and tried not to remember the pain he'd felt that day in her office when he'd learned his buddy had died in an ambush.

"You were so broken up," she continued. "But then you went on like nothing had happened. You even signed on for another four years."

Because you rejected my proposal that afternoon, he thought.

"How can you do that?" Her tone was more accusatory than questioning. "I mean, if I were you I'd be terrified the same thing would happen to me, and I'd be a basket case on the job."

Where was she going with this? "I won't pretend it's a walk in the park, but there are other soldiers counting on us so we have to move on."

"Then there's your family," she said as if she was speaking her thoughts aloud instead of really talking to him. "I can't imagine what it's like for your mom and dad or even your sister. They must worry all the time, living every day knowing the danger you're in. Wondering if today is the day that…" She jumped to her feet and started pacing.

"Hey." He went to her and turned her to face him. "What's this all about?"

She looked away.

He tipped her face up and found concern and—dare he hope?—caring in her eyes. "Are you worried about me?"

"Maybe. If we…" She paused and inhaled deeply. "I don't know how…"

He replayed their conversation and linked her worries with the day Jeter died. Had she connected Jeter's death with their future, wondering how she might handle it if he were killed in action, too?

He had to clarify even if she shut him down again. "Are you saying, if we were together you wouldn't know how to handle being with someone who faces danger every day?"

She nodded. "My mom handled it just fine, but then Dad hadn't deployed to war-torn countries. So with you…" She shrugged.

He led her back to the sofa and kept her hand in his, reveling in the fact that she didn't try to remove it. "I know it's hard on my family. It's hard on *all* military families when a loved one deploys to a dangerous area. But Special Forces isn't just a job to me. It's like a calling. I can't see the wrongs of the world and not try to right them. My parents made me who I am today, so they understand that."

"Isn't there another way?" she whispered. "A safer way to do the same thing?"

"Maybe, but right now it's a good fit for me." *At least it was until I discovered how much it bothers you.* "Plus, it helps that we're a family of believers. We try to remember God has a plan and trust Him. Then we let it go."

"You make it sound so easy."

"Easy? No. There are days when bad things happen and I question everything. But if I let my feelings change my path then I'm not walking in what I believe is God's will for me."

"I thought I did the same thing. Until tonight." She bit her lip for a moment. "Julie, of all people, pointed out that I've failed to trust God since losing my dad." She jerked her hand free and twisted her fingers together. "After he died, the pain nearly broke me, and I wasn't going to go through that again. So without even thinking about what God might want for me, I swore off dating."

His mouth fell open. "What about us? We got together after that."

"We were a mistake," she jumped in quickly. "I didn't mean for it to happen. Quite the opposite."

A mistake. He was a mistake? Stunned at the fresh anguish ripping through him, he sat back.

"I'm sorry," she said sincerely. "That's how I felt at the time."

"And now?" He forced the question up a dry throat.

"Now? I'm not sure." She got up and, hugging her Bible like a shield, she walked out of the room in much the same way she'd once walked out of his life.

EIGHT

Claire tugged her coat closed against the howling wind outside Alan Burns's house. Temperatures had dropped to the twenties overnight, giving Claire the first real feeling that Christmas was only a few days away. Despite the danger she was facing, she loved this time of year and wanted to get a tree and finish decorating. She'd ask Travis to help her pick one up at the end of the workday.

She climbed into his car and took a final look at Alan's house, which was devoid of Christmas decorations. Inez just didn't have the strength for anything extra. She'd sat on the sofa, a blanket clutched around her frail shoulders, while Claire asked her questions only to learn that Alan had a good alibi. He'd been holding Inez's hand while nausea from her treatment racked her body.

Claire looked at Travis. "I feel bad for bothering Inez when she's so sick."

"Me, too." Travis cranked the heat up. "Now bothering Sylvia Norton? That I don't feel bad about at all."

Claire thought about their earlier visit to Kent's acerbic wife. "I never thought I'd feel sorry for Kent, but every time I see Sylvia, I do."

Travis shook his head in bewilderment. "She has everything money can buy. Diamonds. Expensive clothes. A decorator condo. And yet she wants more. I couldn't wait to get out of there."

"What do you think about her claim that Kent's been working nights at the institute?"

He glanced at her. "We both know there aren't any night shifts. So either she lied to us or Kent lied to her about where he's been at night."

"How do we figure out which one of them is telling the truth?"

"Doesn't matter. What's important is where he's been going. I'll follow him tonight to find out."

Claire hated the thought of Travis going out again tonight, but at least he wasn't going to some warring country. "Maybe Kent's leaving home to get away from her."

"Could be." He slowed for a stop sign and looked at her. "It's equally as likely that he's working a second job, trying to make enough money to keep her happy. And that makes him an ideal person to steal and sell an expensive prototype."

Travis's dire tone settled over her as her phone rang, making her jump. She looked at Caller ID. "It's the police department." She pressed the button to answer using the speaker setting.

"Ms. Reed, this is Detective Purcell." His voice was filled with tension. "We've finished running the tests on the cloth recovered at your house after the break-in. As we suspected, it was saturated with chloroform."

Travis had suggested this might be the case, preparing Claire to hear such news. Still as the memory of the man's hand hovering over her mouth came rushing back, her unease ratcheted up. "So we're looking for someone with access to chloroform then."

"Unfortunately it's readily available. It's often used as a solvent in laboratories." He paused for a moment. "Perhaps you know someone with access to a lab."

A lab? Her heart sank.

"Can you hold for a second?" She muted her phone and looked at Travis. "Mike minored in chemistry in college. Maybe he has access to a lab through a friend or an old classmate. Should I tell Purcell?"

"No." Travis met her gaze, his intensity scaring her even more. "If you tell him, he'll question Mike and that might spook him. The last thing I want is for that creep to move up plans that we can assume are meant to cause you harm."

Travis was right. They were barely staying one step ahead of the creep trying to abduct her. He'd come close to harming both her and Travis, and she wouldn't to do anything to cause him to escalate these attacks.

Travis resisted letting his mouth hang open and left his meeting with Colonel Lynch. The meeting hadn't gone as he planned at all. He'd expected the colonel in charge of the institute to ask for an update on the theft. He never expected him to offer him a job. But he had. A full-time one. Right here at the institute. With Claire. Not like it mattered. After her abrupt departure last night, he doubted she'd want him around.

But if God wants you to be together, it can happen. The thought came out of nowhere.

Travis had spent a restless night pondering her revelation about ignoring God. Maybe Travis had been doing the same thing. He'd been certain that being a Green Beret was the life God wanted him to lead, but had God really led him there, or had Travis decided for himself? And was it possible that this was the point where God wanted him to take a different fork in the road?

Valid questions needing answers, when he had time to sort them out. Later. Much later, when Claire wasn't waiting for him. He started down the deserted hallway to Claire's office so he could drive her home.

She looked up from stowing her laptop. "Right on time."

"On time for what?"

"To escort Julie, Eric and me to pick out a Christmas tree."

All thoughts of a possible future together fled at the mention of her stepping into a potentially dangerous situation. "That's not a good idea, Claire. You'll be too exposed. Anyone could attempt an abduction."

She wrinkled her nose at him. "Julie's the only one who knows where we're going, and you can be sure no one follows us."

She had a point, but… "Can't this wait until the thief is apprehended?"

"Who knows how long that'll take? We're no closer to resolving this case than when we started, and I won't let it ruin my Christmas celebration." She took a stubborn stance.

He gritted his teeth before her adorable expression had him yielding without thinking this through.

She took a few steps closer to him. "Next you'll tell me I can't go to church on Christmas Eve if this isn't over by then."

"Now you're just trying to make me feel guilty."

An impish smile crossed her face. "Is it working?"

"Yes," he reluctantly admitted.

"So we can go?" She came even closer, the plea in her eyes making him want to give in.

Despite the heady effect she continued to have on him, he wasn't ready to concede. Not without doing a bit of recon first. "Is there a particular place you want to visit?"

"A big lot on the outskirts of town. I've gone there every year since I moved here, and if it helps, I know it's fully fenced."

It helped some. "Give me the address. Let me check satellite photos and do a quick drive-by. If I think it's safe, then we'll go."

A jubilant smile brightened her face, and she threw her arms around his neck, hugging him hard. She felt warm and soft and smelled of springtime. He should push her away until he could be sure God really was telling him to go for it again, but he couldn't think straight with her in his arms.

His heart ached to have her in his life again. Ached for sunshiny mornings with her smiling up at him in a cozy home. *Their* home, with cookies baking in the oven and children with Claire's luminous smile sitting down to sample them.

For the first time since she'd sent him packing years ago, hope filled his heart. Nothing was clear yet, but he was willing to edge closer to a leap of faith. Claire was more than worth it.

Travis kept Claire by his side as he waited at the refreshment stand for her hot cocoa. Eric and Julie had insisted on driving separately to the tree lot and had arrived several minutes ago to stroll off arm in arm to look at trees. Travis had seen the longing in Claire's eyes as she'd watched them. Despite her comments last night, he knew she really did want a relationship, though he doubted she'd accepted that yet.

She shivered violently and ran her hands over her arms.

"I'd have thought after growing up in the north that thirty degrees would seem like beach weather to you," he teased.

She cast him a playful grin. "That was before I moved to Orlando and acclimated to the sweltering summer temperatures. Now I get cold when it drops to the sixties."

"Lightweight." He pulled her under his arm for warmth.

Yeah, right. For warmth.

She rested her head on his chest and his heart burst with happiness.

She suddenly jerked her head up. "Do you see it?"

Her urgent tone sent a bolt of apprehension through him. "See what?"

"Over there." She pointed across the lot. "The perfect tree."

A tree? He sagged in relief and dug out money to pay the cashier for the drinks. "Is there such a thing?"

"Yes and someone else is about to claim it." She shot away from him and across the lot.

He charged after her, but a family of five stepped in front of him and she disappeared behind a row of trees.

Fear sliced along his nerve endings. "Claire!" he shouted as people gave him funny looks. "Claire, where are you?"

He rounded the corner just as a hooded man dragged her through trees lining the fence.

"Stop!" Travis drew his weapon. "I'm armed and I won't hesitate to fire."

People nearby gasped and rushed away as Travis raced for the trees. He plunged through the trees that slowed him down, knocking them off their stands. He found Claire sitting dazed on the ground like a discarded doll, a soaked rag lying next to her. Likely more chloroform. He spotted a gaping hole in the chain-link fence behind her and Claire's abductor disappearing through it. He wanted to go after the guy, but he needed to check on her even more. He dropped to his knees as a powerful engine roared to life on the other side of the trees.

"Claire, honey." He took her chin in his hand and looked into her confused eyes. "Are you all right?"

She nodded woozily. "Go after him."

He evaluated her for another moment then raced to the fence. He eased through the opening in time to see a white van squeal onto the main road. The same white van from Claire's original attack? Likely.

Travis grabbed his phone and reported the incident to a 9-1-1 operator. Hoping to avoid a misunderstanding with the responding officers, he mentioned his military status and added that he was armed and had drawn his gun in the crowd. By the time he got back to Claire, she'd come to her feet and was clutching a tree to remain upright.

He held her elbow to stabilize her. "You doing any better?"

"The fog has cleared some, but I..." She shivered, and he knew it wasn't from the cold.

"That was a close call." He stepped closer to her, needing to touch her and prove to himself that she hadn't been harmed. Not shifting his focus, he drew her toward him, giving her every chance to pull away. Her eyes warmed instead, and he couldn't help himself. He dipped his head and claimed her lips. Soft. Warm. Like he remembered. He put his heart and soul into the kiss, making sure she knew how he felt. She returned it ounce for ounce.

He wanted to simply enjoy it, but this could end so badly. She was responding to him now, but was it out of love or just a need for connection after a frightening event? He knew that he loved her...but could he trust her to love him back? Could he give her the power to break his heart again?

Would they have a chance to find out? Because before their love could ever have a chance, he needed to make sure her tenacious attacker didn't lay his hands on her ever again.

Standing with her friends and Travis, Claire could still feel the tingle of his lips on hers, and she wished they were still kissing. The intensity of her emotions shocked her. She couldn't believe the sense of belonging and oneness with Travis she felt. And she wanted more. Much more.

Enough to let go of her fear? To trust that even if she got hurt again, God would get her through it?

"Claire," Travis said, drawing her back. "I made sure we

weren't followed so do you have any idea how this creep found us?"

"No," she said, trying to concentrate on anything other than how full his lips were. "We certainly didn't tell anyone we were coming here."

"Claire...I..." Julie wrung her hands. "I mentioned it to a few people at work. But that was okay, right? I mean surely your stalker isn't someone from the institute."

"Let's talk about this later," Claire said before Julie asked additional questions and Claire was forced to lie. "I'd like to pick out our tree and go home."

"What?" Travis's voice shot up. "You still want a tree?"

"Of course."

"Why don't you let us choose it?" Julie offered. She tried to look cheerful, but Claire saw the toll these attacks were taking on her friend. Eric slipped his arm around her and she snuggled closer to him.

Claire felt a sting of jealousy and couldn't even look at their happiness when her heart ached so badly.

"Thanks, Julie," Travis said. "I want to get Claire out of the open. We'll meet you at the house."

Claire swung her focus to him and planned to argue, but his eyes were steeled with resolve and Claire knew she wouldn't change his mind. She said good-bye and he escorted her to his car.

Once they were on the road, she faced him. "I'd like to tell Julie what's going on. This last attack might put her over the edge. She deserves to know that she's not in any danger."

"I'll call my CO the minute we get to the house and ask for permission."

Surprised at his easy acquiescence, she continued to watch him. Or maybe she just wanted to watch him. Maybe touch him. Experience the warmth between them again.

"I can feel you looking at me," he said without taking his focus off the road.

"I didn't think you'd agree so quickly."

"Despite what most women think, men aren't oblivious to *everything*. I saw how upset Julie was, and I'll help if I can."

"Thank you." His kindness had always been something she'd admired, adding another check mark in a column that had filled fast in his favor.

He didn't say anything else. Maybe he was replaying the incident and trying to figure out their next move. Or maybe he was thinking about the kiss that told her he still had feelings for her. Deep feelings like the ones she was experiencing.

Was she foolish for continuing to shut him out?

A vision of Travis hitting his head and losing consciousness in the attack at her home flashed before her eyes. Even in a sleepy suburb of Orlando, Travis could've been killed in the blink of an eye.

How ironic. She'd chosen not to get involved with him because of the dangers of his job, but danger lurked all around. Car accidents. Burning houses. Plane crashes. He could die anywhere. Anytime. His job increased the odds, but there was no job that would leave him completely safe.

She looked at him and for the first time in two years, she let her feelings for him flow. Her heart felt full and whole as she was sure God intended for her. She wanted to embrace it. Be happy. Be content, but she couldn't change six years of running from pain in an instant, if she could change at all.

NINE

Wishing coffee could bring him to life after his late night, Travis downed the last swallow and rinsed out his cup. He'd hung outside Kent's house until 3:00 a.m., but Kent didn't leave home. A major disappointment. It was bad enough that Travis sat in a freezing car for endless hours, but seeing Claire's expression fall this morning when he'd told her they were no closer to finding her attacker? That cut right through him.

"One good bit of news is now that Julie knows the truth, she's not afraid anymore," Claire said. "Thanks again for getting permission for me to tell her last night."

"You're welcome," he replied, wishing he could do something to alleviate Claire's fear, too.

She finished loading the dishwasher. "We should get going."

He dug car keys from his pocket and headed for the door. He took a good look around the area before escorting Claire to the car and climbing behind the wheel. She immediately lowered her visor to the ever-present Florida sunshine and settled back in her seat.

Keeping a vigilant eye on their surroundings, Travis drove through her subdivision. Deflated snowmen and Santas lay on the grass while the sun's rays caught lights strung on palm trees. The incongruent sight made him smile, but the smile disappeared the moment he turned onto the institute's street and caught sight of the overflow parking lot filled with copious vases of red roses.

Odd. He could see poinsettias at Christmastime, but roses? Concerned, he slowed to take a closer look.

Claire leaned forward. "Is that Mike?"

Travis searched the far side of the lot, where a man dressed in a black tuxedo had his back to them. He was attaching a vinyl banner to the fence. He glanced furtively over his shoulder then turned back to his work.

"It *is* Mike," Claire said. "What in the world is he up to?"

"Whatever it is, you stay here while I check it out." Travis turned off the car and reached for his door handle.

Claire grabbed his arm. "Be careful, okay?"

"Hey," he said, "Don't worry. I'm trained to handle myself in dangerous circumstances."

"Still." She squeezed his hand. "Be careful. For me."

"Of course."

He may have played down this situation for Claire, but as he jogged across the road, he kept his hand firmly seated on his gun. The biggest mistake he could make would be to underestimate his enemy, and Mike was the enemy until proven otherwise.

Travis stealthily moved in, and when he was five feet from his target, he said, "Hello, Mike."

Mike spun. His gaze quickly ran over Travis then lit on his rental car. He promptly ignored Travis and with a big smile, he started for the road.

For Claire.

Mike slipped his hand into his coat pocket.

Gun! Travis's mind screamed and he reacted without thought, tackling Mike to the ground and straddling his back.

"What the—?" Mike mumbled as he squirmed. "What're you doing, man, and what's my girl doing in your car?"

Travis slowly turned Mike over and jerked his hand out of the pocket. A black velvet box lay in his palm. A ring? He was going to ask Claire to marry him?

"This is your grand gesture?" Travis stifled a burst of hysterical laughter threatening to escape. "Flowers and a proposal?"

Mike's eyes narrowed. "What business is it of yours? And I'll ask again, what're you doing with Claire?"

"I'm doing some testing for the army while I'm in town and she's working on the project."

"You didn't mention that the other night."

Travis released Mike's wrist and stood, keeping his hand

on his gun just in case. "What are the odds that the Claire I work with and the Claire you mentioned are the same person?"

Mike scooted back. "Fair enough, but what's with the tackle?"

"Someone attacked Claire the other day. I thought you might have a gun," Travis answered truthfully.

"Me?" Mike's mouth dropped open. "I'd never hurt Claire. I love her."

"I know that now, but…" Travis shrugged. "You should probably get the lot cleaned up before they arrest you for trespassing."

"But I haven't asked Claire to marry me yet."

Travis eyed the guy, putting a healthy measure of warning in his gaze. "She's not available."

That evening, Claire ran her vacuum over the carpet to keep herself occupied while Travis followed Kent. With Mike ruled out as a suspect they'd spent the whole day digging into Kent's background. His military background proved he was a formidable foe and she didn't want Travis anywhere near him.

"Face it," she mumbled. "You also don't like that Travis isn't here and you're alone."

I really, really don't want to be alone. The sudden thought caused her feet to still.

She'd loved being with Travis. In the past *and* since he'd come to Orlando. Loved every minute of it, even the tense, raw moments, because the way he made her feel proved she was alive. Fully alive and not the shell of a woman she'd been since her dad's death. She'd simply been going through the motions of life, but not really living. Except when she was with Travis. He brought out her desire to live life to the fullest. Something well worth the risk of losing him.

Convinced to tell him how she felt as soon as he got home, she continued across the room with a lighter step and noticed her phone blinking on the table. She found a text from Julie.

You won't believe what I discovered about the thief's identity. Can you come to the office so I can show it to you?

Yes, she replied without giving it a second thought, then dialed Travis to share the news. She got his voice mail. She suspected he'd silenced his phone to keep from alerting Kent. She left a message telling him she'd have Harper escort her to the institute and hurried outside to explain her situation to Harper.

"I'll need to drive," she said. "The security booth is unmanned at night and the barcode sticker that opens the gate is mounted on my dash."

He looked uncomfortable with leaving his car behind, but he radioed in the plan, then secured his vehicle.

Excitement over the lead had her chatting nervously about the weather as she drove, and she nearly missed her first turn. She hooked a quick right and Harper eyed her, but she ignored him and placed her focus squarely on the road.

Good thing she had, as a car suddenly pulled from the curb in front of her, forcing her to hit the brakes.

"That guy'd get a ticket if I was in my patrol car," Harper mumbled.

The car slowed more and soon a large SUV pulled out behind them and raced toward her bumper.

Harper swiveled to look behind them, and his expression shifted from surprise to grim understanding. "It's a trap. They're gonna squeeze us until we're forced to stop." He drew his gun. "Try to go around the car."

Anxiety making her hands shake, she swerved to the side. Both cars reacted quickly and kept her sandwiched between them. The SUV revved its powerful engine and slammed into her bumper.

The car in front jerked to a stop and she stomped on the brakes but couldn't stop before crashing into it. Her air bag deployed, slapping her in the face and knocking the breath out of her. She heard Harper's bag inflate, too. He shoved it away.

"Stay here." He eased out. Staying low, he slid along the side of her car, heading for the rear.

A gunshot split the night.

She struggled out of her seat belt and dived for the passenger's seat. She stuck her head out just in time to see Harper drop to the ground.

"Are you okay?" she screamed, but he didn't move or reply.

She had to check on him. As she slipped out, she saw a man jump from the front vehicle.

Was he coming to kill her, too?

Harper's gun. She had to get to Harper's gun.

She scrambled toward him, but hadn't gotten three feet when she was jerked back by the shoulders. An arm clamped around her waist. She bucked and kicked, twisting with all her might.

"Give it a rest, Claire," a familiar voice sounded in her ear. "Don't scream or the chloroform comes out again. Got it?"

"Eric?" His name eased past the lump in her throat.

"Surprise." He lifted her up and walked to his car as if he was carrying a small child.

Julie's Eric was behind this? Was Julie involved, too? Was that why she'd sent the text?

The sting of betrayal bit hard, but when Eric opened his trunk and dropped her inside, her thoughts turned to survival. She could scream but they were on a deserted stretch of road and it wouldn't do any good. But clearly Eric wasn't taking any chances. He bound her hands and feet then gagged her before slamming the trunk.

Darkness settled in. Cloying. Fearful. Black. She had to get out of here. She just had to.

The car roared to life and her heart raced as she struggled against the ropes. The rough fibers tore at her skin and panic settled over her, cutting off her air.

Save your strength, she warned herself.

She'd need every ounce of energy if she was going to get out of this alive.

TEN

Disgusted, Travis headed for his car. Kent was having an affair with a woman from the institute, which explained his whereabouts and his lies to his wife. It made Travis sick. If he was ever lucky enough to have a wife, he'd never sully his vows that way.

He dug his phone out to view his messages and discovered a call from Claire and one from the institute. Maybe she'd gone to the office. He didn't like the thought of her going anywhere without him and worry nagged at him as he listened to her voice mail. She *had* gone to work. At least Harper was with her. Still, Travis would head straight to the institute to make sure she was okay. As he neared the building, his phone rang. Caller ID declared the institute.

"Claire," he answered.

"No, it's Julie. Claire's been in a car accident."

His heart plummeted. "Is she okay?"

"I don't know. We don't know where she is."

"Then how in thunder do you know she's been in an accident?"

"She's testing a new phone app we're developing for military vehicles. If she's in an accident and her phone's mounted on her dash, the app senses the collision and starts the video recording on her phone. Then it sends an email to Peter Fisk who's the project supervisor. He's downloading the data now. We'll know more soon."

"I'm right outside. Meet me at the gate to let me in." He cranked the wheel hard and jerked to a stop until the gate lifted. Within minutes, they were in Peter's office with introductions out of the way.

"I've already had a chance to review the video, but honestly, it's too dark to get any idea of where the accident occurred."

Peter ran a hand over his head. "I've already used her phone's GPS to try to locate her, but she doesn't have it turned on."

Feeling helpless, Travis peered at Peter. "She was afraid her abductor was using GPS to keep tabs on her so she turned it off. Can you track the email and get a location of where it originated?"

"Not without the help of her cell phone service provider." Peter held up a hand. "Before you get excited about that, even if I could find someone to talk to me at the phone company, they won't share private information with me. It would take police involvement to get a warrant for it and that could take time."

Which they didn't have. "Then let's look at the video to see if we can figure out her location."

Peter started the video playing and tapped the screen. "That jarring of the camera you see is the point of impact. Since Claire was hit from behind, her front-facing camera caught this video of the back of her car."

The camera settled, displaying a large SUV forcing her car forward then the screen suddenly changed. Travis wished for sound to hear Claire's voice, but they only had video.

"Now she slams into the car in front of her," Peter said. "And the phone changes to the rear-facing camera, which catches everything in front of her car."

A smaller sedan came to a complete stop, which in turn jerked Claire's car to a stop. The sedan inched several feet ahead, but Claire's vehicle didn't move.

"So it's a minor fender bender," Travis said, his senses still on high alert. "I don't understand why she didn't call me."

"Keep watching," Peter said.

The driver's door opened and a man climbed out of the sedan. He raised a gun and rested his arm on the roof, his face shadowed in the darkness of night. The muzzle flashed and the man's arm jerked.

Travis's heart stopped. He could almost hear the gunshot reverberate through the night. Feel the recoil of the weapon. See the target fall.

"Did he just shoot someone?" Julie's voice skyrocketed high.

"Looks like it," Travis said, but kept his eyes glued to the screen, dreading confirmation that the gunman had shot Claire.

Weapon pointed ahead, he marched toward her car. He crossed between the vehicles and disappeared from the video then he returned with Claire clamped in his arms. She was kicking and thrashing, but he managed to get the trunk open and drop her inside.

"She's alive," Julie said on a whispered breath.

Relief flooded through Travis, but Claire was still in extreme danger so he kept his eyes riveted to the screen. To Claire. Headlights from her car caught the terror in her eyes, making Travis furious and light-headed at the same time.

He waited for Harper to come to Claire's rescue, but there was no sign of the officer. Which meant he'd been incapacitated. Likely he was the one who'd been shot.

Travis flashed a quick look at Peter. "Would you call 9-1-1 to report the shooting?"

"I did the moment I saw the video. They're already looking for Officer Harper."

"Good," Travis said and hoped the police had some way of tracking their officer. Maybe finding Claire, too, but it looked as if her abductor planned to take her from the scene.

He retrieved a rope then wound it around her wrists and ankles, drawing it tight. He closed the trunk then turned, the headlights clearly illuminating his face.

Julie gasped and dropped into a chair.

"Eric?" Travis spun on her. "Did you know about this?"

"The abduction? No."

"But you had something to do with the theft."

She cringed but said nothing.

Travis advanced on her, giving her a look guaranteed to break even the most reluctant subject in one of his interrogations. "If you know what's good for you, you'll tell me everything."

"I stole the prototype," she admitted, trying to back away from him, "but not to sell it—honest!"

"Then why?"

"I'm so tired of living in Claire's shadow. Always being

second in charge when I'm just as qualified. I wanted to take Claire down a peg so the people in charge of the institute would look to me for once. When Eric suggested stealing the prototype to make her look bad, I went for it."

"And you let your boyfriend attack her?"

She shot up a hand. "No…no…wait. I didn't know he was behind the attacks. You have to believe me. I thought she was being stalked. At least until she told me you believed the attacks were related to the theft." She wrung her hands. "Then I talked to Eric, and he promised he wasn't the one responsible."

"And just like that you believed him?"

"Claire said you had no proof of who attacked her, so I thought you'd made a mistake. And besides, he was with me at the tree lot when she was attacked, so it couldn't have been him."

"Good point, but with two cars involved in this abduction he's obviously working with someone."

"I didn't know that at the time."

"You didn't send the text to get Claire over here, did you?" Travis asked as his thoughts cleared and he started to process his next steps.

Julie looked at her phone. "I can't believe he did this." She paused for a moment and lifted her head in thought. "Maybe I should've seen the signs. He's having financial issues. His parents have money and could help him, but they refused." She wrapped her arms around her waist. "I didn't know he was this desperate. I just didn't know."

Travis didn't want to believe her, but he thought she was telling the truth. He'd met Eric and didn't suspect the guy, so why wouldn't a woman blinded by love fail to notice his duplicitous behavior? Either way it didn't matter.

Eric had Claire, and Travis needed to find her. "He'd take her someplace private. Anywhere come to mind?"

Julie tapped a finger on her chin as precious seconds ticked by.

"Think!" Travis shouted, making her jump. "Where would he take her?"

"His family has a private compound on the outskirts of Orlando."

"Tell me about it."

"They have several thousand acres with a few cabins near a lake. His parents have their own plane so there's an airstrip. The rest of the land is swampy."

The perfect place to hide someone—and maybe even dispose of someone. "Tell me how to get there."

She rattled off directions. "It's very remote with only a narrow lane leading to the cabins so if he's there he'll see you arrive."

"Which might make him panic." Travis ran over the scenarios he might employ for a rescue. "You said there's an airstrip. How close is it to the cabin?"

"Maybe a half mile."

"Far enough away for someone to parachute in without being seen?"

"I guess so."

Travis dug out his phone to call his CO and arrange for a helicopter to the compound.

Let me be doing the right thing here, Lord, he prayed. *And hold Claire safely in Your arms until I can get to her.*

The helicopter rotors thumped through the night, bringing Travis closer to the compound.

"Going black." The pilot's words carried over Travis's headset, and the chopper went dark except for the faint glow from the instrument panels.

His heart racing, Travis signaled for his pilot to bank right and drop him nearby. He would've liked to fast-rope down instead of free-falling, but the sound of a helo hovering close to the ground would alert Eric.

He checked his gear a final time then looked through his night-vision goggles to confirm the police and an ambulance waited out of sight for his command to move in.

The door opened, and Travis signaled his readiness before dropping into the night sky. Gravity pulled him downward. The wind rushed up to meet him, and he directed his chute toward his landing target. He caught a glimpse through his goggles of Claire bolting from the cabin then racing across the lawn, heading straight for alligator-infested swamps.

A man darted outside behind her. Eric. He carried a rifle and moved at a rapid clip. He was soon hot on her tail.

With Travis's rifle strapped to his back, he could do nothing to help her from his altitude, and panic threatened to swamp him.

Keep it together, man. Eric needs her alive.

Or does he? The thought broke through, sending terror to his heart. She might've already provided Eric with the specs, meaning his goal could be to silence her forever.

And Travis was powerless to stop him.

ELEVEN

Claire pounded over the spongy ground, her every sense attuned to the night hanging thick and heavy overhead. To the slight breeze carrying fetid smells from the swamp. The insects buzzing. The darkness suffocating and paralyzing as she raced through it. No matter her fear, she had to keep going. Her life depended on it.

Eric said he'd lost money in an investment and needed a quick infusion of cash. He'd borrowed it from a loan shark, and when he couldn't pay it back, he'd conned Julie into stealing the prototype. He turned it over to the loan shark, who soon learned it had no value without Claire and he demanded Eric abduct her. The loan shark had even helped—driving the van that had rear-ended her. When she wouldn't give him the information tonight, he'd threatened to kill Travis if she didn't give up the specs.

She couldn't let the man she loved die, so she'd told Eric what he needed to know. He immediately called the loan shark and when she heard them discussing how to get rid of her, she'd bolted for the door. She'd heard Eric snatch up the rifle on the table then charge after her.

He was gaining on her now, his footfalls pounding closer.

Panic raised its ugly head. She tried to pick up speed, but swampy gunk sucked at her feet and threatened to take her down. Her only hope was to hide. But where?

Think, Claire, think.

She slowed and searched the area. A pool of stagnant water lay ahead. As a native Floridian, Eric had to know water meant gators. If she took to the water, he'd never follow. She'd rather chance making it safely to the other side before Eric spotted her than stay on shore and risk a certain bullet to the back from his gun.

She held her hands high to keep the slimy water from her wrists rubbed raw from her attempt to escape the ropes and plunged in. Thankfully, her ankles hadn't suffered the same injury or the pain might slow her down. She'd traveled about thirty feet when she heard movement to her side.

A gator? Probably. She imagined a large alligator swimming toward her. Water sluicing off his rough hide. His beady eyes skimming over the surface and fixed on her. His jaw poised and ready to snap.

Terrified, she picked up speed and the foul water churned. She saw a dark form about ten feet away.

No, oh, no.

She dug her shoes in and pushed with all her might. The quicksand of a bottom captured her feet. The water shifted more.

Now only three feet away.

Please, not this!

A crack split the night and the gator stilled. She spun. Saw a man on the bank with some sort of goggles on his face and a rifle to his shoulder.

Eric? Or maybe his associate? But she hadn't made it safely to the other side where she could hide. If it was Eric, he had to be able to see her. So why would he kill the gator when he could've put the same bullet in her back?

"Claire," the man called out as he lowered the weapon.

His voice wrapped around her like a blanket. "Travis. Is that you?"

"It's me."

"You found me." She started sobbing. "You really found me."

"Shh, honey. You don't want to attract any more of those shoes in the making, do you?" He laughed, and it rumbled through the mist helping her gain control of her tears. "I'll keep an eye out for another one while you hightail it over here."

"Be careful," she warned as she slipped toward shore. "Eric's after me and he has a gun."

"Not anymore."

She heard the certainty in his voice and couldn't believe this

wonderful, amazing man was in her life. The man who readily gave of himself so others might be safe. Gave of himself
so *she* might be safe. The man she loved and wanted to spend
the rest of her life with, if he'd have her. And she planned to
tell him that just as soon as she escaped the swamp without
becoming a gator snack.

Claire's plan to declare her love had been a good one, but
police sirens and a very demanding police officer stepping between them preempted it. Travis gave him a quick rundown
of the events and offered the location where he'd bound Eric
to a tree.

"Promise me you'll secure the stolen prototype and specs
before going after Eric," Claire added. "I don't want to risk
him getting away and taking it from the house."

The cop nodded. "First, we need to separate you two until
we can take your statements."

"No," Travis growled, and fired a look that would make
Claire run for the hills.

The officer widened his stance. "It's protocol."

"I don't care about protocol. I'm not leaving this woman's
side ever again."

Detective Purcell joined them, his gaze shooting between
Travis and the officer then settling on Travis. "We can let protocol slide this time if you and Ms. Reed agree not to discuss
the incident before we take your statements."

"You have my word," Travis responded quickly.

"Then after the medic clears Ms. Reed for travel, I'll give
you both a lift to the station." He focused on the cop. "Let's
give them some time alone."

"Wait," Claire said. "Before you go, I wanted to ask if Officer Harper is okay."

"He took a bullet, but he made it through surgery with flying colors." Purcell and the other officer departed.

Claire blew out a breath of relief before scooting closer to
Travis. Even in the dark, she tried to telegraph her feelings for
him in a single look. "I hoped you'd come."

"Did you now?"

She nodded. "Next time don't wait so long, okay?"

With a laugh, he swooped her into his arms and held her tight. She wished the police would finish setting up their portable lights so she could get a better look at his face.

"I love you, Claire," he said, tightening his arms even more. "And I promise there will never be a next time as long as I have anything to say about it."

"Promises, promises," she joked, suddenly too uncertain to voice her own feelings until the arc from a flashlight caught his face and she saw unfettered love in his eyes. "I love you, too, Travis."

"I knew that."

"Did you now?" She mimicked his earlier comment.

A floodlight clicked on next to them, letting her see the confidence fleeing from his face. "Let's say I hoped you did."

She looked deeply into his eyes and made sure her love burned as brightly as the floodlight. "I do. So much. Don't ever doubt it."

She laid her head on his chest and sighed out her happiness. A sudden breeze kicked up, and despite his nearness, she shivered.

"Let's get you to the ambulance so we can get out of here. Can you walk?"

"I can, but…" She snuggled closer.

"Freeloader," he joked, and carried her to the ambulance, then gently set her on the bumper.

The cheerful sound of Christmas carols played from the medic's phone mounted on her belt. "Let me know if you want me to turn the music off. I'm not supposed to have it on, but sometimes this job gets me down and music picks me up."

"Please keep it playing," Claire said, fully embracing the Christmas spirit now that her ordeal was over for good.

"I agree." Travis rested a shoulder on the vehicle. Claire noticed his eyes didn't leave the medic while she disinfected and bound Claire's wrists, then checked her vitals.

"You're good to go." The medic climbed into her vehicle to stow her supplies.

Claire looked up at Travis and found him watching her carefully, that uncertainty she'd seen earlier in his expression. She took his hand and twined their fingers together. "I want you to know that I don't care how dangerous your job is. I'm not going to send you away again. Ever."

He looked deeply into her eyes. "Not that I'm not pleased, but why the sudden change?"

"These last few days have shown me that I can't eliminate danger." She ran her finger down the side of his face. "The only thing I ask is that we try to find a way to communicate in your long deployments."

"About that." He joined her on the bumper and settled her on his lap. "I was thinking I'm ready for a more stable job. One where I'll be around for you and all the little Chapmans we might have."

"You can't do that for me. The army needs you."

"And they'll have me. Did I mention Colonel Lynch offered me a job at the institute?"

"You know you didn't." She playfully punched his shoulder and he grinned.

"Ah, guys?" The medic pointed at a sprig of mistletoe hanging from a shelf. "Feel free to use this if it helps the cause."

Claire felt a blush creep over her face, but she didn't care. She was going to kiss this man now, and no medic or even the officers escorting Eric to their cruiser were going to stand in her way.

She looked into Travis's eyes. "I suppose this means you're going to have to kiss me."

"Oh, yeah. Now and copious times every day for the rest of our lives." Smiling, he lowered his head.

As his lips claimed hers in a bruising kiss, Claire heard strains of "The Most Wonderful Time of the Year" coming from the medic's phone and she knew without a doubt every time of the year would be wonderful now that her Green Beret was home for good.

* * * * *

HOMEFRONT HOLIDAY HERO

JODIE BAILEY

You were running a good race. Who cut in on you to keep you from obeying the truth?
—*Galatians* 5:7

Dedication

For the brave men and women of the military and their loving families who support them at home.

ONE

Kelly Walters hit the snowy ground by the road with a thud that knocked the wind from her lungs. The crack of the gunshot echoed off the trees surrounding the parking lot of the Fort Campbell Family Resource Center, shredding the December midnight air.

"Hey!" The shout followed the gunshot and a body leaped over her, pounding footsteps crunching in the fresh snow that had fallen that afternoon. *Get it together, Walters.* Her fingers dug into the chilled ground and she pulled in a deep breath, the residue of gunpowder tickling her nose. She assessed the damage as she focused on the brittle stars. Toes moved. Fingers moved. She turned her head from side to side. Neck fine. But her bicep... With a sudden rush, the adrenaline ebbed and the pain kicked in. Her fingers flew to her right arm and came away warm with blood. Her blood.

Somehow all of that seemed faraway. This wasn't happening. She was outside the Family Resource Center on Fort Campbell, not in a war zone like the soldiers whose families she aided as a Family Readiness Support Assistant. Her job involved connecting dependents to resources and holding hands when times got hard, not dodging bullets.

Surely she'd fallen asleep wrapping that mound of presents for tomorrow. That had to be it, because there was no way she was shot by some punk kid who'd flagged her down in the crosswalk to ask for directions.

The footsteps came back, slower this time, a slip in the gait. Major Tyler Rainey took a knee beside her, grimacing as he did. "You okay?"

"Mostly." Blood smeared across her jeans as she dragged her fingers across her thigh. The whole scene receded, as if she was watching it on a movie screen instead of living in the moment. "Nicked my bicep instead of drilling my shoulder, thanks to you." If he hadn't pushed her out of the way... She shuddered, then shoved aside the *what if* like her father had taught her. Emotion got you nowhere. If she gave in to emotion, she'd curl up in a ball and whimper like a kicked dog. "Did you get a license plate?"

The dark crossover had pulled up as she and Tyler stepped into the crosswalk on their way to the parking lot. Kelly hadn't hesitated to lean in when the young man in the passenger seat asked for directions. She'd turned to point down the road when Tyler threw her to the side and the world cracked with a gunshot.

"No. They were gone too fast, but the guard gate will have something on them." Tyler dragged his hand across the slight wave in his short dark blond hair. "They had to have just come in. The gate's not even a half mile up the road. That's what drinking and carrying a pistol will get you." Dropping to a sitting position, he pivoted and waved his fingers toward himself. "Let me see your arm."

"Flesh wound." It burned like fire, but she held it out toward him, anyway.

The minute the pressure of his fingers hit her elbow, she looked away. Something about that touch overwhelmed the pain and shot a whole different kind of warmth through her body, one she'd been trying to avoid for months. It was not good when the FRSA couldn't stop thinking about one of the rear detachment commanders. It was her job to be here for the families left behind during deployment, to be the liaison between them and Tyler as he led the soldiers and civilians supporting the push on the front lines. Tangling the two could get more complicated than twisted parachute lines.

Reluctantly, she pulled herself away. "It's really just a flesh wound."

It didn't seem as though Tyler wanted to believe her, the way he studied her face, but, finally, he turned his attention to the guard shack. "You're right. He nicked you, but having it looked at in the E.R. wouldn't hurt." Discussion closed, he pulled out his phone. "Yeah, this is Major Tyler Rainey. I'd like to report a shooting at the Family Resource Center."

His voice was so calm, it was almost like he was asking for a weather call over the radio. But the words... *A shooting.* Kelly pulled her knees to her chest and held on with her uninjured arm. It could have been so much worse. *Keep it together, like Dad taught you.*

Tires screeched around the corner, cutting Tyler off in midexplanation as his head whipped around. "They're coming back." He was up faster than his knee should have allowed. Shoving his phone into his pocket, Tyler dragged Kelly to her feet by her good arm. "Can you run?"

She eyed his knee, focusing on anything other than immediate danger. "Can you?"

"Watch me." He gripped her hand and pulled her forward, setting a faster pace than she could handle even on her best days.

They were halfway up the walk to the Family Resource Center when the first bullet spit dirt behind them. She swallowed a shriek. Three more irregular shots, then silence as they rounded the corner of the building.

Kelly pressed her back against the brick and strained hard, listening, while searching for a place to run. Streetlights left few shadows. Leafless tree branches shifted in the breeze. There was a wide expanse of fresh snow between them and the road, which would make their tracks easy to follow. Without a key to get back inside, they had nowhere to hide.

The engine drew closer, humming to a stop under the building's overhang. She turned to Tyler to see if he'd found them an out.

He scanned the trees, the nearby road, the other side of the building... Likely, he saw what she saw. Nowhere safe to run. They were trapped.

He leaned closer, blue eyes intense, his whisper barely audible. "There are two of us and two of them."

"And they have a gun." Not to mention the disadvantage of her wounded arm and his recently reconstructed knee.

"Well, there's that." The humor fell flat in light of the foot-

steps crunching slowly closer. *One* set of footsteps. Kelly hoped
the driver wasn't circling around the back of the building to
surprise them from the other side. Her heart beat faster, drowning out every other sound.

Until sirens lit up in the distance.

From a few feet away, a muffled curse, pounding feet, the
squeal of tires...then nothing.

Tyler released a long breath and bent at the waist, hand
braced on his good knee, exhaling loudly. "I think you're safe
for now." He looked up at her, face grim. "But I also think we
passed the point where you can call this random."

The ancient faded-green desk chair squeaked as Tyler
dropped into it, propped his feet on his desk and crossed his
arms behind his head. His whole body ached from adrenaline
and, not that he'd admit it out loud, the brush with fear.

Someone had taken a shot at Kelly Walters. And they'd
come back to finish the job. He shut his eyes against what
might have been, but his imagination burned with blood and
tragedy, anyway. She could have been killed. Like...

Pressing a thumb and index finger against his eyelids, he
squinted hard and shoved the images back into a dark corner,
wishing his body would relax enough to let him sleep. But
the adrenaline hadn't quite let go yet. He wanted to go park
his truck outside of the apartment Kelly rented off post and
stand watch, but she hadn't asked and that was a boundary he
wasn't ready to push. Not with a civilian coworker. So here he
sat, in his office at work, waiting for dawn. In the morning,
he'd call and offer to escort her back to the Family Resource
Center for the big day.

How he'd gotten roped into volunteering to work behind the
scenes at the community's annual holiday toy giveaway, he'd
never know. Well, actually, he did know. Because Kelly had
been the one to ask. Had it been anyone other than the petite
brunette with the ready smile, he'd have said no. Tyler opened
his eyes and frowned at the ceiling. Too bad he was only here
until his knee healed. After that, he was back to his battalion

in the mountains of Afghanistan. That fact alone made any talk of being more than colleagues kind of tough.

His life was a soldier's life, and the last thing he needed on the battlefield was to be torn between family and mission, or to leave a family behind if the unthinkable happened. He'd already seen that firsthand. He balled up a piece of paper and bounced it off the ceiling, catching it easily. As soon as he got the doc to sign off on his knee, he was headed right back where he should be. In the proverbial trenches, not standing behind a curtain and passing out wrapped gifts to the children of deployed soldiers.

And certainly not spending hours on a Friday evening wrapping hundreds of presents next to the woman who stole way too many of his thoughts.

The frown returned for an encore. Okay. So that part hadn't been so bad. But it still wasn't what he was trained to do. No matter how much they'd laughed and talked and learned even more about each other than they had over the past six months they'd spent working together. And no matter how glad he was he'd stayed hours after the other volunteers left, since it meant he was there for her when she was attacked.

His feet hit the floor with a thud, drawing a wince as his knee reminded him he'd pushed it too far tonight with the running. The pain was worth it, though. If he hadn't been there, there was no telling where Kelly would be tonight.

He checked his watch. She should be wrapping up at the hospital by now, getting her arm bandaged up. If they'd been more than colleagues, he'd have insisted on staying with her and taking her home afterward, but she'd blocked his every maneuver to do that. After he'd finished telling his part of the story to the military police, she'd practically forced him to leave, insisting everything would be okay.

Speaking of stories… Tyler yanked open his top drawer and dug through the clutter until his fingers found the business card he'd tucked away a few months ago. Kelly's dad had dropped by the battalion a week or so before he'd deployed with another unit in the 101st Airborne. Sergeant Major Jackson Walters was a no-nonsense kind of guy, a man Tyler had served under seven years earlier at the 82nd Airborne.

The minute the sergeant major recognized Tyler, he'd pulled him aside and slipped him the card with his personal international cell number on it. *Keep an eye on her. She's all I've got left.* It wasn't a request typically made, but Tyler had promised, tucking the card away and certain he'd never need it. What kind of guy called the father of a grown woman to report on her welfare?

That was long before tonight. And it was certainly before he'd started to think of Kelly as more than the coworker he consulted with on family issues, accompanied to way too many funerals and, more recently, had lunch with at the Post Exchange.

He shook that thought off once again and tapped the card against his desk. Did this merit a personal call to a war zone? She'd barely been nicked, and if those guys hadn't come back, he'd have sworn it was a random act. But they *had* come back, which meant they likely wanted something more.

The card crumpled in Tyler's balled fist. He checked the time and did the math. It was midmorning in Afghanistan. Intel said the sergeant major's unit was gearing up for a massive joint offensive. It probably wasn't the time to interrupt his day with upsetting news.

Tyler slipped the card back into his drawer. He'd keep an eye on the situation and wait. Everything in him hoped this whole thing was two guys who'd hit the town a little too hard in their search for pre-Christmas cheer.

He whipped out his phone and called a buddy of his with the military police instead.

The phone only rang once. "Captain Shorter." He sounded more brusque than usual.

"Shorty. It's Rainey."

There was a light chuckle on the other end of the phone. "Rainey, your name came across my radio not too long ago. What were you doing at the Family Resource Center with your FRSA at midnight?"

The heat that rushed into Tyler's skin made him grateful this wasn't a face-to-face discussion. "Believe it or not, wrapping

Christmas presents for the deployed soldiers' kids. Her other volunteers ducked out early, so I stayed behind to help. The big community toy giveaway is tomorrow." The nearby town of Hopkinsville rallied around the soldiers' families every year, heaping toys and food on the spouses and kids left behind.

"Check out the Good Samaritan. What's up? You picked a crazy night to get tied up in other people's shootings."

"That's why I called." Dropping back in the chair, Tyler propped up his bum knee and ran a finger along the edge of the pain, wary of massaging the tender places too hard. "Wanted to see if you had any special intel on the two yahoos who took a shot at Kelly Walters."

"Not a thing yet. It's going to take a while to get footage from the gate. There are more pranks and mischief going on tonight than I've seen in ages."

"Yeah?" Tyler chewed the disappointment out of the word. What he really wanted to hear was those two were safely in handcuffs so he could maybe get some sleep without worrying about where they were lurking. "Like what?"

"Petty messes. Couple of broken car windows. Some spray paint. A front door kicked but not breached. Kids with too much time on their hands now that it's Christmas break."

"I don't envy you." That kind of nonsense drove Tyler up the wall, but it happened sometimes when dads were gone for long periods of time and moms were stretched thinner than they'd ever dreamed.

"You're jealous and you know it. You'd love to be in any kind of action at this point. Even rescuing pretty girls from handguns."

"We're done now."

"You only say that because I'm hitting too close to home."

"Out." Tyler pressed End and tossed the phone to his desk. Sometimes Shorty was too intuitive for his own good. Made him a good cop but a terrible friend.

The phone vibrated, rattling a coffee cup on the desk.

Tyler snagged it, checking the caller ID. Surely the man hadn't thought of another way to harass him.

The number on the screen made the adrenaline surge again.

He swiped to answer. "Kelly. You okay? Need a ride from the hospital?"

"I'm home." Her words were hollow, unbelieving.

Tyler sat straighter. "What's going on?" If those men had found her, he wouldn't be able to answer for what happened to them.

"My apartment." She pulled in a shaky breath. "It's been trashed."

TWO

The Christmas lights hanging from balconies around the apartment complex glowed surreally against the fresh snow. Even at four-fifteen in the morning, squares of illumination from surrounding windows filtered dimly through the dark. Apparently, the ruckus at Kelly's apartment was keeping the neighbors up, too. This was probably not earning her high doses of Christmas cheer from her neighbors, most of whom had young children.

Kelly let the blinds drop against the window of her first-floor apartment and steeled herself before turning to face the mess behind her. The gray couch lay on its back, stubby wooden legs exposed. Every picture and award had been ripped from the walls, glass ground into the carpet. Dishes, pots and pans lay scattered and strewn around the room, but nothing was missing, not even the laptop she'd left on the coffee table. Everything was simply a mess, calculated to be as disruptive as possible.

Coupled with the gunshot that still echoed in her ears, the fear was close to winning. It was one thing to be the victim of a random act, another very personal thing to know someone had been in her home and touched her things. If she turned around fast enough, it almost felt as though she could catch them still in the room, watching her. It was too much for one night, the coincidence almost unthinkable.

We passed the point where you can call this random. Tyler's assertion rattled in her head, even though she wanted to silence it. It had to be a coincidence. There was no reason for anyone to target her. She'd spent the better part of the past hour racking her brain as she watched the police comb through her apartment. Nothing stood out except the one thing she hated to admit.... She'd feel a whole lot safer when Tyler showed up.

"Ma'am?" A tall policeman, slim in his uniform, stopped in front of her. "We're finished." He talked her through the next steps, handed her copies of paperwork she wasn't ready to read yet and left.

All Kelly wanted was to put things together enough to go to bed, but after the evening she'd had, she knew sleep would not be an option. No sleep meant a long day of smiling through the weariness tomorrow. For weeks she'd looked forward to the toy giveaway. All she wanted was the best for those kids, but now the day ahead felt like torture.

A crunch of feet on glass, then a voice drifted from the doorway. "I passed the police on my way in."

Tyler. Something around her heart cracked, and she let herself revel in the relief of his presence. She couldn't have it for long, but right now she was too exhausted to fight the tremor that quivered in her stomach. Swallowing her sigh of relief, she looked up at him, trying to keep her voice level. "They just left." She swept her hand to encompass the whole room. "Now there's this."

Tyler winced and stepped into the room, pulling the door shut behind him before he stepped over a pillow from her bedroom and an overturned kitchen bar stool to meet her. "They did a pretty thorough job." His exhale was hard enough to move the bangs on her forehead. Either that or he was standing closer than he usually did. Not that she minded at the moment. Given the situation, it was all she could do not to give in to an impulse that had been building for months, to lean against him and let him wrap his arms around her. Even with him close, she felt as though she was facing this beast of a night alone, and she could use whatever comfort she could get.

Kelly straightened and took a step back, her thigh brushing her overturned couch. She knew better. People would fail her every time, wouldn't be there when she needed them most. Tyler himself had made it no secret that he wasn't here to stay. It was God she should be trusting, not a six-foot soldier with shoulders that looked broad enough to bear every one of her burdens.

"You zoning on me, Walters? Is this day finally getting to you?"

Let him believe it was that. It was way better than the truth. "Probably. This day started twenty-three hours ago when my dad called."

Something in that sentence apparently piqued Tyler's interest. His muscles tightened. "You talked to your dad today?"

"Yeah. Something strange about that?"

"No." There was a forced nonchalance in the words as he tipped his chin toward her couch and leaned over. "Not at all. Just…surprised."

Kelly joined him in moving the couch back into position. "He won't be able to call on Christmas. Lets his guys have all of the phone time, so he thought he'd send his love a couple days early." Her voice strained as they lifted together, righting the sofa. "I'll talk to him after New Year's."

"Hmm."

"That's it? One syllable?" Nudging the couch back into place with her hip, she hazarded a look at Tyler. "For that kind of moral support, I could have called the zoo and asked them to send a chimpanzee over." What she needed right now was the Tyler Rainey who told jokes over Chinese food at the P/X food court and managed to tease a grin out of her when days got too long—not this closed-off, stoic Rambo, who seemed intent on keeping her at arm's length. *Where you should be.*

"Hey, that begs a question." Tyler turned away from her and started stacking broken picture frames, collecting them on the heavy wood coffee table. "What made you call me?"

Momentary weakness. She was scared and realized she felt safer when he was around. "You were the only friend I could think of who'd still be awake." Kelly eased a half step toward the open kitchen when he turned back to her. If he was going to act as though it was perfectly natural for him to step in and start setting her apartment to rights, so be it, but she didn't have to let him touch her heart. Glass rattled as she swept it from the counter into the trash can. "And you're failing at the whole friendship thing."

"Sorry." There was a twitch in his eye, almost like a wince.

"I doubt I can make things all better, but I can tell you you're in good company tonight." With an expression Kelly couldn't decipher, Tyler went back to righting furniture, lifting her recliner off its side. It would be nice if he quit doing that. It made his biceps stand out under the long-sleeved shirt he wore, pushed his shoulders up in a way that showed the power there.

"How am I in good company?"

"Talked to a buddy of mine who's an MP. Apparently, we're having a bit of Mischief Night in December. Yours is the only incident I know of off-post, though."

Something cold ran down Kelly's back, raising the hair on the back of her neck. Shuddering, she straightened, still holding the pan she'd intended to put back in the cabinet. "What happened?"

Tyler's voice was tight. "Some spray paint. A few slashed tires. A door kicked open, but no intrusion."

"Sounds like a bunch of kids with too much time on their hands."

"That wasn't a kid who shot you. What did the doc say?"

"That I'm one blessed girl." Kelly tried to keep sarcasm from stinging the words as she settled the pan into a cabinet by the stove. "That the biggest thing I'll have to worry about is infection if I don't keep the wound bandaged up. Though I'll have to go and buy a new jacket." She turned her shoulder toward him so he could see the tear in the jacket she still wore. "Think insurance will cover that?"

Tyler paused, a slight smile on his face. "You're something else." His gaze stayed on her longer than it had since he'd walked in, searching for something she couldn't quite understand.

"Seriously." Her voice dropped lower, the emotion behind the words tearing away the smile she'd flashed a moment before. "Thanks for staying late with me tonight. If you hadn't been there and seen what was happening…" Fear gripped her at the idea of where she might be right now had Tyler Rainey not pulled her out of the way. "I could be—"

The rest of her words muffled against his chest as he dropped the couch pillow he was holding and crossed into the kitchen to pull her close. Her arms slipped around his waist of their own accord, even though her mind knew they shouldn't. For one minute, she'd allow herself this feeling of not being alone in the world, of being protected by someone else.

Only for a moment, though, because she was the protector, and this interlude would only make her want things she couldn't have. But boy, was she going to enjoy this moment, listening to Tyler's heartbeat, feeling his chest move as he breathed. Feeling the warmth of his arms holding her close in a place safe from flying bullets, kicked-in doors and a shattered apartment.

"There's something you have to consider." His voice rumbled in his chest, a deep throb against her ear. "Everything on post might appear to be random, but your attacks seem targeted." He set her away from him, hands braced on her shoulders, and tilted his head to capture her attention.

Green eyes scanned his, back and forth as if reading the words on his mind. As long as she didn't see the ones beginning to form on his heart. Her muscles stiffened, triceps tightening under his fingers. With a sniff, she shoved him lightly. "Why on earth would someone come after me? I know no secrets, other than a few spouses have told me and, believe me, none of them merit this." She swept her hand from her injured arm to her living room then stepped out of his grasp to lean against her counter.

Frustration pounded under Tyler's skin. She shouldn't be so nonchalant. There was no way she could miss that she'd been attacked twice, much more violently than any other family. The question was why. His fists balled at his sides. Let him find out. He'd take care of the problem before anyone could hurt Kelly again.

He pulled in a deep breath, seeking perspective. *Stay on course, Rainey.* He wasn't going to push this line of thinking, not when he was wheels up as soon as his knee was cleared for duty. Someone else would have his office, his job, working with the Family Readiness Group and Kelly to aid the families in their battalion while he was half a world away. Getting invested in her problems wouldn't be fair to either of them. "I'm just saying—"

"There are plenty of families hurting on post tonight, wondering why someone damaged their property. There's no way I'm going to hole up in my house crying 'why me.' As soon as we get cleaned up, I'm going to try to sleep then head back to the Family Resource Center to hand out presents to some kids who need a little bit of joy." She pushed off the counter and backed away from him, squaring off from what she must have deemed a safe distance. "That's my job. It's what I do. I'm here for others, not for myself. The last thing I need is you trying to put all of the focus on me."

Whoa. Okay. Tyler held up his hands in surrender. "Maybe you're right. Maybe I'm tired and this mountain is really a molehill that I need to step around." Not that he fully believed that, but if it would take some of the fury out of her expression, he'd go with anything.

Her shoulders relaxed, though her face remained hard. "Maybe."

The sudden softness made Tyler want to reach out and pull her to him, although at this point all it would likely get him was a boot heel to his instep. His toes curled involuntarily.

Tyler was about to suggest that they might be better off if they called a full truce and went back to cleaning when there was a light tap at the door and a young woman peeked in. She wore a sweatshirt over fleece pajama pants, and her dark brown hair sat in a high ponytail. Tyler's eyebrow quirked even as he stepped between Kelly and the newcomer. Right now, he didn't trust a soul he didn't recognize.

The younger woman took in the room. "What in the world…"

Kelly wasted no time shoving Tyler aside and stepping around him. "Stephanie. What are you doing here?"

She hugged the woman before Tyler could react, but that didn't stop him from holding his breath until they broke apart and he could see that Kelly was still in one piece, no new bullet holes or stab wounds. Maybe Kelly was right. If he was suspecting twentysomething women in Snoopy pj's, it was probably time to hit the rack for a couple of hours.

"I'm glad to see you already have company." There was a teasing lilt to the new girl's voice that made the back of Tyler's neck burn.

Kelly heard the implication, too. When she glanced at Tyler, her cheeks pinked. With a tight smile, she shook her head. "This is Major Tyler Rainey, the Rear D commander over at 2nd Brigade. We work together. He's offering moral support—and some grunt labor with the heavy lifting."

The grin that tipped Stephanie's lips said she didn't quite believe Kelly's story, but she didn't force the issue. "Tasha, who lives a couple of buildings over, said something was going on here, so I thought I'd check on you. I tried your cell phone first, but you didn't answer."

Tyler stepped forward, still not quite sure he trusted the petite brunette. "I'm sorry. I didn't catch your name." Sure, Kelly had said it, but Tyler needed some control of the situation.

"Oh." Stephanie held out her hand. "I'm Stephanie Anderson."

The look Kelly shot Tyler let him know she knew his thoughts to the letter…and she wasn't happy with them. "Stephanie is my Point of Contact with my dad's unit." Her voice was warm, but there was a chill underneath meant for him and his wariness. "You know how that works, Major. The Family Readiness Group passes down information through spouse volunteer POCs who check on family members, make sure everyone is in the loop and doing well. I'm sure you're familiar with the process."

Okay. So this Stephanie girl wasn't someone random off the streets. Kelly didn't have to be sarcastic about it. Her tone cut him down to three feet tall, and a retort flared in his chest. He swallowed it and shook her extended hand. "Nice to meet you."

Kelly seemed unfazed by the underlying tension, turning instead to Stephanie. "Really. I'm fine. You didn't have to drag out of bed in the middle of the night to check on me."

"It's okay. Jason called just before I got word about your

apartment. We were video chatting and I was up, anyway. I was worried because you always answer your phone."

"I shoved it in my purse after I called Major Rainey. It's probably still on vibrate from a briefing earlier today." Kelly's forehead creased. "No telling who called needing something." She shook her head. "Speaking of needing something... Have you heard any more from Tasha Pope, other than my house was a crime scene?" She graced Tyler with a quick look. "She's a wife in Dad's unit, one of the other Points of Contact. Married her husband right before the deployment and volunteered immediately. There was an issue with her husband's pay."

"As in he withdrew it all before she got a chance to pay the bills. Two months in a row." Stephanie clamped a hand over her mouth. "I'm sorry. I shouldn't have said that out loud, Major." She flicked a mortified glance at Tyler.

He dismissed her concern with a wave. "Nothing that hasn't happened before. Some of the guys get into some high-stakes poker games when they get bored. She get it straightened out?"

"Major Pinser, his battalion's Rear D, is on it." Kelly patted his arm. "You can't save the world, Major Rainey."

There was nothing Tyler hated more than being patronized. Nothing. And Kelly Walters well knew it.

She'd already turned away. "All is well here. Why don't you go home and get a couple of hours of sleep, and I'll see you later?" Kelly was guiding Stephanie toward the door before Stephanie realized what was happening. "See you in a little while. You're still coming to the toy giveaway, right?"

"Yeah." Stephanie hesitated in the doorway. "See you later."

As her footsteps faded, Tyler checked the time. "It's nearly 0500. If we hurry, we can at least get some of this back to rights and grab some breakfast before we have to play Santa's helpers. I'll drive you, keep you from having to be alone."

Kelly's index finger tapped against the side seam of her jeans. She searched the living room, the kitchen, and the ceiling before she answered. "Okay. Breakfast is a date. But I'm driving. I've ridden with you one too many times, and I'd like to live till Christmas." She was in motion, swiping more broken glass into the trash before the word *date* registered, and Tyler doubted she realized it had been spoken.

Although everything in him wished it were true.

"Now that was almost worth not sleeping all night." Tyler shoved his plate away and stretched back over the booth, arms behind his head, red T-shirt pulling tight across his chest.

Kelly caught herself staring and looked away, downing what was left of her orange juice before she spoke. "Almost, but not quite." She surveyed the room, looking anywhere but Tyler.

Eagle's Nest was the epitome of a mom-and-pop diner. Situated off post on the Kentucky side, the small restaurant had been around since before either of them were born. Appreciation plaques from brigades, photos of soldiers and banners clogged with signatures from deployed units papered the sunny yellow walls. A brightly lit tree stood in one corner, while metallic garlands in a riot of red and green dripped from the ceiling. It ought to be chaotic, but the eclectic mix added to the atmosphere set into place by scattered square tables covered in red-and-white-checked vinyl cloths. Two waitresses bustled in and out of the open kitchen by the small counter, from which the scent of frying bacon and brewing coffee drifted through the room.

Kelly sat back in the vinyl booth and let the everyday down-home smell of country cooking soothe the knot that had been increasing in her stomach ever since the gun smoke cleared. No matter what Tyler said, she couldn't make herself believe there was anything special about her. She was a girl, living out her calling, helping other families. Surely it was just mischief, like the other cases.

Or... The acid from the orange juice burned, and she gulped water instead. Kelly forced more negative thoughts away. She could not, would not, believe this was anything more coordinated than a bunch of kids running wild without their daddies home to rein them in.

She dropped her forehead into her hands. "I have got to get some sleep."

"You and me both."

"Think if I racked out right here in this booth, they'd have a problem with it?" Kelly peeked between her fingers at the nearly empty room, where only two other young men, civilians from the look of their hair, sat at a table in the corner. They avoided her gaze. "They definitely have the room."

"Wait until about 0800. This place will be hopping."

"Can't believe I've never been here before. I keep hearing about it, but I never seem to make it over." Kelly drew in a deep breath and forced her mind to the present.

"A lot of the joes come here. Good coffee. Homemade biscuits. And, of course, there's bacon." The words should have transmitted humor, but they fell flat. While he was talking to her, his focus was shot.

She knew that look, had seen it on her father after deployments, had watched many soldiers sport it when they came home. It was vigilance, a trained eye for threats. Kelly pulled in a deep breath and asked the question she really didn't want answered. "Okay, Rainey. What's running through your head?"

"Is it that obvious?" Wrapping his hands around his thick white coffee mug, he rotated the cup back and forth between his palms. "Very few people read me that well."

Kelly cleared her throat and looked away as a young man stepped through the door, fingering his baseball cap as he took a seat between them and the two men in the corner. No way would she cop to learning every facial expression in Tyler's arsenal. That would tip him off that she'd been paying attention. It didn't stop the blush from warming her cheeks, though. "I've spent a lot of time with a lot of hurting people. I'm pretty good at telling when someone's smiling through the pain. It's similar enough to what you're doing right now." She pulled her lower lip between her teeth, hoping he'd buy the story.

Apparently, he did, though he never looked up from the coffee cup he palmed. "Just watching…and sitting here thinking I should call Shorty."

Her eyebrow quirked. "Sounds like a mob hit man. I'm pretty sure a busted front door and a mess in my house don't merit a call to the mafia."

"Don't forget the shooter. That worries me a whole lot more."

Kelly wanted to wave off his concern, but he pinned her in a gaze that said more than she wanted to hear. He was worried. About her. Specifically. All of a sudden, she couldn't swallow. A look that intense was not something she should be on the receiving end of. This could not be about her. "So." The word choked and died, so she downed half of her water and tried again. "Shorty?"

"Captain Shorter. My buddy I was telling you about with the military police. I'm itching to talk to him since your house got hit after you were shot."

"Grazed."

"Call it what you want. Someone aimed at you and pulled the trigger."

The water she'd chugged turned to ice in her stomach. The more he brought that up, the more he tore down her convictions that the events of last night were random.

That, and he'd showed his protective streak. This was getting too familiar, and she suddenly regretted calling him last night...and inviting him to breakfast in a moment of weakness this morning. She tore the edges of her napkin into fringe, anything to keep her hands busy, to distract her from her thoughts—and from the man sitting across from her.

Oblivious to her edginess, Tyler kept talking, intent on scanning the room, as if there was a plan that only he could see written in the air. "I'm thinking a call to him could help connect the dots, maybe put some gas to this fire and get the investigation rolling a little faster."

Behind Kelly, the door squeaked open, bringing a rush of cold air into the room.

Tyler followed the movements of a young soldier who stepped into the diner, rubbing his hands against the cold. "You don't need to be flippant about what's happened to you."

"And I don't need to jump to conclusions, either."

Tyler didn't seem to hear her. Instead, he reached across the table and laid a hand on her fidgeting fingers, the muscles in his face tightening. "Listen to me. I want you to get up and walk out ahead of me right now." Releasing her, he pulled some bills from his pocket and dropped them onto the table.

"What—"

"Come on."

Kelly slipped out of the booth as Tyler blocked her view of the rest of the room, then rested his hand on the small of her back and urged her forward. They cleared the door and the glare of sunrise on snow stole her vision for an instant. "What's going on?"

His pace didn't slow as they crossed the small parking lot toward her car. "Call me paranoid, but there was something about that guy who came in earlier." He pressed her faster. "He knew I was watching him and still eyed you, like he was daring me to confront him."

For the first time, a real sense of danger leaked over Kelly's skin. She couldn't swallow, and she stumbled, trying to look over her shoulder.

There was no pause in their footsteps until they reached the far side of her SUV, out of sight of the restaurant's door. Tyler held out his hand. "Give me your keys." His voice was hard, allowing no room for argument.

Kelly reached into her coat pocket, cold fingers fumbling for her keys, which clattered to the ground. She bent low to grab them, then straightened so fast she backed square into Tyler's chest, her feet almost slipping from beneath her.

He gripped her biceps, steadying her, though she hardly felt it. All of Kelly's focus was on her front tire, where the thick handle of a knife protruded from the sidewall. It was as though her peripheral vision fell away and there was nothing else but that rubber-gripped metal.

Tyler's fingers dug in tighter, then he unlocked the car and shoved her in. "Stay here and lock yourself in." The SUV rocked as he slammed the door and was gone, vanishing inside the restaurant before Kelly could turn to track his movements.

Her pulse pounded so loud in the silent vehicle, it was a wonder the mirrors didn't vibrate. She scanned the street in front of her, the backseat, constantly in motion, constantly waiting for someone to throw themselves against the door like a bad scene from a low B horror movie.

It was probably only a minute before Tyler reappeared at the entrance of the restaurant, but it felt like three lifetimes had passed for Kelly. He pulled gently on the door handle before she opened it, then he gathered her against his chest as though he could block the rest of the world from seeing her.

It seemed to work. With him holding her tight, it felt as though no one could touch her. "Where did you go?"

"That guy... He took off out the back of the restaurant through the emergency exit as soon as we were out the front. The owner's calling the police." He eased back to scan her face. "Now do you believe that someone's after you?"

THREE

The air in the Family Resource Center crackled with excitement and voices. Familiar Christmas songs piped through the room. The sounds should have been comforting, but Tyler couldn't think over the onslaught of high-pitched childish giggles. The line of children waiting for Santa snaked until the end was impossible to see. He wanted to find joy in the scene, but all he could see was trouble, too many things that could go wrong.

Against Tyler's wishes, Kelly worked the crowd, stopping here to chat with a small group of wives, pausing there to share hugs with a group of children. At the moment, she'd stopped to applaud an impromptu concert by a toddler rocking out on a cardboard guitar. She'd been uncharacteristically quiet since they'd found the knife, hardly uttering a word on the ride over, but to watch her now, no one would know anything had happened.

On the other hand, Tyler could not stop fidgeting. From his post by the entrance to Santa's room, he could see half of the area, and the idea that someone dangerous could be lurking in the half he couldn't see had every one of his nerves on high alert. What he wouldn't give for a platoon to patrol this room and be his eyes. He knew exactly who he'd choose, too, if they weren't busy overseas....

After changing the tire and speaking to the sheriff's deputy from Christian County, Tyler had tried calling Shorty, but the call went to voice mail. Likely, he was catching a few hours of sleep after last night's excitement. Well, Tyler sure had more to add to that plate. He'd left a terse message, wondering if he should place a call to Sergeant Major Walters, though there was nothing the older man could do from half a world away.

Helplessness ate at him. He couldn't do anything to stop this. Tyler felt one step behind.

His leg ached an accusation. Maybe he was only half the man he thought he was.

He tossed the thought away. A bum knee wasn't stealing his tactical mind. A brunette with a force of life all her own was. *Lord, focus me.*

"Ready?" Kelly's voice at his shoulder nearly shot him out of his skin.

"How did you sneak up on me?" The words were harsh, but the fact she'd done it underscored the need for the very prayer he'd been praying.

"Not hard with you staring at the ceiling." She smiled, ignoring his attitude, but the lines around her mouth were too tight, the creases in her forehead too pronounced. The knife had been a signal Kelly couldn't ignore, though she was clearly trying. She tipped her head toward the door Tyler guarded. "You're off crowd control. Two of the other volunteers came down with strep and they need us behind the curtain. They'll give us a gender and age, and we'll dig out the appropriate package to pass to Santa. Think you can handle that?"

"And then we all go home and sleep?" As if that was going to happen. He'd pull guard duty on Kelly's apartment, probably, whether she liked it or not.

"Sounds like a plan." She slipped open the door and motioned for him to follow.

It wasn't long before Tyler's knee ached from kneeling to dig through the mound of presents. He was getting soft with all of this time in the States. Used to be he could pull forty-eight hours on patrol without blinking. That involved movement and thought, though, while pulling gifts out of the pile grew more monotonous with each moment.

"Where'd you leave your Christmas spirit, Scrooge?" Kelly hip-checked him as she took the package he held out, double-checked the tag and passed it to another volunteer.

"Somewhere in your apartment about 0430 this morning." Straightening he rolled his head to ease the tension in his neck. "How can you act like nothing is going on?"

Something flickered in her expression, then she gripped his wrist to stop him from grabbing another package. "I can't change what's happening, but I can focus on now. Right now, I'm safe." She pulled him closer. "Stand still and listen."

Tyler straightened, instantly alert. "What am I listening to?"

"Christmas spirit. Joy in a crazy world."

Tyler pulled in a deep breath and let it out through his teeth. They had a mission. Pass on gifts, not stand still, but her grip on his wrist stopped him. In fact, her touch seemed to burn through to his muscles, paralyzing every movement. "Listen, we—"

She laced her fingers with his. "Shh."

Well, when she put it that way… Tyler tried to ignore the feeling of her hand in his, focusing all of his attention on the blur of noise on the other side of the curtains that hid them from the rest of the room. The hum filtered and became individual sounds. Moms laughed. Giggles punctuated childish chatter.

Tyler forgot knives and guns and trashed apartments. Out there, kids whose dads wouldn't be home for Christmas received joy from strangers who'd poured it into this project, to give them something special for the holiday.

Kelly was right. There was more to this than simply passing boxes around a curtain.

A grin itched the corner of his mouth, and he turned it on the petite brunette at his side. "Okay. Every knee-twanging, back-aching moment is worth it."

She grinned up at him and squeezed his hand. "See? Didn't I tell you last week you'd enjoy this?" A rogue piece of hair straggled from her ponytail and tickled her cheek.

Tyler reached up to tuck her hair back, letting his knuckles trail her cheek. All of the sounds she'd had him focused on died away. Man, was she beautiful with that joy on her face, already melting into something different. With that tenacious refusal to let the events of the past twelve hours drag her away from her mission to deliver Christmas cheer. His breath caught in his chest and he knew he'd never be able to deny it again. He was in trouble. As his fingers crept their way to the soft hair beneath her ponytail, he really didn't care. All he knew was he wanted to kiss her. Right now.

"Hey, guys?" A frantic female voice sliced the moment. "You might want to speed things up."

The words might as well have been a bucket of cold water, forcing him out of the moment. Probably for the best.

They seemed to have the same effect on Kelly, who dropped his hand and stepped back, like she was waking from a dream.

Tyler snatched up the nearest box and gripped it a little too tightly. His grip grew even tighter when he looked down at it.

Kelly started to step away, but he grabbed her elbow, eyes never leaving the box. His breathing picked up. "Tell me you remember this wrapping paper from yesterday." Although why she'd choose it, he had no idea. The black paper was flat and dull, a sharp contrast to the sparkling red ribbon threaded around the sides to end in a pointed bow on the top. A glittering tag was anchored under the bow.

Kelly's ponytail brushed his arm as she flipped the tag over. *For Kelly Walters.* Her gasp drowned out every other sound.

Tyler swallowed hard, feet already moving toward the emergency exit. "Clear the building. Now."

What a nightmare. Kelly dropped her head to the steering wheel of her SUV and stared at her hands, too discouraged to watch. Those poor children, caught in the middle of her nightmare. Explosive Ordinance Disposal had been called in, halting the toy giveaway. The children were more disappointed than concerned, but she'd seen the looks on worried mothers' faces. They understood the implications, and they were scared to death.

Kelly had spent the past hour defying Tyler's command that she stay somewhere secure, because she had to keep moving, to stop thinking. She'd circled among bewildered families, doling out smiles and promising the kids who hadn't been through the line that their gifts would be delivered by evening. And they would be. Even if she had to rewrap every gift that EOD had unwrapped and deliver them herself. No child would suffer because some faceless coward toyed with soldiers' families.

Kelly had tried to quash the whispers that ran among the wives, but the collective voice of rumor was quicker than her lone voice of truth. She'd heard *terrorist* whispered more than once, and she couldn't blame the spouses for thinking it. After all, she'd thought it herself.

Even if she still refused to believe it.

A knock on her passenger window made her jump with a silent shriek.

Stephanie waved grimly.

Kelly popped the door locks, and Stephanie slipped in beside her, rubbing her hands against the chill as Tasha Pope got into the backseat.

"It can't get much colder out there." Tasha blew into her gloves and tucked her hands under her thighs.

Kelly turned on the SUV and cranked up the heat, knowing it wouldn't do much good.

Stephanie shivered. "At least there's no wind in here."

"True." Kelly sat back and crossed her arms over her chest, angling so she could see both women. "Why are you two still hanging around? I figured everyone was pretty much gone once the MPs cleared them to bolt."

Stephanie sniffed a short laugh. "I've got no kids to drag back home. Tasha and I helped some of the wives pack up their kids then decided we'd stay and see what can be done in the aftermath."

Tasha leaned up between the seats, dark hair forming a curtain that covered one of her chocolate eyes. "The volunteers took names of the kids who didn't get toys. There are only a dozen. Steph and I wanted to see if we could get those presents delivered."

"I know you well enough to know that's what you were thinking of doing and didn't want you here alone." With a sly grin, Stephanie poked Kelly's elbow.

For the first time since the gunshot cracked last night, Kelly felt warm, as though she had allies other than Tyler. "Thanks." Maybe it was exhaustion, but tears threatened. She blinked twice and stared out the front window. Never would she cry in front of wives who had so much more on the line than she did. Other people needed her too much for her to break down. She cleared her throat. "What's the latest word?"

"EOD is about done, but I only know that because I saw them loading up the trucks. Major Rainey is in the middle of everything, so he'll probably be here any minute to brief you. As soon as they clear the building, we'll go back in. There are other volunteers still here, so prepping those gifts will be fast." Stephanie tapped Kelly's arm again.

Tasha pulled a knit hat low over her ears before chiming in. "Go home. We can take care of this."

Any other day, Kelly would have argued that this was where she needed to be, but sitting in the truck, she began to doubt she even had the presence of mind to drive home. She pulled in a deep breath and said the hardest thing imaginable. "Okay." Guilt ate at her, but she'd be no good to anybody if she didn't rest. She'd think later about what could happen when she was home alone.

Stephanie chuckled. "I know that was hard." She pointed out the front window. "Here comes Major Rainey."

Kelly followed her finger to see Tyler step into the crosswalk, a tall, chiseled man with him. They were speaking grimly as Tyler motioned with his hands, mimicking the size of the box he'd held.

Kelly's stomach tightened, only it wasn't from fear. Once again, he'd been there when needed. What would have happened if a child had ripped into that box?

Even from this distance, she could feel him watching her. In spite of everything that had happened since, she still felt the warm shiver of his touch, the look in his eye when they'd been alone behind the curtain. He'd have kissed her had they been anywhere else.

And she'd have let him.

Her fingers gripped the steering wheel. Absolutely not. He'd made it clear he wasn't staying. Tyler would be like her father, constantly one foot out the door, never able to fully give to his family.

"You okay?" When Kelly looked at Stephanie, a knowing

look formed. "So. Major Rainey?" A smug grin took the place of her curiosity. "I thought so."

"Really?" Tasha poked her head between them. "Nice pick. He's a cutie."

Not the word Kelly would have chosen for the six-foot man whom she knew had biceps of— No. Her brain could take a vacation and stop this nonsense. "No way. He has a knack for being in the right place at the right time. That's all."

"That always seems to be wherever you are." Tasha wouldn't let it drop.

Kelly held up her hand in Tasha's face. "No. Don't go starting rumors."

"Our lips are sealed." Stephanie twisted an imaginary key and tossed it over her shoulder.

Kelly wanted to argue there was nothing that needed to be sealed, but Tyler and the stranger had arrived at her car, and she reached for the door.

Blessedly, Stephanie said her goodbyes, motioning for Tasha as she said, "Call me if there's anything I need to know." She was gone before Kelly even opened her door.

Tyler didn't wait for her to step out of the vehicle. "Well, there's good news and bad news."

There was no way Kelly could handle more bad news. "Start with the good."

"The package wasn't a bomb." The man with Tyler stepped forward and held out his hand. "Captain Shorter."

Kelly gripped his hand, then stepped back, eyeing the man who stood at least two inches taller than Tyler. In spite of the day, she managed a wry grin. "*This* is Shorty?"

Tyler grinned and winked.

Yeah. That was enough to skitter her right back to the conversation at hand, amusement dead. "So what was it, Captain?"

"Assorted wires. A few rocks for weight. Nothing that's going to hurt anybody unless your name is David and you're carrying a sling." His attempt at humor fell flat.

"I assume I know the bad news."

Pulling in a deep breath, Tyler shrugged as he shoved both hands in the pockets of his black fleece. "You probably do."

"Well, I know my name was on the package." She leaned against the hood of the SUV.

"There's more." Captain Shorter stepped forward, tugging his beret tighter over short cropped brown hair.

Tyler looked away at the crosswalk where she'd been targeted the night before. It was almost as though he wished this part didn't have to be said.

Kelly felt her remaining strength flag. "I don't think I'm ready for more."

"We reviewed last night's security footage from all of the gates. Your shooter came in Gate One around 2130. An MP spotted him pulled off to the side of the road around forty-five minutes before you were hit." Shorter tossed his chin over his shoulder toward the gate a half mile away. "Right over there. It looks like he never went farther. He waited specifically for you."

Kelly dipped her head, pinching the bridge of her nose. This would be easier if she could stick her fingers in her ears and hum to keep from hearing things she preferred to ignore, the way she used to as a child.

"I'd like to sit down with you and conduct an interview, see if—" The buzzing of the cell phone at the captain's hip stopped him. He held up a finger as he pulled the phone to his ear. "Shorter."

Tyler reached for her hand, forcing her to look at him. "We'll figure this out."

"I'm not so sure it'll be that easy." Shorter slipped his phone back onto his hip. "Dispatch is getting calls like mad. There are more suspicious packages on front porches all over post. They're all families that were at the toy giveaway today."

FOUR

"Take me back to the Family Resource Center." Kelly leaned across the seat, regretting the stupid decision to let Tyler drive her to her house to get clothes. The plan was for him to take her back to the battalion to sleep in her office, where staff duty could keep an eye on her. She'd been too defeated to argue at first, but now she was wide awake.

The call had come in that they were bringing affected families back to the Family Resource Center until the bomb squad could investigate every package. The number stood at seventeen. The first three investigated had been harmless, but that didn't mean anyone dropped their guard for the rest.

Helpless and feeling out of control, Kelly gripped Tyler's arm where it rested on the console between them. "I have to be there for those families. They're scared. More than anything they want to talk to their spouses and they can't. That makes this all a hundred times harder."

Tyler's eyes never left the road in front of him. "They've called in counselors and chaplains. Trust me. Nobody is alone. You need to sleep. What is it you always tell your volunteers? The thing about the oxygen mask?"

Kelly huffed back in her seat and crossed her arms, not caring that she looked like a pouting two-year-old. "Not the same." Wives only had to worry about themselves and their families. It was her job to take care of them. *All* of them.

"Say it, anyway."

Sucking her lip against her teeth, Kelly sighed in defeat. "If you're on a plane going down, you put your oxygen mask on before helping anyone else. Otherwise, you run out of air and nobody gets helped."

"So, take care of yourself first? Is that what I'm hearing?" Tyler cocked an eyebrow. "You need sleep. And if I have to,

I'll bunk down outside your office door to make sure you don't sneak out." He held up a hand against her protest. "Don't argue. Somebody needs to keep an eye on you until we know what's going on."

"I'm not the only target."

"You're the only one I care about."

Kelly's chin snapped up, pulse pounding in her ears.

Knuckles whitening on the steering wheel, Tyler shook his head. "You're the only one I know personally. I'm worried about other families, too, but they're not personal."

Her usual arguments died. Leaning on Tyler would only lead to disappointment, but she was too tired to fight him. Once she got some sleep that load would transfer right back to her shoulders. Her families needed her.

"Shorter and his guys are the best. And they've brought in Criminal Investigations and Homeland Security. They'll get to the bottom of this."

Kelly sat up, exhaustion gone. "Homeland? They're viewing this as terrorism?"

"They're not ruling it out. Terrorists deal in terror, not just killing. Fake bombs, shootings and veiled threats fit the bill. Someone's trying to scare military families, and they seem to have a special agenda involving you." He tapped the steering wheel with his thumb. "I'm not even sure I like you being at your office, even with soldiers there 24/7."

"Where else do you want me to go? My dad's in Afghanistan. My mom's who knows where. And I won't risk anyone else by running to their home to hide."

"What do you mean about your mom?"

"What?" The abrupt change in conversation rocked Kelly's indignation.

"Your mom. You said she's 'who knows where.' I always assumed… Never mind."

"You assumed she died?"

"Yeah."

"Might as well have." Kelly watched the bare trees, branches iced with fresh snow. "She took off when I was five. Couldn't handle army life." She sniffed bitterly. "That was the early nineties, when army life was a piece of cake compared to now. No major offensives after the first Gulf War. No long deployments. But the idea that Dad could go anytime, the way he disconnected when he was gone... Add to it that she was still pretty much a kid."

"If you were five, I doubt she was much of a kid."

"I was born when both of my parents were fifteen."

"Oh." There it was. That slight shock tinged with the smallest bit of condemnation. "Makes sense. If I'd have thought about it, I probably would have figured it out based on your dad's time in service."

Hmm. He was so...pragmatic. The fact he hadn't judged, coupled with stress and zero sleep, loosened Kelly's tongue into weaving a story she didn't normally tell. "They were kids from a tiny town in Idaho." She gripped the silver cross on the thin chain around her neck and slid it back and forth. "As far as jobs, there was nothing for them, so when he turned eighteen, Dad joined the army against my mother's wishes. She wanted him to stay in that town—doing what, I have no idea. He'd been in a couple of years. They'd already moved once after he left basic and were looking at another move. Dad had been gone more than he'd been home, training and going to school, and when he was away, he totally forgot we existed. He was the kind of guy who couldn't be a soldier and a husband." The years since then had changed her dad, matured him into someone who could be there for his men and his family, but by then it was too late for his marriage. "My mother left me with a neighbor while Dad was on a two-week temporary duty assignment and never looked back." Kelly gripped the cross so tight it dug into her palm. "No further contact. She told my grandmother once that if I hadn't been born, Dad never would have joined the army and she never would have left him."

"Kelly, you can't listen—"

"That's old news." She didn't need his sympathy. She'd long ago dealt with the fact her mother's issues weren't her fault, though she'd learned the lesson of her parents well. Depending on people was foolish. "My dad did a better job of being a dad than being a husband. I turned out fine. I wouldn't have it any other way."

"Wow." Tyler breathed the word so quietly that Kelly barely heard it. "I knew your dad was a stand-up guy, but…wow. He raised you as a single soldier father? Where did you stay when he was deployed?"

"He didn't go much until after 9/11." She'd never forget that day. She'd been drifting, unsure what she wanted to be in life. After hearing about the attacks, she'd frantically tried her dad's cell, scared he'd go wheels up for parts unknown immediately. She'd prayed, cried, stared at the TV wishing there was some way to reach out to the ones hurting worse than she was, the ones in pain as they watched their lives crumble. She'd volunteered with the Family Readiness Group, went to school to be a counselor and later decided what she really wanted was to help other families. "That was also the day I decided I wanted to be a part of all of this."

"And the army created the Family Readiness Support Assistant position."

"I figured if I worked with the families maybe…" This was something she'd never said aloud.

"Maybe you could keep other moms from getting overwhelmed and taking off like yours?"

"Something like that." New fire surged. "Like right now. Days like this are precisely when I'm needed there."

Tyler was clearly frustrated with her. His shoulders squared as he shut down the ignition of her SUV. Funny how natural it seemed to let him drive it. She shoved the thought aside.

"We're not rehashing this. We'll both get some sleep and I'll take you back." He reached for her, then stopped and grasped the door handle instead. Seconds later, he was out of the car, walking up the sidewalk without waiting for her.

Slamming the door, Kelly followed, the need for her pillow warring with the need to be where her calling dictated. She found Tyler in front of her door, looking down. He took a step back as her gaze followed his.

A black box with a red ribbon. Like the one at the Family Resource Center, but this one sat in plain view on her doorstep.

* * *

This one's live.

Kelly dropped her head back against the cinder block wall of the small room at Tyler's battalion usually reserved for soldiers who bore "special scrutiny." She shifted on the hard cot and wished she could erase the words, could stop seeing the look on the EOD tech's face. The lines creasing his forehead, the veiled anger in his voice. She knew that look, that fierce surge of protectiveness. He felt it toward Kelly as he delivered the news to Tyler, never looking in her direction. Likely he couldn't. He knew the news he delivered changed everything.

Live.

Over half of the thirty packages discovered on post were already searched. None held bombs except the one on her doorstep.

The coffee the staff duty officer had handed her when Tyler ushered her through the door two hours ago crystallized in her stomach. She'd never had an ulcer before but wondered if this was what it felt like.

If nothing else, this was what being a prisoner felt like. She cracked one eye open and peered around the windowless room. Pasty, chipped, painted cinder block walls and institutional tile floors held an ancient cot covered in an army-issue sleeping bag. Yep. Prison. Tyler had hustled her here as soon as the tech said her bomb was for real, then he'd vanished.

"Why me?" The groan was louder than she'd intended, and she dropped her forehead to her bent knees.

"I think I can answer that."

Tyler's voice jerked her to attention, sending a strange mix of relief and tension coursing through her. He'd come back. For her.

He'd changed into his uniform, the sight familiar, though the determination in his jaw was new. Kelly wanted to throw herself at him where he stood in the doorway, arms crossed over his chest, but she held herself in place. "They caught who's doing this?"

"I wish." He nodded to the space beside her, and she slid

over to make room. The cot sagged under the weight of his muscular body, the firmness of his bicep pressing slightly against hers.

How she wanted to lean in and let him support her. God. God alone was her support. People eventually left. She cleared her throat and pulled away, though she could still feel the heat of him through her long-sleeved T-shirt. "What answer have you got for me, then? When can I get out of jail?"

Tyler chuckled bitterly. "Think of it as protective custody. Shorter thinks you're better off here than at your office. Hopefully, no one will think to look for you at my battalion." He tugged at a bootlace, then ran his hands down his thighs. "I'm staying, too."

The words gripped her. "But it's almost Christmas."

"Where else would I be going? Family's all in California. I was going to eat in the chow hall. I'll bring my presents here if need be. Open them with you."

Kelly focused on the wall. What would that be like, Christmas Day with Tyler? A tree. Dinner. Sharing a home… Her eyelids popped open. *Never going to happen.* "Tomorrow night's Christmas Eve. I have a solo in the service at Main Post Chapel."

"No way." Tyler shook his head. "Not until this is over."

Kelly pushed herself from the cot and stared down at him, fists digging into her hips. "Yes way. People are depending on me."

Tyler stood, using his considerable height to his advantage. "You will back out as long as there's a target on you." He planted his hands on her shoulders. "We know what's happening. We just don't know who's behind it."

Kelly blinked twice and sank to the cot, trying to get away from his gaze. "What is it?"

Tyler sat beside her, rested his elbows on his knees and clasped his hands. He stared at his laced fingers. "What I'm about to tell you is under wraps, got it?"

Kelly could only nod, the seriousness in his voice stealing her thunder. Something bigger than her was happening.

"Your dad's unit is about to embark on a major offensive. It's been in the planning stages for months."

"But it's winter in Afghanistan. The insurgents back off." Everyone in the military knew winter was "hunker down and hold your ground" time in that mountainous terrain, where snowfall often came down in feet.

"Precisely why higher planned for now. The insurgents shouldn't see it coming. Problem is we think they got intel." Tyler gripped his fingers tighter. "It looks like they're trying to hit the unit's morale. Since they can't fight over there, they're bringing the fight here."

Kelly's fingers and toes chilled. "What do you mean?"

"Every incident has been aimed at families in your dad's battalion."

Kelly sat back hard against the wall, realization tracing icy fingers down her spine. "As the sergeant major's daughter, I'm a high-value target."

"Afraid so. Your father is the highest ranking guy over there who has family here in town."

"That's why everything aimed at me has been elevated. If they can demoralize the chain of command, they can demoralize the entire unit."

Tyler slid back on the cot to lean against the wall. "I've been with Shorter some of this afternoon. Nobody thinks they're out to kill anyone. Yet. There's no leverage if you're already dead, just more reason for our men to get angry and fight harder. But the threat of death, the threat of injury… That'll take a guy's mind off the battle, make him wish he was home, make him grumble about coming back."

"Does the battalion know?"

"They've been put on blackout. No calls or emails in or out. It's better that way, because the soldiers can't do anything from over there to protect their families, and it will keep their focus on the mission. Most of the guys have been through blackouts before. They understand the need."

As cruel as it seemed, it was the right thing to do. Even if they did pack up the whole battalion and bring them home, there was no guarantee the attacks would stop. The parties involved might even escalate. Kelly stared at the ceiling. Until they found who was behind the threats, there was nothing anyone could do.

Tyler balled his fists and planted them on his knees. With all of his training and experience, he'd never felt more helpless. "I'd trade places with any of the guys overseas in a heartbeat to put a stop to this whole mess."

Kelly laid a hand on his arm, lightly at first, then with more insistence. He hazarded a look at her, something he'd been careful to avoid doing since he walked into the room. That fierce need to wrap her tight in his arms and shield her only grew with every incident that happened. He had to fight the instinct. His real job lay eight thousand miles away in the rugged mountains of Afghanistan, not in a cinder block room holding a pretty girl in his arms, even if she was in danger.

One look at those green eyes told him something had shifted with his words. *His* frustration with the situation had taken the edge off *hers* and given her something to focus on. As victim, she had no control. As comforter, she was firmly in her familiar role. The confidence in her expression said more than words.

She smiled that soft smile he'd seen her practice on family members a hundred times. "You're not Rambo. You can't go over there as a one-man army to defeat every insurgent who pokes his head out of a hole."

"It would feel a whole lot better to try than to sit here doing nothing." Tyler usually didn't talk about how he felt. It wasn't done in the army. It made him feel powerless. But it was worth it to see how she was drawing strength from leading him. He'd tell her every deep thought he'd ever had if it would keep that look of fear off her face.

"I doubt you're as helpless as you think you are."

Tyler sniffed his derision, failure burning in his gut. "I left my guys two weeks after we got over there. They're embracing the fight while I sit here in my climate-controlled office and dole out advice to rear detachment soldiers and spouses. Not exactly soldiering, am I?" He hadn't meant to truly air his bitterness, but the way Kelly fought to understand him unraveled his resolve. "Stupid knee."

"You know—" Kelly settled back and leaned her shoulder against his "—in all of the months I've known you, you've never told me anything other than you took shrapnel during an 'incident.' What happened?"

No one had ever asked before. Most people ignored it, figuring he didn't want to talk about it. Even his mom never mentioned it. Likely, she didn't like to think about how close she'd come to losing her only child.

Tyler stared at the wall and let his vision go fuzzy. "Not much to tell. We were going on joint patrols with the unit we were replacing so they could give us the lay of the land and brief us on where the insurgents liked to play hide-and-seek, that kind of thing."

In the time since, Tyler had tried not to think about it. Since no one asked, he set it aside, hoped the memories would fade. Suddenly, the idea of saying it out loud seemed cathartic, as if it would heal that hole he'd buried deep behind his heart. "We were on a dismounted patrol, working our way across a pass." He lifted his hands and spread them arm's length apart. "Afghans like to wall in some of their routes. We were walking along single file, watching the wall above us, the ground below us, everything, trying to be vigilant, but you can't see everything."

"Must have been claustrophobic."

"Like you wouldn't believe. You know that phrase 'shooting fish in a barrel'? Felt kind of like the fish that day." He'd gripped his rifle tighter and wondered how the soldiers they were replacing had spent a full year patrolling the area without going insane from the narrow focus and tough-to-defend position. "I was following Major Jorgenson, big old blond dude from Minnesota. His shoulders almost brushed both of the walls. If that passage had been any narrower, he'd have gotten stuck."

Tyler grinned, until he thought about that last second. "He turned around to say something to me right as the road opened up and the wall ended. Never got to find out what was so important." Whether someone tossed a grenade or Jorgenson stepped on an improvised explosive device, Tyler never knew. He shook his head. "There was this wall of sound. I mean, it was so loud it took over every bit of the world, even blinded me, because my brain was so full of the noise it couldn't process any other senses."

The room faded in the memory as the smell of dirt and smoke, the concussion of unfiltered explosion took over. "Next thing I knew I was flat on my back staring at the bluest sky you ever saw. Not a single cloud, no sound. I actually wondered if I was dead."

Kelly leaned harder against his shoulder, then reached for his hand and gripped it tight. "I'm glad you weren't dead."

"Me, too. Most days." He wouldn't tell her about the nights he'd stared at his ceiling, unable to sleep because the pain in his leg reminded him that he, a single guy with no kids, could still feel the pain while Jorgenson, a husband and a father of two preschoolers, wouldn't ever feel again. He probably hadn't even felt the blast that yanked him out of the world.

Tyler exhaled loudly, shoving the picture of that last look from Jorgenson out of his head. "You know those war movies where the guy gets hit and there's silence, then all of a sudden there's this rush of chaos? It really did feel like that. Everything whooshed in. I got a rush of adrenaline like you wouldn't believe. I couldn't feel a thing and, for a minute, I thought I was paralyzed. Then I realized I could move my fingers, could sit up. When I saw the blood, I thought I'd lost half my body. I was covered in it. Most of it was his." He shook his head to clear the vision and gripped Kelly's hand as if she was the one good thing in his life.

Maybe she was.

Another thought he had to shake away. He pushed aside the emotion, going back into that matter-of-fact box where he liked to live, where he didn't think about the emotional pain, just focused on the physical recovery. His voice grew stronger. "They thought I'd lose the leg, but they were able to repair it in Germany after the surgeon dug the shrapnel out. Know what it was?" He smiled bitterly. "It was a bullet from Jorgenson's gun. The blast was hard enough to fire his ammo at me. I got shot in the knee by a dead man's bullet."

"You survived for a reason. You know that, right?"

"Only reason I can think of is to go back and make short work of the guys who ripped a daddy from his family."

Kelly didn't look at him, and he felt gratitude he'd never be able to express. He'd left his guys, left a man's killer behind to come home and enjoy comfort while they slogged through. "There are nights I think I ought to sleep in the backyard to suffer like my guys are suffering."

"Not one of them thinks that. I guarantee it. You didn't shoot yourself in the knee to get out of serving. You're no coward, Tyler. You're a soldier. I respect what you've been through and what you've done to recover. I respect your determination. I respect what you've accomplished here as rear detachment commander, working with these families. More than once, I've been glad to look up and see you there. It's…comforting."

For the first time Tyler realized her head was on his shoulder. He'd felt it, but the intimacy of it hadn't struck him. Her shoulder, her bicep leaned into his. Her arm crossed his as her fingers laced with his on his injured knee. There was warmth, comfort, something he couldn't define swirling deep in his stomach. It was a something he wanted to keep on feeling. So much so that he pulled his fingers from her grasp and shifted to drape his arm around her shoulders, drawing her closer.

Kelly nestled her head into his chest as though it was the most natural thing in the world.

He swallowed hard. She had to feel his heart pounding and know this embrace was affecting him more than he wanted it to.

She draped her arm across his stomach and settled in, her head growing heavier. "You may not see a reason for being here, but there is one. I'm sure of it."

"I'm going back." He said it more to remind himself than to inform her.

"I know." Her voice was thick, exhaustion taking over.

Slowly, he lifted his free hand, fingers hovering above her temple. With a light stroke, he eased the hair from her face and let his fingers trail down her cheek as her breathing grew deeper and she fell into the sleep Tyler had been urging her to get all day.

Yes, he would go back. It was where he belonged.

But for the first time, he wasn't one hundred percent sure he wanted to.

FIVE

Safe. It was the first thought to drift across Kelly's mind as she inched into wakefulness. Safe and right. Where she was right now was exactly where she was supposed to be.

Except it wasn't.

Every muscle in Kelly's body tightened as her mind surfaced from sleep so heavy it was a tangible presence. Or maybe that was Tyler's arm around her. What had she done? Kelly fought the urge to bury her face in Tyler's chest. She'd fallen asleep on his shoulder in the middle of their conversation. Dying right now and saving her pursuers the trouble actually felt like a viable option. In all likelihood, he was as mortified as she was, probably thinking she'd thrown herself at him.

"Tyler?" She whispered the name and prayed one of the soldiers on staff duty wouldn't pick this moment to poke his head in the door.

Tyler didn't move. The rhythm of his breathing said it all. He was as far gone as she'd been a few minutes earlier.

Allowing herself an exhale of relief, Kelly pulled her arm back from Tyler's stomach and tried to ease away from him without waking him. Her neck ached from the awkward angle she had lain against his shoulder. She dragged a hand down her cheek, fingering the crease pressed into her skin from a fold in the shoulder of his uniform. Great. She was a marked woman.

Tyler mumbled something in his sleep and felt for her hand but didn't wake up. How had she missed how long his lashes were? At some point, he must have run his hand over his head, a habit she'd noticed he had, because the slight curl at the ends was mussed. For a moment, she almost laid her head on his shoulder again, missing that feeling of security, of rightness she'd felt on waking, but that would be the height of stupidity. He wasn't hers and never would be. The army had him first.

A scrape in the doorway brought her to her feet as one of the soldiers on staff duty cleared his throat. She heard Tyler stand right behind her.

How long had Specialist Miller been standing there? Kelly had never wanted to bury herself under the floor before, but now felt like a good time to start. What sort of rumors would this spawn?

Tyler ran his hand back over his hair. "What do you need, Specialist?"

The specialist looked unfazed, as if he saw the FRSA asleep on the rear detachment commander's shoulder every single day. Meanwhile, the heat in Kelly's face probably made it obvious to everyone that she wasn't used to the situation at all.

"Major Rainey." The specialist stood a little taller, never acknowledging Kelly. "You're needed at the CQ desk." He turned and left before receiving a response.

Kelly tugged at her sweatshirt, refusing to look at Tyler. There was no telling what he thought of her. She turned her watch around on her wrist. Just after five in the morning.

"I'll be back." Tyler was gone before she looked up.

Dropping back to the cot, Kelly pulled from underneath it the backpack she'd thrown together at her apartment. What she needed was a hot shower to clear away the fog. When Tyler didn't come back immediately, she slipped into the hallway and headed for the locker room, glancing out the broad wall of windows that opened onto the quad. Her own reflection, wrung out and sleep wrinkled, stared back. She grimaced and kept walking, trying to ignore the fact that Tyler had seen her that way.

He was waiting when she returned, damp hair stringing to her shoulders, a fresh flannel shirt over a tank top keeping her warm in the chilled room.

"Feel better?" He leaned in the doorway, arms crossed over his chest.

"I feel human now." She stopped in the hallway, reluctant to squeeze past him. There was no reason for her to feel awkward about merely walking through the door, not after she'd slept on his shoulder, but the thought of touching him made her toes tingle. She cleared her throat. "Any news?"

Finally, Tyler stepped out of the doorway, swinging his arm to usher her inside. "None you'll want to hear."

Her steps halted half in and half out of the room, no longer caring that she stood only inches from his chest. She swung her gaze up to his, heart double-timing at the tone of his voice. "What's wrong?"

"Not counting the package at the Family Resource Center, there were exactly thirty bombs. All but yours were on post. All but yours were decoys."

This wasn't surprising. "What else?"

Gripping her shoulders, Tyler dropped against the door frame to put them eye to eye. "That was the MPs at the desk. A few minutes ago, a routine patrol found a guy skulking around in the parking lot. He bolted."

Suddenly, Kelly couldn't swallow. She gripped the strap of her backpack tighter.

"Because of what's been going on, they swept the area and found another bomb…under my truck."

Kelly's mouth went completely dry. Her backpack hit the floor with a dull thud and her hands crept around his waist, looking for something solid to hold on to, something to stop the world from spinning. She couldn't even form a prayer. She stood, gripping tight, pressing her forehead into his shoulder. "They came after you." Her voice muffled against him. For the first time, she realized the danger Tyler was in and how much she'd miss if he was no longer in her life. For six months, she'd sat beside him in chapel, counted on him to back her up when casualties happened in the battalion, laughed at his crazy jokes whenever they shared a volunteer position…. And he'd been the first person she'd called when she was in trouble.

She couldn't stop it any more than she could stop breathing. She was in love with Tyler Rainey. And now was the worst time ever to figure it out.

It seemed as if time stuck right where it was for the space of a few breaths before he gently eased her from him to look down at her. He tried to look her in the eye, but she evaded his gaze, staring over his shoulder, trying to stop him from reading her expression.

He didn't let her evasiveness stop him. "He didn't come after me." He exhaled loudly, tipping his chin toward the ceiling. "He came after you. He knew where you were and he knew who brought you. We have to move you somewhere else. Look at me."

She couldn't. Her mind was incoherent, swirling in the confusion of more bombs, more danger, more emotion focused on a man she couldn't have. Pressing her hands against his chest, she took a step back. "I can't—"

A crack echoed in her ears as glass shattered. A scream tore from her throat as the wall between them seemed to explode.

Tyler hooked Kelly around the shoulders and dragged her through the doorway to the floor of the small room, slamming the door behind them as shouts echoed up the hall. He gripped her cheeks between his hands, swiping dust away with his thumb, searching her face as he did. No blood. "You okay?"

"Yeah. Yeah." She shook off his touch and pulled away, drawing her knees up to her chest and wrapping her arms around them. It was the exact opposite of what he wanted her to do. If he could hold her close, maybe he could keep her safe.

No. He'd failed miserably at that. His guard had been completely down when he'd nearly kissed her, even though he knew better. If she hadn't broken their moment and backed away when she did... His breathing picked up and he balled his fists, willing away the thought. That right there was the exact reason he needed to focus on being a soldier and nothing else. He couldn't be two people.

Scrambling to his feet, he inched the door open and came face-to-face with Specialist Miller.

Miller's jaw had squared in that look Tyler had seen hundreds of times before, the game face of a soldier who knew he had a job to do. "Is everyone okay, sir?"

Tyler stepped through the door and shut it behind him. "We're fine. What happened?"

"Sounded like a gunshot. And there's movement outside."

Tyler was running, boots thudding the tile as he called over his shoulder. "Stay with Kelly." He pushed through the door and didn't stop until he hit the quad. The cold air slapped him in the face as his breath vaporized in front of him in the pre-dawn darkness. From the other side of the building, voices rose as the MPs investigating the bomb in the parking lot headed toward him.

He pushed out the sound and focused on what was closest to him, scanning the area in the glow from the streetlights. He checked out the bushes in front of the headquarters building and came back. Something shifted, a dark shadow moving against the snow.

Common sense said he should wait for the MPs to get here, but he was past common sense. Without worrying about the consequences, he launched himself toward the building as the shadow stood and ran across the open area toward the main road.

No way would Tyler let this guy go. With his breath harsh in his ears, he pushed harder than he'd ever pushed, knee screaming that this was a bad idea.

The figure stumbled, giving Tyler a chance to catch up and throw himself forward, dragging them both to the ground with a thud in a tangle of arms and legs. Tyler came out on top, pinning the shooter to the ground, hand at his throat, giving Tyler his first good look at the man who had tried to steal Kelly from him.

The eyes that looked back at him were as blue as his own and filled with terror. He couldn't have been more than a college kid. For a second, Tyler's grip slackened, then he tightened up, driving the kid's chin up and the back of his head into the ground. "What were you thinking?"

Boots thudded behind him as several MPs raced up. Tyler had no time for them. He needed answers. He pushed harder as the kid's eyes widened. "Why did you try to kill Kelly Walters?"

A hand on his shoulder shook him out of his rage. "Ty. Back off." Shorter knelt beside him. "We can take it from here."

Tyler pulled in a deep breath, then eased up to his feet with Shorty's help, reluctant to let the shooter go but knowing his anger would only get him into trouble if he didn't obey. The minute he put his full weight on his knee, it gave under him. Pain blurred the scene. Only Shorty's hand under his arm kept him from thudding to the ground. He eased down and fought the urge to curl into the fetal position. No. Not this. Not now.

Shorter took a knee beside him. "Talk to me, Rainey. Did he—"

Words had to fight their way past nausea. "I'm fine."

"No, you're not." Shorter stood and waved another man over as two MPs hauled away their suspected shooter. "Get the medics over here. They need to get Major Rainey to the hospital."

Tyler shoved him to the side. "I said I'm fine." He had one purpose at the moment, to get back to Kelly and make certain that she was really okay. With every ounce of his strength, he pushed himself up and stood, testing his knee. It hurt from his hip to his toes, but he'd walk on it if it were the last thing he ever did. Nobody was carrying him out of here on a stretcher when Kelly needed him.

"If you aggravate the damage to your knee, it might not be fixable. You're risking your entire career."

There wasn't time to answer. An MP jogged up, calling Shorter's name. "You have to see this. They found the other guy."

The room seemed to shrink the longer she paced it. It felt like hours since Tyler had bolted from the room, leaving her with Specialist Miller, who'd stationed himself right outside her door. Every time she tried to peek, he urged her back inside, and she'd long ago given up dialing Tyler's cell phone.

She counted her steps across the room again. And again. It might not actually be shrinking, but it was hard to convince her mind of that.

Dropping to the cot, she pressed her fingers against her eyelids. *Lord, keep him safe. And let this be over soon. I can't take any more.* She'd run out of the denial that had been fueling her since the first gunshot cracked. Someone was trying to kill her, and all because her father was a leader of men.

Voices in the hall pulled her to her feet, and the door jerked open. Tyler stood there, eyes locked on her like she were the only thing in the world. She took a step toward him and stopped. No matter what that look said, she *wasn't* the only thing in his world. The army would always come first. She kept the space measured between them. "What happened?"

"It's over."

It took a second for the words to register, and when they did, her shoulders sagged with relief. "Really?"

He nodded, still looking grim. "They have the guy who shot at you in custody. When they patted him down, he was armed. Small caliber handgun, probably the same one he used on you. They found a rifle in the bushes by HQ building. But they caught him, and he's talking. They picked up his partner waiting around the corner in the same car from before. They confessed to being the only two involved." He sniffed bitterly. "A couple of college kids. They were trying to impress a terror cell, get their names recognized. They hatched the whole thing as a way to make a name for themselves, and now that they realize the stakes, they're scared to death. If they keep running their mouths, they might lead us to something bigger than the two of them."

Somehow, the idea that she could walk out of here and back into her normal life seemed surreal. "If it's over, then what's the matter?"

The space between them vanished in two strides, and he towered over her before she could back away. He gripped her chin between his index finger and thumb, forcing her to look at him. "If..." His jaw tightened as he glanced to the right then met her gaze again, a whole other look there.

It wasn't entirely new. She'd caught a glimpse of it last night, when he knelt beside her on the ground outside the Family Resource Center. Only now it was more intense, focused, a blue laser aimed straight at the core of who she was, to a part of her no one had ever seen before.

His thumb trailed her lower lip, eyes following the motion. "If things had gone any differently—" his voice dropped lower "—I'd have lost you for sure."

She wanted to say he ought to be more worried about the fact that there had been a bomb under his truck and he could have lost his own life, but the words died under the gentle motion of his thumb, back and forth. Her lips parted, but no words came.

Tyler must have sensed it as an invitation, because his chin dipped, his thumb dropped away, and his lips brushed hers, lighter than she'd expected, as if he wanted her to agree, to take the next step.

She let go, sinking against him and deepening the kiss. It was everything, heart and soul, poured into the space between them. For the briefest moment, she lost herself in a world that was just Tyler, all she needed. All she wanted. Tyler, who'd been the only one by her side in recent memory.

Tyler. Who would leave her for the battlefield as sure as he was standing here kissing her now.

With a whimper Kelly didn't want to acknowledge, she backed away and broke the connection.

He dropped his arms immediately, questioning expression saying so much more than words as confusion cooled whatever else had blazed in his eyes.

Kelly stiffened her muscles against the pain she was about to inflict. "Did Shorter say when I could go home?"

"Kelly, I—"

"When?" If she let him talk, she'd cave, fall back into that incredible moment when she didn't stand physically alone. When, for the shortest second, she'd known what it meant to be someone else's whole world.

"As soon as you're ready." His voice held something that sounded like regret.

"Now. I want to go now." Kelly stepped away, into the room, started shoving her clothes into her bag. "It's over."

It's over.

Tyler groaned and leaned back in his desk chair, its squeak of protest grating on his raw nerves. The sky outside his office windows pinked slightly through gray clouds, promising a glorious Christmas Eve sunrise.

He turned his back to the window, feeling every ounce the Scrooge. All he had to look forward to in the next two days was chow hall cooking and opening a couple of presents from his mom under his pathetic little tree in his cramped apartment. The silly present he'd gotten for Kelly mocked him from across town. He'd bought her an umbrella after he'd seen her hand hers over to a grieving widow at a funeral.

How stupid had he been to think even for a moment that he could spend the holiday with Kelly Walters. He'd kissed her, and she couldn't get out of his arms fast enough.

Proof positive that he needed his knee healed because he sure didn't belong anywhere but the battlefield. He wasn't a lick of good here. Kelly was sure to start keeping her distance from him now, and the small amount of joy he'd found in rear detachment was snuffed.

"You know, when word gets out about the past couple of days, you'll be a hero."

Tyler sat straight up at the voice, feet thumping to the floor with a knee-jarring rattle.

Captain Shorter stood in the doorway, looking as worn-out as Tyler felt. He aimed a finger at the couch on the other side of the desk. "Mind if I sit? I'm warning you. I might not get up again for a few hours." At Tyler's nod, he dropped onto the fake leather. "If I start to snore, throw your stapler at me."

Tyler sniffed. "I'll be over here drowning you out. What are you doing here, anyway? I thought you left when they took your terrorists in."

"I did." Shorty stretched out his legs and leaned his head against the back of the sofa. "Came by to tell you the kid we grabbed let slip that they were hired by a cell out of Nashville. This is going to pull down an entire sleeper cell. I also wanted to make sure EOD had a handle on the explosive so you can get your truck and go home."

"They finished yet?" Nothing sounded better than driving his truck back home and racking out for a whole day, maybe forgetting that Kelly would probably never speak to him again after that kiss.

"Not yet, but I can run you to your place if you need a lift."

"Nah." The thought of going home to an empty apartment

left him cold. Tyler stretched his leg out, knee protesting. He winced against the pain.

"How much longer have you got before you're healed up?" Shorty must have seen the look.

Tyler shrugged as he mechanically flipped a challenge coin between his thumb and index finger. The same thumb that had brushed Kelly's lip an hour ago. He pressed the cold metal of the coin against his skin, trying to annihilate the warmth of her touch. "Another month or so of physical therapy, as long as I didn't mess anything up with my running tackle tonight. I'm trying to speed them up, though. It's time for me to go back, put in some time with my guys."

"Think they'll send you back with only four months left?"

"I'm persistent."

The couch squeaked as Shorty shifted positions. "All I can say is this, man. It's a God thing that you were here for everything that's gone down this week."

The coin stilled in Tyler's fingers. "Come again?" He bent his knees gently, sitting up to face Shorty. The coin dropped to the desk with a clang. "Why do you say that?"

Shorty sat forward, elbows anchored onto the gray of his ACU pants. "Kelly Walters wouldn't be seeing this sunrise if you hadn't been here."

"Somebody else would have—"

"No way, Rainey. These guys were escalating. This last bomb? They meant it. I think when they figured out we'd locked down the unit and weren't giving our guys any information about what was happening here, they decided to go in for the kill. We can keep everyday information from going to the unit, but we can't hold back a death notification. The guys we caught this morning are talking. The goal was to take out the sergeant major's daughter, like we thought, and stop the whole mission." He shook his head. "I doubt Kelly Walters would have been so easily persuaded to go into hiding if you weren't around." He sat forward. "Think about it. You pulled her out of the way of that pistol round. They came back for her, likely to take her. Who'd have been there with her if you weren't? Nobody. And after the false alarm at the Christmas party, she'd have blown off that package on her doorstep without you there. Rainey…" Shorty sat back and spread his long arms along the back of the couch, allowing one finger to stab in Tyler's direction. "Not all wars are fought on the official battlefield. God needed you here. Kelly Walters needed you here."

Tyler picked up the coin he'd dropped to the desk and ran his thumb over the engraving of Afghanistan. The lieutenant colonel had pressed it into his hand before he'd been medevaced out of country, giving him an "atta boy" when Tyler hadn't done anything more than bleed.

Shorty cleared his throat. "It's the Global War on Terror, Rainey, not the war in Afghanistan. You're no less important here. I battled the idea of a stateside assignment myself until I saw how much work there is to do here. You'll be where you need to be when you need to be there."

Tyler finally looked up. "You really believe that?"

"I wake up praying every day to be right where God wants me to be. Sounds to me like you need to practice a little bit of surrender yourself, especially where a certain female is concerned. I'm no rose petal romantic, but there's something there, and you'd better tell her before she gets the idea there isn't." His cell phone rang, and he inched up and pulled his phone from his belt holster, glancing at the screen. "My wife. She has this sixth sense about when I get off duty." He pulled the phone to his ear and stood, throwing a half salute at Tyler. "Had to make a stop. I'm headed home right now."

Tyler flicked him a wave. What would it be like to have someone worried about when he came home? To have a meal together and talk about their day?

As Shorty left, Tyler stared at the sunrise out the window, his friend's words chasing the thoughts in his head.

The heat of conviction nearly broke him out in a sweat. He wrinkled his forehead. Okay. So God always saw the big picture better than he did. *Lord, let me be right where You want me to be. And let me be content to be there.*

The urge to see Kelly took over his thoughts. He stood, ignoring the protest in his knee, and snatched his keys from the desk as he headed for the door. Shorter was right. Before he went home, he had to tell Kelly to her face that he wasn't ready for this to be over.

SIX

"Turn here." Kelly pointed to the entrance that led to her apartment complex, then reached down and hauled her backpack onto her lap, pulling her keys from the front pocket.

The female MP clicked on the blinker and made the turn. "I'm sure you'll be diving straight into the rack after the week you've had."

"I got a little bit of sleep last night." She looked away, feeling the heat creep up into her cheeks. Yeah. She'd slept all right, and probably drooled all over Tyler's shoulder, as well.

"I can go in with you to make sure the place is clear if you'd like."

"Hmm?" Kelly drew her attention back into the car as it slowed in front of her building. "No. I'm good. EOD cleared the place last night, and I feel confident nobody's come back. The men they caught seem to have followed me onto post." The thought threatened to rattle her, but she pushed back the fear. Really, she wanted this to be over. No more sweeps of her house. No more crazy packages or gunshots. Just rest, then she'd get ready for her solo at the Christmas Eve candlelight service at Main Post tonight. She'd worry about tomorrow when the sun rose again.

Her original plan, with her father gone, was to open the presents he'd left for her when he deployed and then spend the day at the chow hall on post, serving other families and talking them through the holidays without their loved ones. It seemed there was always someone who needed an ear, especially at this time of year. Wishing Tyler was by her side shouldn't derail that plan.

She reached for the door handle and flashed a smile at the young MP. "Thank you, Specialist Anderson. Have a Merry Christmas."

"You, too, ma'am."

Kelly shut the car door behind her, watching the MP drive away before she trudged up the recently cleared walk to her apartment.

In the breezeway, she stopped short, gripping her bag tighter.

A slight figure huddled by her door, forehead resting on her knees, a crumpled sheet of paper dangling from her fingers.

Kelly took a cautious step closer, recognition flickering relief through her. "Tasha?"

Tasha's head jerked up, deep creases marring her forehead. "Kelly." She scrambled to her feet, shouldering her huge leather purse. "You're here."

"How long have you been waiting for me? You could have called." Compassion swept through her, shoving away the last vestiges of fear. The girl seemed distraught, broken, the wild look in her eye one of desperation and worry.

"A half hour or so." She held out the paper in her hand, and it trembled and rattled as her fingers shook. "I got this. From Chase." She sniffed, never looking up from the printed words. "Some Christmas present."

Guns and bombs and domestic terrorists all faded as Kelly took the paper from the young wife's hand and scanned it. The heading was a private email address bearing Chase Pope's initials, sent two hours ago, late afternoon Afghanistan time. The email was terse, to the point. He wanted a divorce.

Kelly sucked air between her teeth and scanned the email again. No explanation, just a two-line ending to a brand-new marriage. She dropped her backpack by the door and pulled the girl close as that mothering instinct surged, the one that often rose up when she dealt with these young wives, some still in their teens, who had no idea what they'd signed up for when they married a soon-to-be-deployed soldier. That didn't make the bonds any less sacred, though. "It's going to be okay."

"How?" Tasha pressed her chin into the muscle along Kelly's injured shoulder, shooting pain through the arm.

She tried not to flinch. Instead, she slipped away and rested her hands on the younger girl's shoulders. "Come on inside.

I'll make some coffee. Chances are, he's—" She cut herself off. Chances were high that Chase Pope was getting his first taste of what a real war zone was like and was shocked that it wasn't as romantic as his childhood war games had made it seem. But she couldn't say that to Tasha. The information Tyler had shared about the mounting offensive probably wasn't common knowledge. "A lot of guys cut ties when the going gets tough, then when they adjust, they realize it's possible to be a good soldier and a good husband, as well. Some soldiers think they have to be one or the other. It's possible to be both."

And what about Tyler Rainey?

Kelly gripped her keys so tightly that they dug into her fingers. Yes, plenty of soldiers had found that balance, and Tyler could, too. She'd been holding on to insecurities over her father's issues, expecting Tyler to be the same as the man who'd raised her, unable to be two men at once. Over and over, Tyler had proven himself different, willing and able to be there when she needed him.

And she'd pushed him away.

"I feel like I'm going to be sick." Tasha gripped her stomach, staring at the door to Kelly's apartment.

Fumbling with the keys, Kelly swung the door open and Tasha bolted inside, heading for the bathroom. Grimacing, Kelly shut the door behind her and followed the girl up the hall, tossing her keys on the counter before going to knock on the bathroom door. "Tasha? Do you need anything?"

The door flew open so fast that the breeze sucked the fine hairs around Kelly's ponytail forward. She took a step back as Tasha bolted from the small bathroom, pinning Kelly to the hallway wall and gripping her tight around the neck. "For you to be out of the way."

Kelly struggled, clawed, fought disbelief and a surge of fear as the world faded.

Tyler parked his truck beside Kelly's car, glancing at the dashboard clock as he did. At least she'd stayed home and hadn't headed out for who knew where. He hesitated. She'd only left post fifteen minutes ahead of him. Surely she was still awake. He'd knock lightly and, if she didn't answer, he'd sit right here and wait until she woke up. There was no way he was going anywhere until he'd had a chance to lay everything out on the table and see if there was a way for them to make this work.

It took a lot to keep his gait at a walk when he really wanted to run to her door, but a fall on the ice would only torque his knee and set him back even further in his physical therapy. He might be content to let God decide where he went, but he sure wasn't going to be stupid about it.

As his foot hit the sidewalk, his phone vibrated at his hip. He started to ignore it, then thought better of it. Maybe it was Kelly, and she'd done some thinking of her own.

The number was Shorty's. He pulled the phone to his ear, dread seeping into his fingers. Something deep inside said this wasn't over. "Rainey."

"Consider this a courtesy call. I got called back into work. Once the feds told them the stakes, the younger of our two guys started really talking, and it's nothing like what we thought."

Tyler's feet dragged to a halt. "What?"

"This isn't a terror cell. It's an antiwar group. They want to stop the war, bring the troops home. Their goal is the same, though. Scare the families by bringing some aspect of the war here. Rainey, they knew every move we made."

"How?"

The sound Shorter ground out over the phone was guttural and angry. "They're a small group, five total, following some antiwar professor at a local college. The ringleader is a woman who came up with the idea of marrying a young soldier and working her way into the trust of the other wives. She volunteered with the FRG and got all of the inside info she needed."

What was that woman's name? The one who always seemed to show up for Kelly at the right time? "Let me guess. Stephanie Anderson."

"Who? No. Tasha Pope. She married a Spec-4 out of Sergeant Major Walters's battalion. While we've been focused on the two in custody, she's been free to roam." There was a pause. "I shouldn't tell you any of this."

"She's going straight for Kelly." Tyler gripped the phone tighter and took off at a run that made his knee scream.

"Stay back, Rainey. We've got a team en route."

Tyler clicked the call off and shoved the phone into his hip pocket, steps slowing when he entered the breezeway.

Kelly's backpack lay to the side of the door, but there was no sign of her.

Adrenaline hit his heart so hard it hurt. Maybe she was tired and hadn't wanted to bother bringing it in. Somehow, he knew not, especially at the sight of her phone peeking from the side pocket. She'd never leave that behind, fearful she'd miss the call of someone who needed her.

Staying close to the wall, Tyler crept to the door and tried the knob. Locked.

Careful to stay out of line of sight of the peephole, he listened, wishing he could mute the hum of cars from the nearby highway. For a moment, there was nothing, then a scuffle, a grunt, a short shout silenced as soon as it started.

Taking a step back, he raised his good leg and prepared to breach the door.

As the dark squeezed in, Kelly forced her lungs to pull in air even as her heartbeat roared in her ears, warning that unconsciousness wasn't far behind. With her last ounce of strength, Kelly forced her good arm up. It was like swimming in syrup, but she managed to raise her hand, digging her fingernails into the younger girl's temple and raking them down her face, drawing blood.

With a shriek, Tasha pressed a hand to her cheek and fell back, allowing Kelly to pull in a deep breath. She fought the urge to bend low and gulp air. This fight was nowhere near over.

Before Kelly could fully straighten, Tasha lunged again, fist crashing hard into Kelly's injured shoulder, eliciting a whole new kind of pain. Kelly cried out and went to her knees, trying and failing to sweep Tasha's legs from under her.

With one more kick, Tasha caught Kelly between the shoulder blades and drove her to the floor, driving her foot into

Kelly's injured shoulder. Wet warmth trickled down her arm as the wound tore open. Before Kelly could process the pain, Tasha's knee drove into her lower back, and the girl wrapped the strap of that huge purse around Kelly's neck.

She pulled tighter as Kelly gagged, leaning lower. "Never wanted to have to kill anyone, especially you. But if taking out one can save hundreds, the math's not in your favor."

The world spun out in a whirl of color and a roar in her ears.

But then there was a new sound. A crash. A splintering. The tightness around Kelly's throat eased, allowing her lungs a breath and clearing her vision.

Tyler stood in the doorway, broad shoulders drowning out the light, fists balled at his sides. His hard expression should have paralyzed Tasha Pope.

From above, Tasha cursed and scrambled to her feet. "What are you doing here?"

"Doesn't matter. This time, it's really finished." Tyler's voice held a finality that brooked no argument.

Kelly pulled herself to a sitting position. It was over. Really over.

Until Tasha pulled a phone from her pocket and flipped it open. She held it out toward Tyler, free hand pointing at the leather bag that lay abandoned on the floor next to Kelly. "Major, I'd stop if I were you." Her voice was way too calm for someone whose end game was at hand. "There's one more bomb, and Kelly is sitting right beside it. It's enough to blow all three of us into the next world." She rose and took a step toward Tyler, blood dripping from her chin. "All I have to do is press Send. You let me walk out of here and I'll hand it to you as I pass. But you try to stop me and we're all done."

Tyler glanced from Tasha to Kelly to the bag, then back to Tasha, his jaw tightening as he did.

Kelly shifted sideways, keeping her eyes on Tasha, whose focus never left Tyler. With the last of her strength, she said a quick prayer and swept her leg sideways, catching Tasha across the back of the knee.

Tasha cried out as she pitched forward, phone flying toward the living room.

Tyler was all motion as soon as Kelly moved. He dived into Tasha, pinning her hands behind her and wrestling her to the floor.

Kelly bolted for the phone and snapped it shut, then set it gingerly on the counter and stepped away. She slumped to the back of the couch and gripped her shoulder, eyes finding Tyler's across the room as he kept a struggling Tasha pinned. "Now it's over?"

He nodded as tires screeched to a halt in the parking lot. "Now it's over."

"Well, that should take care of it." The young nurse anchored one last piece of gauze over Kelly's freshly stitched bicep and slipped the chair back to admire her handiwork. "It's going to hurt like you can't imagine when the meds wear off."

Kelly tilted her arm and looked at the bandage. "That's what ibuprofen's for." The words came out in a squawk, throbbing through her bruised neck. Thankfully, scans had shown no deeper damage, though Kelly knew she'd come close.

"It's gonna take more than that." The nurse stood and smoothed the front of her scrubs over the bulge of a very pregnant stomach. She pressed a stack of gauze pads into Kelly's waiting hand. "Change it whenever it starts to feel uncomfortable. Doc's put in a prescription for some heavy-duty painkillers if you want to get any sleep tonight." She smiled down at Kelly. "Merry Christmas."

Kelly pulled her shirt on over her tank top and awkwardly buttoned it with one hand, the dull ache in her bicep proving the nurse was telling the truth about the pain. She wasn't one for meds, but the pain in her throat coupled with the throbbing in her arm said she wouldn't be able to tough it out.

She'd wrestled the last button into place when the nurse stuck her head back in the small curtained room. "There's a hunk of a soldier out here asking to see you. It okay if I let him in? He's been waiting…impatiently."

Kelly felt a smile tilt her lips. "Yes."

It only took a second for Tyler to step in and pull the curtains shut behind him. He stood there uncertainly, hands behind his back, clearly waiting for her to make the next move.

"Come on in," Kelly whispered.

"What did the doc say?" He matched her whisper, stepping closer until he stood over her.

"I'm one blessed young lady."

"I'll say." Tyler brushed a straggling lock of hair out of her eye and let his index finger trail down to her neck, leaving a warm trail of goose bumps in its wake. "Tasha Pope didn't do you any favors." The way he said the name was hard, and a look crossed his face that said more than his words could. "I was almost too late."

"Right place, right time." Her voice was a harsh whisper as Tyler stepped back and eyed her.

"What was that?"

"Right place…"

"…right time." A smile teased the corners of his mouth. "That's what I thought you said." He pulled up the stool the nurse had vacated and plopped himself down, putting himself at eye level. "We need to talk."

Kelly swallowed, trying not to wince. "I can't…" She cleared her throat, ignoring the knot that felt more like tears than pain. "I can't sing tonight."

Tyler scanned her face, confusion knitting his eyebrows together. "That's not what—"

Kelly reached out and let her fingers trail down his face, from his forehead to his chin.

Tyler hesitated, then turned his face so his cheek rested against her palm.

"I think God's trying to tell me something." Kelly managed the words before Tyler reached up and caught her hand, planting a kiss in her palm, then clasping their hands together.

"What's that?" His attention never left her.

"Don't try to be everything to everybody." She tightened her fingers around his. "Enjoy every gift He's given me."

"Including the one that's always in the right place at the right time?" Tyler's voice was husky as he kissed the end of her middle finger, sending a jolt clear through to her toes.

At her nod, he lowered their hands, settling them against his chest, then planted a light kiss on her forehead, her cheek, then a gentle one against her lips, a promise that had only just begun.

EPILOGUE

One year later

The hum of voices drifted in from the small fellowship hall off the chapel, punctuated by the giggles and thudding feet of small children. There was a decided lower key in the harmony this Christmas Eve, with most of the men home from rotations in Afghanistan. Somewhere in that din, her father was probably chatting with Tyler about what shorter deployments would mean to the men and women of the 101st. It was his favorite topic of conversation lately. That, and retirement.

Kelly smiled. Like that would ever happen. Shoving her hands deeper into her coat pockets, she settled back and watched candlelight play on the wall behind the altar. She'd sent the chaplains into the fellowship hall, promising them she'd extinguish the candles after the Christmas Eve service, but the hush of the room and the dim light of the candles kept her in her seat. It was a powerful moment, just her and God on this night of all nights. Gratitude overwhelmed her, but all she could think to say was *thank You,* over and over again. *Thank You.* For her father's safe return home. *Thank You.* For the fact she was alive to see another Christmas Eve. *Thank You.* For Tyler's steady, loving presence in her life. None of it was deserved, she knew, and yet all was a gift by the grace of God.

Like Christmas itself.

She was about to slip out of her seat to blow out the candles and go revel with everyone else, when someone slipped in beside her.

Tyler picked up her hand and laced his fingers with hers. "I was wondering where you'd disappeared to."

"Nowhere. I was about to come and find you."

Slipping his fingers from hers, Tyler stretched his arm across the back of the pew and drew her closer. "It's so…holy in here." His voice was low, letting her know he felt the same wonder that had gripped her. It wasn't the first time over the course of the past year that his thoughts had synced with hers.

"Perfect word."

"So, I'm thinking I should give you your Christmas present now, if you're okay with that."

Kelly angled away from him so she could see his face. "You don't want to wait until tomorrow? I don't even have yours with me."

"Nah. I'm thinking now is the perfect time." With his free hand, he reached into the inside pocket of his jacket and slipped out a folded paper, then handed it to her. "Part one."

The jumble of words and letters was instantly recognizable. Orders. He was leaving Fort Campbell for another post. Kelly felt her Christmas spirit ebb as she scanned the paper in the dim light for his next duty station. Ranger School. Fort Benning, Georgia. With a report date in May. "How is this a present?"

"I said that was part one." Tyler withdrew his arm and turned sideways in the pew so he could look at her. "With me needing that second knee surgery after all that happened last Christmas, the army and I both felt like I could use a longer recovery period. I'll be at Ranger School teaching other soldiers, and there won't be any deployments for three years." He leaned away to withdraw something from another pocket. "I figure that's long enough to get a good start on this." Reaching for her hand, he wrapped her fingers around a small black box.

This time, Kelly was sure her heart stopped beating altogether. "Is this…?"

"A diamond-encrusted invitation to Fort Benning, and to anywhere the army sends me after that?" He popped the box open in her hand, and the solitaire inside caught the candlelight. "I do believe it is." Slipping the ring from its place, he held it out to her. "What do you say? Do you think you want to marry an old soldier and join the ride wherever it takes us?"

Kelly bit back a grin and swallowed tears at the same time. "More than anything."

The words were barely out of her mouth before Tyler had both arms around her, holding her as though he was afraid she'd vanish if he loosened his grip.

She leaned into him and let go the way God had taught her over the past year, surrendering to the fact that life was out of her control, but fully, completely, in control of the God who loved her and of the man who would always be there… no matter what.

* * * * *

COMING NEXT MONTH FROM
Love Inspired® Suspense

Available November 4, 2014

DEADLY HOLIDAY REUNION
by Lenora Worth

Jake Cavanaugh's daughter has been kidnapped by a serial killer, and the only person he can turn to for help is Ella Terrell, a former FBI agent...and his old high school sweetheart.

HAZARDOUS HOMECOMING
Wings of Danger • by Dana Mentink

A found necklace reopens an old missing persons case and changes everything for Ruby Hudson and Cooper Stokes. They must put the past behind them in order to find the truth before someone silences them.

TWIN THREAT CHRISTMAS
by Rachelle McCalla

Long-lost twin sisters have a chance to reunite at Christmastime if they can stay alive long enough to find each other.

SILENT NIGHT STANDOFF
First Responders • by Susan Sleeman

The last person Skyler Brennan wants to spend Christmas Eve with is her FBI agent ex-boyfriend, but she'll have to trust him with her life—and heart—when a bank robber comes after her seeking revenge.

IDENTITY WITHHELD
by Sandra Orchard

A widowed firefighter is determined to rescue a woman in witness protection from her pursuers. But when the criminals involve his son, will he be able to save them both?

PERILOUS REFUGE
by Kathleen Tailer

After witnessing a murder, Chelsea Rogers goes on the run. Can she trust Alex Sullivan to protect her from the killer on her trail—before she becomes the next victim?

LOOK FOR THESE AND OTHER LOVE INSPIRED BOOKS WHEREVER BOOKS ARE SOLD, INCLUDING MOST BOOKSTORES, SUPERMARKETS, DISCOUNT STORES AND DRUGSTORES.

LISCNM1014